LOWRY PEI'S
FAMILY RESEMBLANCES

"Pei splendidly evokes the torpor of a small-town summer, from baseball games on the radio to horseplay at the local swimming pool. He also underlines the connection between heat, sun and sex.... Karen and Augusta are both engaging, three-dimensional creations. We want their story to continue, for the summer not to end."
—PHILADELPHIA INQUIRER

"The encounter between Karen and her aunt is handled masterfully, allowing Karen's attitude to shift slowly from anger over having the knowledge of Augusta's unhappy sex life thrust upon her to comprehension of what it means to be an adult and solely responsible for your own passions, to discover the delicate balance that will keep her from doing too much too soon—or the even worse mistake of being afraid to get intimately involved at all.... [Pei] has a quality that is rare today, a willingness to put sensitivity before sensationalism."
—ST. LOUIS POST-DISPATCH

Family Resemblances

Lowry Pei

Vintage Contemporaries
Vintage Books
A Division of Random House
New York

TO JEAN

FIRST VINTAGE CONTEMPORARIES EDITION, February 1988

Copyright © 1986 by Lowry Pei
Published in the United States by Random House, Inc., New York, and simultaneously in
Canada by Random House of Canada Limited, Toronto. Originally published, in
hardcover, by Random House, Inc., in 1986.

Library of Congress Cataloging-in-Publication Data
Pei, Lowry.
Family resemblances.
(Vintage contemporaries)
Summary: Fifteen-year-old Karen spends the summer with her unusual Aunt Augusta
and learns many things about love, life, and the complexities of growing up.
[1. Aunts—Fiction] I. Title.
PS3566.E32F3 1988   813'.54   87-40101
ISBN 0-394-75528-6 (pbk.)

Author photo copyright © 1986 by John McClure

DISPLAY TYPOGRAPHY BY BARBARA DE WILDE

Manufactured in the United States of America

10   9   8   7   6   5   4   3   2   1

Family Resemblances

chapter 1

On the hottest days, my Aunt Augusta would drive around New Franklin with the windows rolled up, so that people would think the air conditioning still worked in the Buick she had inherited along with the house. Occasionally, when she got to an out-of-the-way place, she'd hit the four buttons by her left hand and all the windows would slide down at once to let in relief, but she may have done this only when I was with her, to accommodate my weakness and youth; alone, for all I know, she never let down her resolve. She almost managed not to sweat, as if a regal bearing would keep her cool. Once, when we were all visiting—my parents and I—my mother, red and hot, told her to her face it was absurd. Augusta, beautiful as she was, looked stony. I could see her in profile from where I sat in the back seat, and I was glad the Buick was big and I didn't have to be any closer to her. Whose side to be on? There was a silence for half a block, and then she finally looked at my mother and said, "What they don't know won't hurt me."

When I was fifteen and a half I went, or got sent, to visit Augusta by myself because my mother couldn't put up with me. It was summer again, and I was unbearable because of a lost boyfriend. His name was Roger Andrew, singular; I called him Rodge; he was sixteen, and touched my breasts, which made me feel as if I might die of self-consciousness. Having touched me there and elsewhere a number of times, he gradually ceased to call me up, and I became—dramatic. I moped extravagantly, talking on the phone all evening to my best friend, Jeanette Markey, sleeping till one o'clock, playing the same 45's until no one could have made out the words but me. My father seemed nonplussed; this kind of bereavement left him nothing to say, even if I had been willing to listen. Parents like mine didn't quite admit to themselves that their daughters, even at fifteen, made attempts at sex; but sex was a side issue. There was no talking to me, about that or anything else, so my mother didn't have to say much when she suggested a thinly disguised exile in the care of Aunt Augusta. In a different mood I might have refused, but I didn't care what she had planned this time, and I knew that part of her plan, always, was to make it hard to resist.

New Franklin, where Augusta lived, is east of St. Louis in the part of Illinois that did not get flattened out in the last ice age, where "corn" comes out "carn" and people talk about combing their hairs. I rode the train down from Chicago to St. Louis and Augusta made the hour's drive to pick me up. On the train I wondered if I should have brought a bigger suitcase, to suggest that I wouldn't mind leaving Evanston for good, or else one that was clearly too small, but no one except me would have noticed. The ride was fast and flat and repetitious—across or down the main streets of small towns so quickly I barely had time to read the signs, and then more cornfields. A couple of times we stopped among the plants that stretched out too far, and I thought how glad I was to be inside where it was air-conditioned. Then another train would go by in a long, monotonous rush and we would slide into motion again. I thought about Rodge, about wanting to be touched; desire demanded a good deal of thought. I slouched sideways across two seats and curled into the smaller me that hadn't yet filled out my body. The upholstery prickled. I was still unhappy, but it was already a relief to know that distance alone would answer the question of why he didn't call me up, as long as I stayed away. How annoying: my mother had been right again.

My parents made a great point of telling me that when I came back was entirely up to me, as if I were suddenly grown up and independent, but what did I know about going away from home? Anyway Augusta's house was only an extension of it, was family. When my grandmother died, Augusta wanted the house and my mother didn't, so that settled that; she moved in, among all the childhood memories, where it seemed to me that no one but my grandparents could actually live. At first—when we next visited after the funeral—almost nothing was changed; different mail lay on the front-hall radiator, a different coat hung from the coatrack, but that was all. Only gradually did the furniture shift and ebb, banished to the attic and basement, sold in garage sales and given away to the thrift shop, and boxes of mementoes got packed perhaps forever and stored—for whom? For me?

I wanted to feel independent, grown up, as I ate lunch in the dining car, but the steward made me sit with a couple my parents' age and their sullen little boy, who looked as if he might throw up just for spite. Family life. They tried to be friendly for a few sentences and then dropped it; the waiter didn't even try. By the time I left the diner I felt about twelve years old, and who ever heard of a twelve-year-old having a grand passion?

As soon as I got back to my seat and took out whichever Ngaio Marsh book I was rereading that week, the train stopped and a boy about sixteen got on and sat down next to me, plunk, as if he had planned it all along while he waited for the train to come. I was so excited I scared myself. "Hi," he said, and I managed a weak "Hi" in response, or maybe I didn't, because he looked at me like, Is this girl all right? I kept looking at his hands and trying not to think what I was thinking, trying not to shift in my seat or sigh or do anything that might be interpreted as the beginning of a conversation, until after ten frozen minutes I managed to pretend to go back to my book. All the rest of the way to St. Louis I rode stiff as a board behind the protection of a dog-eared paperback, cursing myself in my heart. At the very last, after the train had pulled in, he offered to get my suitcase down from the overhead rack, and I thanked him and actually smiled. That was all that enabled me to feel like a human being as I descended to the platform and heard Augusta call my name, the "a" in "Karen" subtly different, countrified, to my Evanston ear.

As usual, everything about seeing Augusta was a little out of joint at first; I always forgot that she looked so much like my mother, and so different, like my mother made seven years younger and stretched a couple of inches. For a second each time we met, her face seemed comically long; after that first moment I found her beautiful. I envied her thinness, her ability to go anywhere in a pair of blue jeans, and most of all her hair, which was reddish-brown and perfectly straight, unlike mine, which was coppery and curled.

Augusta gave me a quick hug under the gray metal heavens of the St. Louis train station; it was too hot for more than momentary contact, and a cloud of steam blew across us from under the train and made it hotter still. "Phewkes," she said, like someone out of a Wodehouse book, and once again I was back to family. "The train was nice and cool," I said inanely.

"I'm glad something is," Augusta said. She made a move in the direction of my suitcase and then clearly decided I was big enough to carry it myself. "Actually, the house isn't bad. I keep the shutters closed all day and drink vast quantities of iced tea. How are you?"

"Fine."

"I've heard you're terrible."

"I can't imagine where," I said, trying to sound sullen and oppressed.

"Well, you'll survive," she said. "I'm sure we both will."

"How are you?" I said. She didn't seem to have heard me; we marched along a few steps in silence. I shifted my suitcase to the other hand and looked up at her. Her eyes met mine and I was scared, but thrilled, to see her look at me like another grownup.

"Terrible."

For a moment I would willingly have gotten on the next train back to Chicago. Most of my life, adults had kept their problems to themselves; couldn't I just concentrate on Rodge's clumsy fingers unbuttoning me on a hot night in a dark solarium and not have to know what came next? Still, I managed the words "What's wrong?"—knowing I could do no less. Augusta looked as if she regretted opening her mouth.

"Forget it," she said. "Your problems are more fun."

I kept my head down, and Augusta said nothing else all the way to the car; once I glanced up and caught her watching me. I could imagine her thinking to herself, Don't put it on her, she's only a kid. The same thought I was having with only the pronoun changed.

I wasn't about to ask again as she piloted the Buick—windows

down—to New Franklin. Augusta asked me a few questions
about how my parents were, which I answered with all the
vague brevity I could manage, while I watched the landmarks
go by—the field of plowed but never planted black dirt with
the signboard in front of it titled THY WONDROUS BOUNTY,
ILLINOIS, the falling-down barbecue shack at French Creek
where I always wanted to stop but wouldn't have dared to go
in, the almost-too-pretty white houses of Lebanon.

New Franklin was the same as ever; what else could it be?
A Midwestern town bisected by the B & O tracks with one
main street parallel to the railroad and another one at right
angles to it, where "department store" meant dry goods and
shoes and "downtown" meant those three or four blocks along
the tracks. Anyone could list the stores without even visiting
the town: grocery, tavern, dry goods, drugstore, auto parts,
appliance, hardware, farm implements. From a row of second-
story windows tenacious silver letters proclaimed the presence
of a dentist. It would have taken some toothache to get me up
those steps.

But the stores seemed like afterthoughts; the houses of the
town were New Franklin. Most of them were brick; they had
front and back porches, lightning rods, garages that were almost
barns. Tin flashed from more than a few steep roofs, and even
a sagging frame house covered with peeling brick-pattern tar-
paper had some kind of a soul inside it, some reason for being
on this earth. I could walk down the street and feel that the
houses were alive.

Augusta's was one of the grandest houses in New Franklin,
giving rise to rumors that she was rich; the truth is that my
great-grandparents, who had built the place, had left their
descendants not much more than the house itself. My grandfather's "department store" had made him a living, a position

for him in the town, but certainly hadn't made him rich; my mother had told us Augusta was crazy to live in that old place, she wouldn't even be able to keep it up, on a schoolteacher's salary. Augusta told her that it was free and clear and the taxes were low and she was moving in.

The house was three stories of dark red brick; the ground-floor windows facing the street were twice as high as I was. In the attic there was an iron cistern, no longer used, that took up an entire room. It was built like a ship, and it terrified me as a child because I kept imagining it crashing through the beams and squashing me flat as I slept. There were white-marble fireplaces, with arched openings flanked by columns, in various rooms of the house, including one in the front bedroom; they were coal fireplaces, too shallow for wood, and the chimneys no longer worked. One, in the parlor, had had a gas heater in it, when I was a child, that leaked slightly and filled the house with the faint odor of gas, the smell of winter visits. On the south side, off the back sitting room, a tiny windowed room stuck out; apparently it was a gesture in the direction of a conservatory, but for as long as I could remember it had harbored nothing but dusty boxes no one wanted to carry up to the attic—for all but two weeks of the year, that was where the Christmas ornaments were kept. I could have drawn every room in the place from memory—could have placed almost every single object: an anvil had sat, for no reason, on the floor of the pantry all my life, and I had tried and failed, on every visit, to pick it up.

As we bumped across the tracks and onto the road that led into town, Augusta rolled up the windows. It was one of those days when my grandmother would have said it was hot enough to hatch lizards. Sweat popped out all over me, and for a moment I was furious, even though I remembered her doing it when we had all visited the summer before. But I noticed that she sped up at the same time, making a sort of dash for the house, where we could get out, and it was only a couple of blocks. If anything could make summer in southern Illinois seem cool, leaving the car after a ride with Augusta would do it.

I turned the knob of Augusta's front door—she never locked it—and let in a long shaft of summer glare, invading the dimness of the hallway and the front stairs. She was right about her house; it wasn't bad at all. The long louvered shutters were closed, and the windows were open, so that air but not light could filter through. The inside was high and dark and quiet; I might have been underwater.

"There's a good deal of gardening to do," Augusta was saying. "I've been meaning to pull out the cabbages, the white flies have ruined them. Somebody has to mow the lawn before it gets too high to cut. Do you want to go to a ball game or not?"

"I don't think so." Augusta had a passion for baseball, which still hadn't struck me as odd.

"Well, they're no good this year, anyway. You can have the other front room, the one across from mine, okay? Do you want something to drink?"

"Yes, please."

"I'm dying for a beer." She moved abruptly toward the kitchen as if she didn't know that I was there yet. All at once I felt just the way I had at home: alone. I stood in the dim hallway and contemplated a print of the St. Louis Exposition of 1904 which I had looked at a thousand times and never liked. Why had I let myself get roped into this? There was nothing, absolutely nothing, to do in New Franklin, no one I knew except Augusta, no one around but a bunch of hicks . . .

"Iced tea?" she called from the kitchen.

"Sure." I made an effort to raise my voice and thought, I'm standing here like an idiot waiting for someone to tell me what to do. But it was still a second before I could get myself moving to join her.

The kitchen was brighter than the front of the house; the shades were not fully drawn. I noticed that the old wallpaper had finally been replaced, and wondered—my mother's daughter —how she could afford it. Augusta handed me a glass of iced tea. For a second we didn't know what to do with ourselves; then we sat down at the kitchen table. I kept coaching myself: Make an effort.

"What else did my mother tell you?"

"Oh—lots. I don't think she wanted me to pass it on, she just needed to get some things off her chest."

"Did she make you invite me down?"

Augusta looked tired. "As a matter of fact, no. I thought of it first, all by myself. I hope you don't die of boredom— anyway, you can always go home." I knew she didn't mean to sound so severe, but that didn't keep me from feeling shriveled up inside. Suddenly I realized that she had been saying hospitable things about what she and I might do most of the way back from the station and I had hardly uttered a word.

"I'll be fine, I really will. I'm just in a bad mood. I'll get over it. It was really . . ." As she leaned her chin on her hand and gave me a slow smile, I ran down, helpless.

"Nice of you to come," she said. "Don't worry about what your mother told me. Let's go shopping. There's not a thing in this house to eat."

I never failed to be amazed that Augusta could leave the keys in the Buick without a second thought when she went into a store. Once, I mentioned it to her, and she said impatiently, "That's where they *belong*," but her impatience didn't seem to be with me—rather with the world beyond New Franklin, where things did not fit to her liking. Everyone in town knew Augusta and the Buick, if only by sight and reputation, and any fool who might have tried to steal it wouldn't have had a chance.

"So," she said in front of the soft drinks, "you have boy problems, is that it?"

I was mortified. I couldn't talk about something like that in the grocery store; someone had probably overheard already. "Sort of," I muttered as furtively as I could.

"According to Cheryl—" Augusta said, meaning my mother, "—no, wait, I wasn't going to talk about that, was I?"

"According to Cheryl what?" I said, feeling daring and bad.

"I'll tell you later." She looked down at me from her superior height of five foot nine. "What do you want for dinner?"

At dinner, Augusta poured me a glass of wine without any comment, and I could have kissed her on both cheeks. Perhaps it made me bolder after a while, or perhaps I was bold enough by nature. "Well?" I said.

"Well, what?" The way Augusta attacked her steak I could tell she didn't take it for granted.

"You said you were going to tell me later—you know, about what my mother said."

"You don't let up, do you?"

"No."

"Well, if you must know, she said she thought he was a very nice boy, but making out with him had given you this crazy idea you were falling in love."

Good God. I could feel myself turning pink. My mother said
to my aunt that I was, quote, making out with him? I didn't
know if I was more embarrassed at the thought of her knowing
or the thought of her saying it.

"Anyway," Augusta said, "I don't think she minded, really,
so much as she just didn't buy it—I mean—well, I guess she
just didn't think he was falling-in-love material, that's all."

"Well, no one's asking her to," I said.

"I know, I know— See? I shouldn't have brought it up at
all, she told me not to because she knew it would make you
mad."

"You don't have to—"

"Defend her?" That hadn't been what I was thinking. Augusta was a little pink herself. She poured me another half glass
of wine, herself a whole one, held up her glass to clink with
mine. "Here's lookin' at you, kid," she said. We sipped. I
thought about how I could never in a million years have this
conversation with my mother.

"Besides," Augusta said after a minute, looking over my
shoulder, "making out gets to be kind of a lost art once you
grow up. You might as well make the most of it."

I couldn't say a word. Tell me more, I thought to her, though
I hoped she wouldn't look me in the eye. Outside, the crickets
were hard at work, cranking up for the night.

She didn't say anything more that first evening, at least not
about boy problems or making out. We drank the rest of our
second glass of wine and finished the steaks, and this time I
listened while she told me what she had been doing since school
let out. She seemed to have very little notion of entertaining
me—apparently I had missed my chance on the ride home. I

tried to feel that self-reliance would be good for my character, but the house was big, and we didn't seem like enough to fill it up. I thought about what it must be like for Augusta living there alone.

"Well, you know where everything is," she said, as we got up from the table. "Don't you?"

"I think so."

"You okay?"

What could I say? "Sure."

She gave me a quick hug that surprised me. "Good to have you here," she said. For a second I felt weepy. I tried to hug her back instead of saying anything, but before I could, she broke away and marched off as if embarrassed, through the dining room to the parlor beyond it. I watched from the kitchen door as she turned on a lamp and picked up a book.

"I put the TV upstairs, if you feel like watching it," she said without looking around. "And maybe you should call your mother." Then she sat down and began to read. It was like being a child all over again, when the adults don't seem to know you're really there.

chapter 2

Later that night I discovered at last how Augusta stayed so thin no matter what she ate: she didn't sleep. At that peculiar hour when any awakening seems violent, I came to, staring at the ceiling of a strange room, and didn't know why until I heard footsteps determinedly pacing the downstairs. They had to be Augusta's. Didn't they? I listened as hard as I could, sent my hearing across the hall and tried to find out if Augusta was still in her bed. If she was in there and not downstairs, what was I going to do? Why were we lying here, a couple of un-protected females in bed, without even locking the door? A car went by, making an unreasonable amount of noise, more noise than cars really made, I thought, and trapezoids of light sped across the walls and ceiling in the opposite direction to the sound. I realized I wasn't quite sure what the room looked like. Calm down, I ordered myself, as the car roared away. If Jeanette were here she'd make a joke out of it somehow. But what if she were here alone? She wouldn't be, she'd have too much sense. Then from downstairs I heard one word, "Damn," in Augusta's voice. Saved—I wasn't going to be raped and murdered after all. But what in the world was she doing?

I couldn't tell.

Then I woke up, and it was morning. Augusta was downstairs already, or still. I could hear her putting a pot on the stove, the back screen door slapped shut and echoed itself, bouncing off the frame and knocking closed again. I felt disgustingly lazy. It was almost as bad as waking up on Saturday morning at home to the sound of my mother talking to her office on the phone and my father, like everyone else on Forest View, mowing the lawn. Children would be practicing pianos in nearby houses, kids on bicycles would be racing each other and yelling about the result, burning up a thousand calories a minute, the whole din making me feel as if all of Evanston would look at me over its shoulder and mutter, God, that Karen Moss, she's finally getting out of bed. And it would be worse if my mother was already out showing houses, talking to customers about mortgages and closing costs and property taxes as if she could think of nothing better to do on Saturday morning than work. If this was what it was all about, I had a distinct feeling I wouldn't cut the mustard. And now Augusta, going her one better. Maybe she didn't make as much money as my mother did, but she didn't even bother to go to bed.

I got dressed as fast as I could—baggy shorts, tennis shoes, and white socks, a blue work shirt with the tail hanging out and tied up in front in a knot around my waist, which was about as elegantly casual as you could get where I came from (if only there had been someone in New Franklin to notice), and under the shirt a most uncasual bra—the body-armor kind that, as far as I knew, all nice girls wore. You would have thought I had as much to hold up as Elizabeth Taylor, or else that I lived in fear of having anything touch me there, neither of which was exactly true.

When I got downstairs Augusta was out in the garden trowling away, with a kerchief over her hair; the radio was forecasting hot weather to itself in the kitchen; and the clock said eight-thirty, which I managed not to take as an accusation. The pot of coffee on the stove was still warm, and the morning itself was plenty hot already. I poured myself a cup of coffee and joined Augusta outside.

The screen door announced me; Augusta turned around and wiped the back of her trowel hand across her forehead, leaving a streak and making me feel too clean. "Good morning," she said.

"Good morning." I took a drink of the coffee and wondered what next.

"Would you just look at the root on that thing?" Augusta pointed at a weed lying at my feet. It was like a dirt-colored carrot. "No matter how deep you dig, there's always a little bit left behind, and then they come right back."

"They grow like weeds, I'll bet."

"Yes." She gave me a sideways look as if to say, Maybe this visit won't be so bad after all. "How did you sleep?"

"Did I—" hear you wandering around in the middle of the night, I wanted to ask, but as soon as I started, it sounded rude.

"What?" She had started cultivating again.

"I slept fine, thanks."

"Have you had breakfast yet?"

"No." I had been wondering if I should start right in weeding. Don't forget, you're not a guest, I reminded myself in my mother's voice, family has to help with all chores.

"Well—it's all there," she said, waving her trowel at the house. "Except juice. We're out of juice. There might be half a grapefruit. You're not on a diet, are you?"

"No, do you think I should be?"

Augusta turned around once more to inspect me. "Good grief," she said, and shook the dirt off an uprooted weed, then threw it at my feet with the rest. "Go eat some breakfast."

For some reason it was easier to get up in New Franklin; we usually managed to eat breakfast before the heat clamped down, as it did by nine almost every morning. I had thought there would be nothing to do, but there was too much; Augusta had enough projects in mind to last two or three summers. Painting the trim was one of the less ambitious items on her list, not as hard as restoring the shutters, most of which had missing or splintered louvers and were covered with coats of unevenly peeling paint. She was determined to fix up the slightly absurd, collapsing gazebo in the back yard or else tear it down altogether. And there was always weeding the garden, watering the garden, extending the garden, picking the crabapples before they got so heavy they broke a limb off the old tree, turning the compost, cutting the lawn—which between sun and thunderstorms could get beyond cutting if it was left a few days too long. That meant fixing the lawnmower, which was supposed to propel itself and was almost impossible to push if it didn't, and which insisted on throwing off the belt that made it move forward. And besides all that, we still had to shop, cook, clean up, and ponder what to do next with the inside of the house. Boredom was not going to be a problem, though running out of energy very well might. Augusta made me feel flabby and spoiled, and though I wanted to rebel against her projects a hundred times, I kept feeling I had something to prove.

Each evening that first week we sat in the kitchen a little longer, I drank a glass of wine and she drank two or three, and she talked as no one had in my presence; I thought that this was the secret talk of adults, just as children have their secret life that no one else can know.

"I was a little older than you, actually. It was during the war. I had this boyfriend who lived about three blocks from here, on Lincoln—I could show you the house, but it doesn't matter. As soon as he got to be old enough, he enlisted; that's what people do in towns like this. Everything was very important then. Now everybody seems to think that was some kind of magic time, but it wasn't; it was frightening and everything felt temporary. So of course he wanted me to sleep with him before he went away, and of course I did. That was part of the way it worked, though people didn't admit it out loud; it was almost like a ritual. Send off the warriors. I don't know if we're really as bloodthirsty as it seemed or if everyone just pretended. Anyway, there was too much involved for us to just . . . do it. I wanted making love to him to be perfect, whatever that means, though of course I didn't know anything about it because I never had, but that wasn't really the point. I mean, sex is a fine thing, but when you start talking about wars and getting killed and never seeing somebody again, it only goes so far. You don't really want to hear about all this, do you?"

I nodded, or some part of me told my head to nod and it nodded, though she was right: I didn't really want to hear it.

"You're really something, you know that?" Augusta said. "How'd you get me into this?"

"*Me* get *you*?" I was afraid at once that I had been insolent. Where was the borderline with her?

She gave me a look, but I hadn't stepped over. "I don't know what good it'll do you, anyway," she said, "hearing about my checkered past just because there's nothing better to do. I hope you don't think I'm going to give you any advice."

"I get plenty of that at home," I said, feeling a little disloyal. But Augusta was family, and within the family you could complain. All she did was raise one eyebrow—a trick I tried to master, practicing in my room with the door shut, but never could. "What happened to him?" I asked.

"Jerry? He made it all right, survived the war; when he got back I was at the U. of I. I was a senior. He went there on the G.I. Bill, but we didn't have much to say to each other, I guess. I only saw him a couple of times after he came back. He still lives around here. In Belleville. He's got a heating business there. I don't suppose we have very much in common except the demise of my much prized virginity."

She stopped talking as if she wished she hadn't said that. Some kind of struggle seemed to be going on inside her; she tapped her knife on the edge of her plate, watching the point of impact.

"I'm corrupting you," she said at last, tapping.

"You're not."

She set down the knife. "Karen—cynicism is a terrible thing. So long as you understand that; no matter what I may sound like, okay?"

I wanted to pat her hand or touch her somehow but there was no right way. "I thought you weren't going to give me any advice," I managed lamely, and to my surprise she smiled.

"I can't be trusted," she said. "Want some more wine? No. I can't go making a drunkard out of you as well. I'll bet the ball game's on, what do you think?"

"Seems to me the ball game's always on."

"Well, then, why don't you go read *War and Peace*, or whatever it is you young hotshots do, and I'll do the dishes."

"But it's my turn."

"It's not a question of turns. Go on. If you stay here you'll have to listen to the Cardinals lose."

"Okay."

Actually, I was in the middle of reading *The Catcher in the Rye*, which I thought was probably the most realistic book ever written, and as I went upstairs to find it I could hear the voice of the announcer over the sound of water running into the sink. "Broadcast of this game has been authorized by the St. Louis Cardinals National Baseball Club, Inc. . . ." Already the words were like a tune I heard every night from somebody practicing a piano in the distance. They were comforting; they saved me from thinking about the things Augusta told me that I didn't entirely want to hear.

chapter 3

Sometimes I wondered if it was right for Augusta to tell me the things she did, as we sat in the kitchen in the evenings. There was something illicit about the secrecy of doing whatever we pleased. I couldn't help wondering as I took walks around New Franklin alone what the town thought of Augusta, a single woman living by herself in a house too big for one person. I was just her niece, my grandparents' grandchild; they said hello and saw right through me to my ancestors. Maybe Augusta was thought of as a person who knew where she belonged. She was George Streeter's girl, Augusta. But she was something else, too: unmarried, thirty-five—in not too long she'd be an old maid or something worse; already, I was almost sure, they considered her an eccentric.

She was no maiden, of course—Jerry had taken care of that when she was seventeen. When I asked her what happened after that, she said, "Nothing," and ate half a dish of ice cream before going on. The amount of chocolate sauce she put on it would have given me pimples for two weeks, but even that didn't make me wish I was thirty-five.

"There was nobody to go out with, and besides, I was waiting for Jerry to come home, at first. Also, I was terrified that I'd get pregnant. My period was late right after Jerry left, and I practically threw myself off a bridge. Anyway, it was almost as though it hadn't happened, or like a strange experience that could only happen once. It wasn't much fun anyway, not that first time—for one thing, we were in a car, for God's sake." She ran a finger around her dish and licked it. "Do people still do that these days, or are things getting less barbaric?"

"I wouldn't know."

"Sorry."

"Do you want any more?" I asked, getting up.

"No . . . just leave the dishes for now, why don't you?"

"It's no problem." I scraped off the plates and piled them by the sink, wondering just what people in fact did, what Jeanette did, for instance, who as far as I knew had never let a boy unhook her bra, and probably thought I was wrong to have done that. I couldn't help it, I thought to her. You don't know about that yet.

"Well, did it matter?" I said, still in the pantry with my back to Augusta. By looking in the window over the sink I could see her wavery reflection sitting at the kitchen table.

"Did what matter?"

"You know. You and Jerry." I wanted to say "making love" but the words wouldn't quite come out.

"Of course it mattered." I sat down again and reached for the iced tea. "Later on, when I was in college, I went out with a boy named Allan. He was 4-F. Diabetic. He was also Jewish. Some of my friends didn't like that very much, and some of his friends didn't like me. But they didn't say that, of course. They'd just get drunk at a party and then get me off in the corner and tell me, whatever else I did, not to go to bed with him."

"And?"

Augusta crossed her arms and stared at the salt shaker. "I didn't," she said after a while. "I don't know why I let them get away with that. But everyone said he couldn't marry a girl who wasn't Jewish. Even Cheryl made a point of telling me that. I guess I just didn't want to take the chance of hearing it from him." She untucked one hand and pointed to herself. "No guts."

"Come on."

"And to top it off, right then was when Jerry came back and thought maybe we'd just take up exactly where we left off when I was seventeen and he hadn't been through a whole war. He was a little scary, I can tell you. That made me mad at the world—seemed as if I couldn't do anything right. I could just see him getting some idea that I was still his girl-friend and punching Allan's face in. To him the word 'Jew' was nothing but an insult."

"He didn't do that, did he?"

"No. He called me some nasty things and then stopped speaking to me." Looking at her face, I thought, not for the first time, that Augusta would be hell in a fight, and I had a feeling that she hadn't let that conversation end without saying a thing or two herself. Things she might even regret.

"Have you ever seen him again?"

"Who, Jerry? He fixed my furnace last fall."

I had meant Allan, but now I didn't know what to say. Apparently the look on my face struck Augusta funny. "What's the matter?" she said. "He does a good job."

"But wasn't it weird, I mean—"

"Well." That eyebrow shot up. "Life's a lot longer than you probably realize. At your incredibly youthful age."

I tried to look resentful and Augusta tried to look conde-scending, but after a few seconds both of us started giggling.

"I still don't see how you could stand it," I said.

"Here's something else you won't get. When I first saw him after he came back, I really didn't like him very much, and I definitely wasn't in love with him, but I had to sleep with him just one more time. For some reason it was a necessity."

"No wonder he got a funny idea you were his girlfriend."

"What do you know about it?" Suddenly she was cold as could be, and scary. She reminded me of how my mother got sometimes, and I wished I was upstairs reading a book.

"Sorry," I said.

"Oh, it's not your fault."

But maybe it was. Maybe I had no business in a conversation like this. Couldn't Augusta tell that? Maybe she was corrupting me after all.

"I don't mean to snap." She wouldn't look at me. "I'm really a very difficult person to get along with, that's a fact."

"No—come on—it's been a whole week . . ."

The wan attempt at a smile she gave me shut me up. She looked at me as if I were someone other than myself—my mother, or who, I couldn't tell—and then I could almost see myself swim into focus for her as me, Karen, her niece.

"Are you having a lovely visit?" she asked, dwelling sardonically on the word "lovely."

I leaned forward. "Divine."

Maybe, I thought after Augusta had gone upstairs to watch a baseball game on TV, the problem was that at home we never talked about anything much at all. Except money, sometimes. Maybe the point about Augusta *was* that she had never gotten married, but not the way the town would have meant it. My parents seemed to have gotten themselves into a position where everything went without saying, or wasn't safe to bring up. Around them there was no way to tell the difference between walking on eggs and the most predictable of routines, not even for me, and I lived there. You would have thought that sex didn't exist, except as a sort of inconvenience; the need to find a meaning for life they seemed to regard as an adolescent social disease which they wouldn't catch if they didn't pay too much attention. Why was I bothering to go to school, I would ask them, but the answer always seemed to be because somebody said I had to. I was getting it over with, like my adolescence. Life seemed to be full of things that fell into that category. What's the point, I kept wanting to say, but whenever I did I felt like the clumsy, ill-mannered cow who started the Chicago fire.

Up until recently, my father had been good for an answer to that question, but no more. Something had gone wrong with our private talks, even before Rodge. That was what evenings with Augusta reminded me of, except with Augusta they weren't in code. With my father I had always had the feeling he was trying to tell me the truth, but he couldn't quite bear to see the look on my face when I got the message. So he told it to me sideways; nevertheless, I could trust him.

In a way my father had gotten me in training for this visit with Augusta during all the hours we had spent together on weekends while my mother was selling houses. I had certainly learned how to do yard work, whether I liked it or not; I had learned that he expected me to help him even if he didn't ask, that he had very particular ideas about compost, and that I was not above shoveling cow manure. He persisted in referring to certain vegetables in the garden as mine, even though he wouldn't let me or my mother touch his precious dirt without his approval; he claimed I had helped him build the bookcase in my room because I had put in a few screws and stood around while he was making it, waiting to hand him a tool that he could have gotten for himself. He called me "Miss" for a nickname, and I couldn't bear it in front of my friends. "My name is Karen," I would say through my teeth, and he would just smirk and tell me to be in by eleven at the latest.

"Miss," he said one Saturday the summer before Augusta, when I was about to ask him for a ride to Jeanette's, "let's go to Loyola Beach."

"Loyola?" We hadn't gone there in five years, not since we moved to Evanston. "I told Jeanette I'd go shopping with her and her mother at Old Orchard."

"You can always do that. Come on, get your suit on, and we'll go to the old place. I'll bet you've forgotten what it's like."

"Loyola's gross, Dad, nobody ever goes there."

"Not grand enough for you anymore? Come on, we haven't gone in a long time."

"No wonder," I said, but I knew I was going.

I had a new bathing suit I had been waiting for a chance to wear, but I wasn't going to waste it on a trip to Loyola Beach with my father, and that was just as well, because it clouded up while we were still driving, and almost as soon as we got to the beach it started to rain. My father didn't seem to care. We sat in the car and ate hot dogs; he would have listened to the ball game, but it was rained out too, of course.

"What a great idea this was," I said with my mouth full.

"Don't you get tired of shopping?" he said.

"No."

"What are you looking for, anyway?"

"Clothes." If he's brought me all the way out here to lecture me, I thought, I'll take a bus home. I really will. Then I remembered I didn't have any money.

He finished his hot dog and licked the mustard off his fingers. "I could go for another of those," he said.

"Me too."

"You sure?"

"Yes."

The stand was about fifty yards away, a white shack under whose eaves a bunch of beachgoers had taken shelter, lumpy and disappointed. My father put on a limp blue gardening hat he found in the back seat, stuck his hands in his pockets, and strolled over almost as if it weren't raining. I couldn't decide whether I admired him or whether he was just a little crazy. He ran back, though; like me, he had a lot of respect for a good hot dog.

"Well, Miss," he said, once we had finished our second round.

"Well, what?"

"Have you ever wished you had a sister?"

I felt choked; he sat staring peaceably over the steering wheel, out at the blue-gray lake. "Is Mom pregnant?" I finally managed.

He chuckled without looking at me. "No."

"I don't get it."

"It was just a thought. A beach thought, now that we're at the beach."

"I don't know," I said, opening the glove compartment and fiddling with his flashlight. "I've got Jeanette and M.J. already. I mean, they're not *sisters*, exactly."

"They're not even related," he said. I knew he thought he was very funny; he deserved to have a flashlight shine right in his eye. That earned me a fishy glance. Rain drummed on the roof of the car. "It looks like all the time off I'm going to get this summer is going to come in a couple of weeks, and I was thinking maybe we could drive out West. I wouldn't want you to grow up believing there's nothing west of Milwaukee."

"Thanks a lot."

"It'd be a hell of a drive, but still."

"You know Mom hates to camp."

"Who said anything about camping?"

I pondered the idea, watching three people in bathing suits run awkwardly from the hot-dog stand to their car. He was right, I was getting bored, but I couldn't imagine going anywhere right then; it wasn't safe. I had a feeling that if I looked away, even for a minute, my friends might slip ahead and leave me still a child.

"In a couple of weeks?"

"More or less."

"Mom's been really busy lately, do you think she'll be able to?"

"I don't know, why don't you ask her about it?"

Because it wasn't my idea in the first place, I wanted to say. He seemed to be thinking about something else altogether, as if he still hadn't said what he came to say. When we drove back I got him to stop at a pay phone so I could call Jeanette, and sure enough she was home. They had put off shopping because of the rain. "You went to the *beach*?"

"Yes. How about if I come over?"

The rain had started to slack off when we pulled up in front of Jeanette's house. "Her mother'll give me a ride home," I said.

"Well, she doesn't have to if she doesn't feel like it. You could always call us."

"Okay." I started to get out.

"Hey, Miss?"

"My name's Karen, Daddy." My right foot was getting rained on.

"Thanks for the outing. It was a great day for the beach."

"Sure it was." I ran up the steps to Jeanette's front porch thinking, My father, and rang the bell. My father what, that was the question.

"But why did you go to the *beach?*" said Jeanette as she opened the door.

"He knows it's totally impractical, that's why he gets you to bring it up instead of doing it himself," my mother said. "You know how he works. What does he think we're going to do, drive all the way to Yellowstone to sleep in a tent?"

"God, I'm sorry I ever mentioned it."

"Don't swear, please."

I left the room. "God."

chapter 4

The central part of the upstairs in Augusta's house was one big open space, with the bedrooms off two of its sides; that was the real living room. It was half surrounded by bookshelves; Augusta had more books, I thought, than any one person could actually need, even if she was a schoolteacher. Row upon row were paperback murder mysteries, which she kept buying, only to discover, sometimes, that she had already read them and knew how the plot came out. I was always in the middle of one of these mysteries, carrying them from room to room and putting them down without noticing where, losing my place, losing track of the plot, wishing the current one would be over with so I could read something better. I kept them in the back pocket of my shorts and sat on them and ruined their spines; Augusta didn't care. "At least they're some use to somebody," she said.

Like a watched pot that wouldn't boil, the humidity remained forever at a simmer, suspending me in a medium that seemed to have an intimate touch. I never went anywhere without feeling the fact of my body, and one afternoon when I was alone on the street a pale face peered from behind a screen and muttered something I didn't quite catch, an invitation perhaps, or nothing more than a suggestion. Maybe I made it up, or the mutter was never intended for me but rather for someone inside that dark room out of the sun.

I took walks until I hardly felt like a stranger anymore; I could follow the progress of other people's gardens. Sometimes I would ride Augusta's bicycle; around dusk, when it began to cool off, was best. Sometimes I would stand in the drugstore for an hour reading magazines that I was embarrassed to buy and take home, like *Mademoiselle* and *Seventeen*. They made me almost unbearably conscious of being a girl. Someone was supposed to fall in love with me, and somehow I had inherited this terribly subtle task of making them do it, letting them do it, telling them to stop . . . exactly what they might do if I didn't stop them was never clear, which gave it a sort of wonder and horror, and I had no idea how I could ever be the cause of something so important.

Nothing I read connected very well with me and Rodge. No one in the magazines ever sat on a sofa in the dark with her shirt unbuttoned and her unhooked bra up around her neck, while her boyfriend's hand worked its way down into her shorts. All the way down. Rodge had to go through the most awkward contortions to get his hand and wrist past my belt, but taking it off was not imaginable. When he finally touched me and brought out of me a sound of pleasure and surprise, he seemed terribly embarrassed, as if I had caught him at something, and he buttoned me up and kissed me profusely and went away, once he had unwound my arm from around his neck, leaving me to stand bewildered and buttoned in the front hall, not knowing why. I had entirely forgotten that my parents might be listening from upstairs. I shuffled back into the living room, hitting my shin on an end table in the dark, and lay down miserably on the sofa across the spot where we had been. My clothes all felt yanked out of place, my lips were sore—had I gone too far? Was that the answer?

You couldn't figure that out by reading *Seventeen*.

Nor could you figure out what I learned one night after the sound of Augusta downstairs woke me up—that I could do for myself some of the things Rodge had done—only better. I wondered if Jeanette and M.J. knew that.

"You know, an idea just occurred to me," Augusta announced late one afternoon. "Are you listening?" We were sitting in the kitchen and I was reading a murder mystery.

I took a gulp of iced tea. "No."

"Don't be a pain, I'm trying to do you a favor. What you ought to do while you're down here is learn how to drive."

I looked at her. "Drive?"

"Is something the matter with you?" In two seconds she would be annoyed.

"But what would I . . ."

"The Buick, silly. There's plenty of places you could learn without smashing into anything."

I had a vision of myself creeping down the streets of New Franklin with the windows rolled up, sweating away and terrified of hitting some kid on a tricycle. "God, that's really— nice, I mean . . . are you sure you want me to do that?"

"Sure, if you wreck the car I'll just wring your neck, that's all." She stood up. "So." It took me a second, even though I knew how Augusta worked, to realize that she was going after her car keys. "Okay?" she said gaily, plucking them from the inside of the cupboard door.

"Do you really want to do this right now?" But I had already put down my book.

"Stop worrying, it's easy. Really."

"It isn't rush hour or anything?"

"Karen . . ."

"Okay."

We marched down the front hall together, and it occurred to me that if I didn't total the Buick I might actually be able to go home knowing how to drive, to stroll out of the house like an adult and put the key in the ignition and go and not tell anybody where. If I could steal a car first. I could just imagine my mother letting me drive the one-year-old Impala she took the customers around in. That would happen the day Lake Michigan filled up with hot chocolate.

The Buick looked much longer than the last time I'd seen it.

"We'll take it over to the high school and you can drive it around the parking lot," Augusta said. She did not roll down the windows.

On the way across town I sweated and watched her, hoping to pick up a few clues before it was too late. Augusta drove in an almost regal way, without effort and gazing straight ahead, and watching her, I began to wonder if perhaps some faculty I didn't know about took over when you got behind the wheel of a car. At least the Buick had automatic.

Quietly we rolled onto the parking lot and stopped. I tried not to pant.

"Well?" she said, agreeably.

"Are you sure this is legal? What if the cops come?"

"Around here everybody knows how to drive by the time they're fourteen. It's no big deal."

We traded places. The driver's door slammed, and it was too late to go back.

"What do I do?"

"Let's see you put your feet on the pedals." That was easy enough. "Move the seat up." Of course; her legs were longer than mine. "There's a button for it on the side of the seat. It's like those things for raising and lowering the windows, just push it forward."

I found it, and the seat glided forward, reminding me of a shrinking room in a horror movie.

"Enough, enough. Now put your hands on the wheel." I did; it seemed bigger around than I had thought. "Can you see okay?"

"I guess so."

"Now. The pedal on the left is the brake and the one on the right is the gas."

"No kidding."

"Look, if you already know how to drive, just say so."

We glared at each other momentarily. "You thought this up," I muttered. I tried the brake with my left foot, avoiding Augusta's eye.

"Don't brake with your left foot," she said.

"How come?"

"Just don't." You're some teacher, I thought. "Now. Don't step on the gas, okay? Take the shift lever and pull it toward you—toward you, that's right—and move it over so it's in Drive."

"Where it says D?"

"Yes." Before she answered I could feel the car engage; the note coming from the engine changed, and inexorably the Buick began to creep forward.

"It's moving," I said, clutching the wheel.

"Step on the brake."

I hit the broad pedal and sent a jolt through the car.

"It's got power brakes, you don't have to press that hard."

Now I was sure I was in trouble—I couldn't even stop without making a mistake. I would have wiped the sweat off my forehead but I was afraid to take my hands off the wheel.

"Now look around you," said Augusta in her teacher-voice. "You've got the whole parking lot in front of you and nobody's here. So all you have to do is take your foot off the brake and very, very gently step on the gas."

I took a deep breath and moved my foot; the Buick started creeping forward again. I rested my toe on the accelerator, pressing as little as I could. Nothing seemed to happen. Maybe I just thought I was pressing. A little more and the engine came to life; an instant later the Buick began to roll, and we were actually driving.

"That's good," Augusta said grimly.

"Now what?"

"Now steer." But the steering wheel didn't feel as if it was connected to anything. Every time I felt myself veering to the left I'd swing too far to the right, and back again; the fence on one side of the parking lot and the wall of the high school on the other felt dangerously close, as if I might hit either one on my next swing.

"It's okay," Augusta was saying, "just don't correct so much, Karen, just take it easy." But I knew she was worried, I knew she shouldn't have trusted the Buick to me, we were both going to regret this, and before anything worse could happen, I hit the brake again, forgetting what it could do. We stopped in a brief, violent screech of tires. Augusta kept her hands on the dashboard, where she had braced herself to keep from hitting her head on the glove compartment. It took me a moment to unclench my fingers from the steering wheel, trying to remember—can I let go? Will it be okay?

"Would you mind if I rolled down the window?" I said.

Augusta exhaled sharply. "No."

There were four switches lined up in a row on the driver's door, and I wasn't sure which to press, so I pushed down on all four. Majestically the windows hummed their way open. Cooler air blew through the car, carrying a slight aroma of burning rubber.

"Well, at least you know how to stop," she said. "Maybe you could kind of lighten up the next time you do it, though." She reached over and moved the shift lever to Park. "You can take your foot off the brake. Now, this time I want you to turn to the left and keep turning until we're heading back the way we came. Maybe that'll be easier than going straight, anyway. You remember how to put it in Drive?"

Obediently I slid the black-knobbed lever over a couple of notches and resigned myself to fate. As we started forward again, I could see that I had painted myself into a corner where the fence met the high school, and I was sure that one or the other would be the end of my driving career.

"Just keep turning," Augusta said. "There's plenty of room."

Whatever you say, I thought, spinning the wheel as far as it would go, and at the same moment hit the gas. The Buick's fat tires sprayed gravel and shot us into a crazy pirouette, tilting and skidding; I tried to correct, to let up, and the wall of the school seemed to bulge in my direction. As hard as before I hit the brake, fully expecting a crunch, the sound of grinding metal and breaking glass, but nothing happened; again we screeched and rocked to a stop. The smoothness of the engine's idle seemed to mock me.

"You know, driving with you is really exciting," Augusta said. "I mean it. Never a dull moment. I have to say, though, that your driving lacks a certain, um, refinement, you know?"

I let myself slump down in the driver's seat and closed my eyes. "You're crazy," I said, starting to giggle.

"That's really very perceptive of you, yes—especially when I think about being in the passenger seat while we drive through a brick wall—"

"I missed, didn't I?"

"You *missed?* God, I hope they never make me teach Driver Ed."

"Make you? They wouldn't let you."

"It's a good thing Cheryl didn't see this," she said, half to herself.

"You're corrupting me again."

"So? There's no fun in being fifteen if somebody doesn't do it. Now, do you want to drive home, or shall I?"

"I think you'd better." Sometimes Augusta still scared me; I wondered if she knew there were limits.

I got out and changed places with her, surprised again to see that there wasn't a scratch on the car, and for a wonder, she didn't roll the windows up all the way home.

"When I was fourteen Cheryl did the same thing to me," Augusta said later on, after dinner. I tried in vain to imagine them, Augusta a kid, probably skinny and awkward, my mother twenty-one, unmarried, not yet my mother. "She'd just graduated from Northwestern and thought she was a really big deal. So did I, for that matter. I was taller than she was, that was about my only claim to fame. Anyway, a week or so after she came home she took it into her head to teach me to drive. We had a Buick then, too—we always had Buicks. Dad had a thing for them. He got a Mercury once, for some reason, but he only kept it two years.

"This Buick was black, and the windows were so high up that Dad used to say you could put a bathtub in the back and take a bath on the street and no one could see you. Cheryl took me out in it and said she was going to teach me to drive. She took me out of town on the road toward Collinsville and told me to try it, which was really dumb, because even then cars went pretty fast on that road and someone was bound to come along. It's just a good thing I was tall, at least I didn't have any trouble seeing over the steering wheel. And don't forget, this one had a stick shift. So Big Sister's going to try to show me how to work the clutch. She couldn't explain it worth a damn. I thought, What's so hard about this? You push it in and then you let it out again, so what?

"Well. So I got behind the wheel and figured out where everything was, and meanwhile every once in a while a car would zoom by. We were kind of halfway off the road because the shoulder wasn't wide enough for the whole car. I finally got the rearview mirror adjusted and seeing those other cars started to make me nervous. Cheryl was telling me to go ahead and let the clutch out, and I was trying to do it slowly, the way she said, and we were just starting to move when a car roared by and honked its horn right in my ear. Startled the hell out of me. I must have taken my foot completely off the clutch, because the car just jumped right into the ditch and stalled. You should have seen the look on Cheryl's face. She bumped her forehead on the doorframe, you could tell it hurt, and besides that, she was scared, and mad at me, when she realized how much trouble she was going to be in.

"She gave me hell. I was the stupidest, clumsiest, most immature, worthless, revolting kid sister in the entire world, and it was all my goddamn fault. The only problem was, it was her fault, and she knew it. So after she finished giving me hell, we got out and walked back to town and got a tow truck to come and pull us out of the ditch. When he asked her what happened, she said she was trying to pull over and just went too far.

"The front fender was a little bent on the right side, and besides, you can't keep anything a secret around here. Dad went to grade school with the guy that owned the garage, for God's sake. You would have thought we tried to burn down the Taj Mahal. Dad was mad enough when he saw the dent, but when he figured out Cheryl had been trying to teach me to drive the Buick without even telling him, he was just speechless. She really got it. 'We thought you were old enough to know what responsibility is'—I remember Mother saying that. She didn't yell, she just said it. They kind of ignored me, it's the advantage of being fourteen. But they kept telling her how disappointed they were in her, until you know what she did?"

"No, what?"

"She went out and sold the watch they gave her for graduation back to the jeweler where they got it and gave them the money to pay for the fender. Everyone was in a wonderful mood after that. She and Dad hardly spoke to each other for a month. But that's the way she was. She just drew a line and said, Okay, that's enough. Only they didn't know it."

Without warning, I was furious myself, miserable with anger, though I couldn't tell if it was at my mother or on her behalf. Nobody said anything for a while, and I remembered how I'd had a party in the eighth grade and she got so angry at me because she heard somebody got kissed. What in the hell was so terrible about that? Was I supposed to do something about it?

Nobody had kissed me, but I wasn't about to tell her that.

"It was really scary," Augusta said, "watching her stay mad

like that. All I could think was, I didn't want to grow up and get that way."

"And?" We inspected each other, wary.

"See for yourself," Augusta said, but I couldn't. Not just yet.

chapter 5

It had been two weeks; I discovered that when my mother called and reminded me that they expected to hear from me now and then. But there didn't seem to be much to talk about—she was selling houses like crazy, trying to get Daddy to cook dinner on the weekends; they had made money off the same people twice because she had sold them a house and Daddy's company had painted it. But how surprising was that? Jeanette had called half a dozen times to ask when I was coming back, a boy had called and hadn't left his name and she thought it was Rodge. That made my heart race even though I didn't more than half believe she was right. She sounded hurt when I said I wasn't sure when I was coming back, but she had been right about sending me there in the first place, so why get mad if I agreed? I knew she and I would still fight, though why we would wasn't clear to me anymore, if Augusta was right and she hadn't minded about Rodge after all.

Only—what if he really had called?

"I'll be back pretty soon, I guess. It's getting really hot down here. Are you and Daddy planning some kind of vacation?"

"Not now."

"Well—I'm glad you called, Mom."

"You could try it yourself some time."

"Right."

"Take it easy on Augusta, okay?"

"Maybe you could tell her to take it easy on me—do you want to talk to her again?" Where was Augusta, anyway?

"No, that's all right."

"Say hi to Daddy for me."

"Of course."

"Bye, Mom."

"Bye-bye, Karen."

I listened to the sound of her hanging up, picturing my mother in her office and the light on the telephone blinking off as she put the receiver down. What was the look on her face?

As always, something hadn't been said. I stood in the kitchen alone, looking around, waiting for New Franklin to come back into focus. Augusta had answered the phone in the first place, but I hadn't noticed when she had wandered off during our conversation. Now I heard her voice from outside. Augusta and someone else, a man. I didn't want to meet anybody right then, but I wandered in their direction anyway, down the front hall, which was always the darkest and coolest part of the house. They were on the porch. I could hear the chains of the porch swing creak, and I stopped where I was, afraid for some reason of them hearing me. They weren't saying anything now. The chains creaked again, and someone's foot scuffed against the porch floor. I was just about to turn around and go back to the kitchen when I heard the man's voice, choked with resentment: "You understand just about everything, don't you?"

His anger stopped me in the dimness, but Augusta was angrier. All she said was "Go away."

"God," the man's voice said with infinite disgust, and I could hear him standing up and walking down the porch steps. I backed away as quietly as I could, toward the kitchen. Just as I reached safety, I heard an engine start up on the street and gravel scratching as he took off. I sat down at the kitchen table and tried to collect myself. Augusta opened the front door, and I had an impulse to run out to the garden or pretend to be taking out the trash, but she went straight upstairs to the bathroom and in a second I could hear water running in the tub. The first thing that crossed my mind was how Augusta had said "Terrible" at the train station when I finally asked her how she was. She did something in the middle of the night. She was crazy enough to let me drive the Buick and to tell me about her old boyfriends and to say she was corrupting me on purpose, and if I had been reading *Lady Chatterley's Lover* or worse, she wouldn't have cared; the books were right there on her shelves. Some fight was going on, so bad she could just say "Go away" to someone's face, and I was living in the middle of it. For a second I thought it was time to go back to Evanston, but I knew I didn't actually want to, and if I wasn't in Evanston or New Franklin, where could I be?

I could hear Augusta sloshing bathwater upstairs, a homey enough sound in itself, but I knew she never took baths—only five-minute showers—and she never stopped working at eleven o'clock in the morning except maybe to drink a glass of iced tea and switch to a different project. Something had to be the matter.

The sloshing stopped, and there were no sounds in the house except the random creaks of old boards and the low muttering of the refrigerator. The day was hot but not unbearable. The sound of a lawn mower swelled up out of the quiet and reminded me of my father, but I didn't know what he could do for me right now. His help didn't always help, anyway. Maybe that was my fault, though—it was hard to tell. Recently he had ̶ ̶ ̶ ̶ deliberate grip when he put his arm around ̶ ̶ ̶ surrounding my shoulder as if he were afraid I ̶ ̶ something; the caution of his touch somehow made ̶ ̶ He liked to tell me to be good to myself, but all I could think in return was, Is that my obligation, too, along with everything else? He probably would do it again if I were to call him now, from Augusta's kitchen—though in fact I wouldn't be able to, because he spent all day driving around from job to job. And what could I say to him, even if I did reach him? If I said I was lonely, which wasn't exactly it, he would just answer, "Come home, then." I didn't want him to figure out that coming home wouldn't help.

The whole apparatus of domestic life that surrounded me suddenly seemed pathetic and thin—if there was anything there to hold on to, it wasn't enough. And out the window the garden looked like more of the same, much as my father and Augusta seemed to love it. Suddenly I couldn't help but think they were clinging to anything they could get. Was that what my mother did, too? And me? Be good to yourself made sense, but how, when I didn't know where to begin?

Augusta had said she had no guts because she didn't sleep with her Jewish boyfriend, but that, like so much she had told me, was easy for her to say. With one look at her I could see that she had courage, and with another I could see I didn't. I would have to get it, and you didn't go to Downtown Market for that.

Outside, the noon whistle blew. I could hear Augusta slosh out of the tub, and then her electric razor. What was she doing? Getting ready for a date?

The thought of Augusta on a date was one to ponder. Whatever he was up to, she was in no hurry to get out of the bathroom. I began to arrange cold cuts and pickles and mayonnaise and bread as I would do any day at lunchtime. Augusta ate remarkable things—sardine sandwiches, pickled peppers, lox in scrambled eggs. She even liked braunschweiger, the bane of my childhood, and would eat it on white bread with mayonnaise squeezing out the sides. There was an old, probably forgotten end of a braunschweiger in the back of the refrigerator, and I placed it on a dinner plate all by itself in front of Augusta's chair.

I was constructing a ham sandwich when she came in barefoot and surprised me. She had a bathrobe on that I'd never seen, a navy-blue thing too big for her; her hair was wound up in a towel on top of her head, and she smelled faintly of perfume. There was red nail polish on her toenails. She didn't look at me, even though I stared, but went straight to the refrigerator and got out a beer. She levered it open with her usual expert flip that propelled the bent cap into the wastebasket by the sink, and took a sip. "Wonderful," she said, her back to me.

"I'm glad to hear it," I said.

She gave me a quizzical look over her shoulder, as if wondering where I came from. Then she sat down with an odd hint of a smile on her face. When she crossed her legs, her gleamingly shaved calf protruding from the bathrobe was as elegant as a model's in a magazine.

"What are your plans for the afternoon?" she asked.

"I don't think I have any."

"Well, I'm sure you can take care of yourself."

"Are you going someplace?"

"Yes." She got up, taking the beer bottle with her, and I heard her marching up the stairs. In three minutes she was in the doorway in a suburban sundress of the sort that anybody else's thirty-five-year-old aunt might wear, but never, in my imagination, Augusta.

"Is there something indecent about this outfit, or what?" she said, after I had stared for a few seconds.

"No, it's just . . ."

"If anybody calls, you can tell them I went out to play tennis." And with that she turned and was gone, down the hall, out the front door; the Buick started and cruised away. As far as I knew, Augusta didn't have a tennis racket to her name.

I ate the sandwich and then, for the first time since I had come to New Franklin, felt at loose ends. Even Lord Peter Wimsey held no attraction for me. I had wished often enough for the privilege of being left alone after a morning of Augusta's projects, but now that I had it, nothing seemed worthwhile.

Aimlessly I wandered upstairs and peered at the pictures on the walls. I didn't like the ones Augusta had put up much more than my grandmother's. But leaning against some Erle Stanley Gardners on a shelf was something worth looking at: a photograph of me and my parents, Augusta, and my grandmother taken four years ago. It was uncomfortable to contemplate myself aged eleven—and, perhaps, everyone else in it. My parents looked younger in the picture, and my grandmother was still alive, and both of those things made me sad; only Augusta looked exactly the same.

The trouble with seeing myself at eleven was that I had looked better then, in a way; if I didn't have a figure, at least I had proportion, I looked all of a piece. The picture made me envious; I felt as if I had grown up as a little girl and then had to start all over from the beginning and grow up again as a woman, and I was sure that would take half my life.

The upstairs was stuffy as well as hot. I wandered into the bathroom to splash cold water on my face and was amazed to see makeup things lying on the rim of the sink—an eyebrow pencil, brand-new mascara, the polish she had put on her toes . . . where did she keep this stuff? I had never seen it before. Even a tiny bottle of perfume: Interdit. I opened it and smelled, passing my nose over it at a slight distance as my mother would do. It was wonderful, but what was in that bottle wasn't Augusta.

Or was it? I felt a way I hadn't felt for years—not since I had been in that picture: I wanted to go through Augusta's dresser drawers, her private things, to spy, to do something shameful. To drag to light something I would wish I didn't know.

I couldn't do that, could I? Before the impulse could take hold I went downstairs, feeling a little sheepish, and lay on the floor of Augusta's study with Lord Peter until I fell asleep.

What woke me was the ringing of an unfamiliar bell. I scrambled up and pushed my hair out of my face. There was the sound of a man clearing his throat, close by. For a panicky moment I didn't realize that it was coming from the porch again; then I hurried into the hall and saw a large dim figure on the other side of the frosted-glass panes in the double front door. The sound, I realized, had come from the old-fashioned crank doorbell which I had never heard anyone use. It seemed to me that strangers had no right invading the private world Augusta and I shared, but I opened the door just as the caller was about to knock.

A middle-aged man in work clothes stood there with his hand raised to tap on the glass and looked at me bewildered; he seemed as uncomfortable as I was, and just as surprised.

"Is Gus here?" he asked.

"Who?"

"Miss Streeter?"

"You mean Augusta? I'm sorry, I didn't—I'm her niece, I'm visiting. She's not home."

"Oh." He looked as though he wanted to get away.

"Shall I"—take a message? You're not on the phone, you idiot, I thought—"tell her something for you?"

"No. It's okay. Sorry to bother you." He turned at once and headed back down the walk to a pickup truck with *Reese Plumbing and Heating* on the side. It took a couple of minutes after he drove away for me to put two and two together. Now I really did know a secret of Augusta's, and I had found it out without even having to spy.

chapter 6

Waiting for Augusta to get home so I could spring my news on her made me too impatient to sit still; finally I decided I might as well cook dinner. Much as I made fun of my father's limited repertoire in the kitchen, fried chicken was about the only thing I could cook, too.

I was putting the chicken into the frying pan when I felt her behind me; the sizzling had drowned out the sound of her coming in. She had her shoes in her hand, but otherwise she still looked as if she were trying out for the part of a suburban matron. I had the impression that the audition was over and it hadn't gone as well as she'd hoped. She leaned in the doorway, watching me; I felt for a moment that I had offended her somehow by cooking dinner, and froze with a drumstick in my hand suspended above the skillet. Fat popped on me and burned my wrist; I jumped back, grabbing a dish towel from the back of a chair to wipe it off. By the time I looked around, Augusta was gone again, and her footsteps were mounting the back stairs. "Smells good," she called down to me.

"Jerry came to see you," I called back.

She stopped. I listened, still holding the floured drumstick.

"Great," I heard her mutter; then, aloud: "And what did *he* have to say?"

"Nothing, he just wanted to see you."

"What did you tell him?"

"Nothing."

"Good." She kept going, up the stairs and into her room, and shut the door. That certainly hadn't been half as much fun as I had expected. For a moment I felt like somebody's ignored wife. "Slaving away over a hot stove"—that was the line, wasn't it? My mother would never say that, though; her idol was Harry Truman, and her line was "If you can't stand the heat, get out of the kitchen." A nice friendly thought to come home to.

Warily, I fitted the rest of the chicken into the pan and waited for Augusta to come downstairs. My thoughts kept going back to Jerry and the thought of her being in love with him when she was seventeen. I kept reminding myself that he was a lot younger then, too; I couldn't get over how much older than Augusta he seemed. His hair was graying, and he had dirt on his coveralls and beat-up-looking hands. It was impossible to imagine him eighteen, or to picture Augusta kissing him. I didn't want to picture anything else.

He seemed nice enough, though. I turned down the fire under the chicken.

Augusta came in wearing cutoffs and sneakers and her favorite top, a blue cowboy shirt with mother-of-pearl snaps. Her hair looked beautiful against it. "How was your tennis game?" I asked.

"Excellent," she said with such finality that I didn't dare pursue the subject. She sat down and unfolded the *Post-Dispatch*. "I'm glad you decided to make dinner, I really didn't feel like cooking tonight." Did I detect the message that it was about time? "Just tell me if there's anything you want me to do," she said absently, reading.

Wait a minute, I thought, I'm not in charge here, who's kidding who? Nevertheless, I searched the vegetable bin for something to make into a salad, feeling for a moment the way I thought my mother must feel when my father sat in the kitchen reading the paper and waiting for dinner to be ready. The joke was on him this summer.

Wasn't she going to say *anything*? Well, it was none of my damn business.

"There are some frozen peas if you want to have them," she observed, turning to the sports page.

I got out the peas. Two can play that game, I thought, picking up part of the paper. If Augusta noticed me fuming she didn't give any sign.

If I hadn't already felt sufficiently put in my place, eating my own cooking would have done it, even though Augusta dutifully praised the chicken. Neither of us said much during dinner. The air turned cooler as we were eating, and the curtains started to sweep inward on gusts from the west. Rain was on the way; when I finished I went upstairs and closed the windows, leaving a crack under each one for the precious coolness to find its way in.

When I came back down she poured me a glass of wine; she had one in front of her already.

"So Jerry came back, did he?"

I nodded. So he had been the man on the porch the first time, too. What in the world was she so mad at him about? But apparently I wasn't going to find out. Augusta made the wine in her glass slosh in a circle, almost over the rim.

"A few years ago," she said. Then she looked straight at me for the first time since she had come home. "Aren't you tired of hearing my stories?"

"No." I took a sip of my wine. I was learning to like the stuff, not just to drink it because it made me look grown up.

"A few years ago," Augusta said, "I did something extremely foolish." She thought for a moment, where to begin. "Jerry wanted me to marry him, but . . . I didn't. That's not what I'm talking about, though. In fact, that wasn't a mistake at all." She stopped again. He and Augusta married? It was unthinkable. For some time now my mother had been asking no one in particular why Augusta didn't get married, but did she actually expect her to say yes to Jerry?

"Cheryl thought I was nuts not to marry him," she said, giving me chills as she did every time she read my mind. "But that's her problem. She's always thought of herself as my second mother. Even after I left home. She was the one who put the hex on me and Allan, really. The rest of my friends and his could all have gone to hell as far as I was concerned, but she couldn't get used to the idea. 'I've got nothing against Jews,' she kept saying, 'but you're asking for a world of trouble.' That was much more than Mother ever said. I kept wondering if she was Mother's mouthpiece, but I guess she wasn't, she always had plenty of opinions of her own. What finally did it was, I invited him home for Thanksgiving. His family lived in Washington, D.C., and he couldn't afford to go home. Cheryl got here a day ahead and cooked the dinner, and you know what she put on that table in there? A ham. It was the only time I can remember that we've had anything but turkey on Thanksgiving." She picked up the salt shaker, inspected it, knocked it against the table to dislodge the grains of salt that were caked by humidity in its holes.

"What did he do?"

"He took a piece when she offered it to him, and then he sat there and looked at it. Then he looked around at us. He had a great deal of pride, Allan did. I told him he didn't have to eat it, and he said he knew that. My father started to say something, trying to pass it off as a misunderstanding, I guess, but Allan interrupted him—politely—and excused himself from the table. I went too.

"He tried to get me to go back and join them, but I wouldn't, so we both left the house. I don't think they expected it—I could hear everyone arguing in whispers in the dining room—but when he picked up his coat, I grabbed mine too, and we left before anyone could say anything else to us. I'll never forget seeing them in the dining room from the sidewalk: my father was looking over his shoulder at the front hall, Cheryl was trying to see us out the window, my mother was getting up out of her chair. We had sort of pinkish wallpaper in those days. The dining room and the parlor were all lit up like one of those dioramas in the Museum of Natural History—well, you can imagine it. I'd have lit a match to the whole thing in a second. Mother came to the door and called, but I said I couldn't stay, and we kept going.

"Neither of us felt much like Thanksgiving after that; we went to Litzsinger's and drank coffee, and he kept telling me to go back home. I wouldn't do it, I said I couldn't face them. He said I had to face them, they were my family, but finally we both caught the Greyhound and went back to Champaign. It took most of the night; we kind of slept on each other's shoulders, and it was the only night we had ever spent together. I've never been so unhappy in my whole life. When we finally got there, I asked him if we couldn't go to his apartment and go to bed together, and he said no, because he said I had too much to prove. He was just as much in love with me as I was with him, but he had his pride. I don't know what the hell I had. My parents called about ten minutes after I got back to my room. They were frantic. 'Tell

Cheryl to call me,' I said, and hung up. That was one thing she didn't have the nerve to do."

Augusta leaned back in her chair and looked up at the ceiling. "It must have been something bringing the two of us up."

I could only glance at her, wanting to avoid her eyes, torn between the need to hear and the need not to.

"We didn't write each other or anything for six months. Then I got a note from her one day that said, 'I went too far.' That was it. She never really did say she was sorry. I think Dad and Mother gave her unholy hell for what she'd done. They didn't really understand it until it was too late, you know; they lived all their lives in this town, what did they know about being Jewish?"

What did I know about my mother, that was a lot more pressing question to me.

"Maybe Cheryl didn't quite understand it herself," Augusta said after a moment, but I could tell she was only trying to be fair. "Maybe she thought she was being subtle. I really don't know."

She looked me over until I had to meet her eyes; Augusta semed tireder than I had ever seen her. "I'm sorry," she said. "I didn't mean to tell you all that. That wasn't even what I started out to talk about."

She seemed to be waiting for some particular response, but I didn't know what to say. "It's all right," I managed finally.

"I really—I'm sorry. I shouldn't burden you with stuff like this about your mother."

"She's your sister," I said, annoyed at the idea that I couldn't take care of myself. In a way I just wanted her to keep quiet so I could think. Did you have to forgive people no matter what they did?

"Okay," Augusta said. For a minute or two we sat silent, lost in our own thoughts.

"The angel passed over," Augusta said.

"What?"

"The angel passed over. That's what happens when everyone stops talking at once. And see? It's almost twenty after. Usually it happens at twenty after or twenty of."

"You're really strange, you know that?" I said.

"What I was thinking of was something totally different."

"The extremely foolish thing?"

"That, yes. Do you like hearing about other people's mistakes?"

"They're more fun than my own, anyway."

"You haven't even made any yet, you're too young. You see? Only an incredibly juvenile person would stick out her tongue like that."

"So what was the big grown-up mistake?"

"Having an affair with a married man."

I was shocked, and before I could collect myself, I knew it showed on my face. Finally I understood. Augusta was nervous, afraid of what I might think of her. Mostly I was embarrassed for her, and I realized at last how much she needed someone to talk to, that maybe she had invited me down just for this. Maybe I was doing the favor and not the other way around; but how could I help anyone when I couldn't even figure out what to do with myself? It was too soon, I wanted to tell her, but I had my pride, too, and I couldn't.

"I imagine you weren't expecting that." She sounded halfway defiant and apologetic.

"No." To me adultery seemed like VD or drinking liquor in

the morning, a terrible confession that surely nobody connected to me would ever have to make.

"Well, I wasn't either, it just happened. You think you know exactly what's right and what's wrong until something happens to you instead of to somebody else. There's no controlling who you're attracted to, you know, it's just . . . passion, it's a force all by itself. The Greeks made a god out of it, don't forget. Do you have any idea what I'm talking about?"

"I'm not sure," I said, thinking of me and Rodge, but it was more the word I wasn't sure about than the way I had felt. Passion seemed too big for me, like wearing my mother's high heels when I was ten years old.

"He was the father of a kid I taught—this man, Jim—that's how I met him originally. It was right after I didn't get married. He came to parents' night without his wife. She was sick or something. He had a son in my class who never said much, kind of a moody kid. I remember he had a habit of biting his pencils until they were nothing but teeth marks all the way up to the eraser. I used to wonder if the paint wouldn't do something to his brain. It was obvious Jim was worried about him, and he cornered me right away and started asking me to tell him what the matter was; in fact, he acted as though I knew the answer and I was going to tell him whether I wanted to or not. I didn't know, of course. There were too many kids in the class and his son never caused any trouble, so the truth was, I didn't think about him much. You don't tell that to someone's father on parents' night, though. Jim was so . . . earnest. He wouldn't let me out of the corner. His son came into the room and I felt uncomfortable, but I didn't know why exactly, I just didn't want him to see his father and me talking that way. Jim had his back to him and he was in the middle of saying something; he saw me trying to get away and put his hand on my shoulder—that made me even more uncomfortable.

" 'Kevin's right behind you,' I said. He looked so guilty he almost jumped, and for a second I felt we'd both been caught at something, but I didn't get it, not right away. You don't want to get something like that, it's too confusing."

I was trying to do arithmetic in my head: Augusta taught the ninth grade, and if Jim had a son in ninth grade a few years ago, how old must Jim have been, how much older than Augusta? That was the kind of problem I always had trouble with—and I couldn't even remember if Augusta had always taught ninth grade or if she changed from year to year.

"If he hadn't come back for a conference nothing would ever have happened. He called me up and made an appointment. I didn't want to see him, but you have to, it's part of the job. It was a cold day and it had been raining all week and I was tired. The kids had been in a bad mood for days. I was sitting in the empty classroom trying to think of what I was going to tell him when he tapped on the door. I hadn't even heard him coming down the hall.

"He seemed like a different person, much quieter, not so ferocious. He didn't seem as if he was going to browbeat me into submission this time. He wasn't even very anxious to talk at first. There was that funny feeling you get in classrooms after school hours, kind of lonely and sad, especially on a rainy day like that. In a way it's like breaking a rule just to be there. I I didn't know what to say to him; he wouldn't sit down, he kept wandering around the room with his hands behind his back, looking at the pieces of artwork I had tacked up on the walls. Finally I said to him, 'Look, I'm sorry, but I don't think I can tell you much more about Kevin than I could a couple of weeks ago.'

"That didn't seem to bother him. He started to talk and it seemed as though he couldn't stop, about how he and Kevin hadn't gotten along recently, all the little things Kevin did at home that had Jim worried. He knew the kid was unhappy and he had no idea what to do except tell somebody. Might as well be me. I was the kid's teacher, and everyone knows teachers take care of just about everything. After a while I didn't really listen. He was in pain, that was clear enough. If you don't exactly listen to people's words, sometimes you can hear them saying the same thing over and over by the tone of their voice.

"When he stopped talking, I said, 'You're angry, aren't you?' He looked at me as if I had landed from Mars, and for a minute I thought, Now you've done it. Then he said, 'I'm so mad sometimes I want to punch people in the nose just for walking down the same sidewalk as me.' But he said it so quietly you would have thought he was talking about someone else.

"He sat down on top of one of the desks—he was too big to fit into the chairs—and we both didn't say anything for a minute. It was still raining, and if the second hand on the clock had stopped moving I wouldn't have been surprised. There wasn't a sound except the rain. Then he said, 'I guess I'd better go.'

"He stood up, and I stood up from behind my desk. I took my coat off the coatrack and turned out the lights. When I turned toward the door he was in front of me—he seemed to be able to move around without making any noise—and he put his hand on my shoulder again, but this time he was doing it on purpose and we both knew that. He didn't leave it there long, but I didn't have any doubts. You think after a while that you're old enough to know the score and not get rattled by anything, but it's not true. When he took his hand away I saw the wedding ring on it and thought, Thanks a lot. I wanted to get mad at him and tell him off, but I couldn't. He didn't give me a chance, anyway; he thanked me for the conference and shook my hand and left.

"I watched him go out to his car in the parking lot through the rain and began thinking that maybe I was making things up. He did look back, though; I don't know if he saw me or not, but he wanted to. I couldn't forget that—the way he looked out there —even though I tried."

Augusta had finished her glass of wine during the telling of this, and now she poured herself another.

"I did try. It's important to remember that," she said. I thought that she was no longer talking to me at all, had not been for some minutes now, but rather to someone she would probably never address, or to whom she could never say these words. They sounded as if she had said them a hundred times in her head. Perhaps that was what she did in the middle of the night.

"It was impossible, though. It stuck, that moment did—that and him putting his hand on my shoulder. I would find myself thinking about those two things in turn, first one and then the other. It's not easy to be honest with yourself, but if you are, sometimes you find out that you know exactly what's going on. I didn't want to, but . . . it was a fact, we were going to see each other again somewhere, we were going to be attracted to each other, we were going to do something about it—I knew it just as if he'd called me up and asked me to meet him.

"I was nervous all the time, I jumped on the kids in my class for the slightest infraction. I felt I'd had a warning that everything was going to change for me, and it could happen at any time, just like that, and I didn't have a choice. Since when was I fantasizing about someone else's husband? Everybody knows you're not supposed to do that, you just *don't* do it, it's not thinkable. Decent people don't let themselves feel that way, so they say. How can you let yourself or not let yourself feel some way, I'd like to know. If anybody had ever explained to me how that was done, it would have made my life a lot simpler, right from the start. But no one ever tells you that, they just try to scare it out of you.

"There's plenty to be afraid of in a town like this, you know. I'm surrounded by people who knew me when I was ten; there's no escape, ever. I knew it would be that way when I moved here, and I almost didn't, for just that reason. But home is home. The alternative is worse. You reach a certain point, and you think—" She paused, seeming to weigh too many possibilities at once. "Well, you think, at least I can be at home.

"Cheryl didn't think much of that idea either, but, you know, she looks at a house and sees real estate. It's her business, I don't blame her. It's falling apart, the roof needs fixing, so what, nobody notices that. I've kept it going." There was a grimness about her jawline that defied me to say otherwise. "You have to, you know. You don't suppose I like driving around with the windows rolled up, do you? But Dad and Mother used to, and I don't want anyone to know what I can and can't afford. In a place like this you never give away an advantage. It's just a good thing I teach in Collinsville and not here. I think that would have driven me crazy. And at least Jim didn't live here. But people find out everything eventually."

It occurred to me that this had only been a few years ago, and that if Augusta was right, then everyone still knew, and Jim himself perhaps still lived somewhere nearby—his kid still went to her school. How did she stand it, I wondered.

"He did call me, finally. Asked me if he could talk to me after school someday. He didn't say it was about his son, or anything else, for that matter. When he came I didn't know what to say, but I knew I had been right about what was happening the second he walked in. I had to say something, so I asked him what he did. He has a store, sort of like Dad's was. He was telling me about it, stumbling over his words, and I was sitting behind the desk staring at him—we must have looked like lunatics. I was listening as hard as I could for any sounds from the hall, because I was scared to death someone else might be in the building and find us. He ran out of something to say—I couldn't pay attention anyhow—and I thought to myself, Augusta, if God knows what's in your heart, it's already too late. So I got up and walked over to him, stood right in front of him. I looked him in the eye and held still. That's all you have to do, you know. And he got the message right away."

chapter 7

Augusta didn't look at me as she went on. "It wasn't easy. The first thing he said after he had kissed me for a while was that he had never been unfaithful to his wife before. I said I'd never helped anyone be, either; it was almost as if we were having a fight. But we knew what we were going to do.

"For days I did what you're supposed to. I made an effort. I thought about how it was wrong to do this to his wife—I had actually met her once at the beginning of the school year. She didn't deserve this. If he would do it, he must be a crumb. I didn't deserve it myself, I was going to get hurt, hate myself—whatever you can say to yourself I said. Nothing worked. You can't argue desire away.

"The first time, we didn't have any excuses cooked up, or any story to tell anybody, but I don't think anyone noticed. He met me here when I came home from school. The only time I've ever locked the front door is when we've been here together."

The angel passed over again, but it was not twenty of or twenty after. Outside, it had begun to rain, not hard, but as if it might go on all night.

"We said we wouldn't be lovers again after the first time. But it didn't work. Anyone could have predicted that, except maybe me. Doing something like this teaches you what you're made of. How far you'll go. I'm not a nice person, you know. And desire isn't nice, either; it's unscrupulous and selfish, and it won't let go. You don't want somebody because it's a good *idea*, and you don't not want them because it's a bad one. And it wasn't a case of the grass being greener on the other side, either. Those are just words. The truth is, people don't know how to say what they want or even what the hell it is."

From the depths of my ignorance and inexperience I could testify to that, and I thought despairingly, Doesn't it ever change?

"Seems to me I said I wouldn't give you any advice when you came out here. I guess I lied."

"I won't give *you* any, I promise," I said. She favored me with a wan smile.

"Want some wine?" she said, surprising me.

"No, thanks."

She poured what was left of the bottle into her glass. "Cheryl doesn't know about this," she said, looking me in the eye to make sure I paid attention. "I don't suppose it would do much for her view of my illustrious life, so perhaps she shouldn't find out." I wondered if I'd be able to keep the secret, or if I wanted to be in a kind of complicity with something so clearly taboo.

"*She* might not think so," Augusta said in a new tone, "but Cheryl and I are actually very similar people in some ways, no matter what it may look like. That's the real reason she wouldn't like hearing about this. Too close to home. For one thing, we're both selfish. Me more than her, though. She got married, after all, she brought you up, that's more than I can say for myself."

For once I felt myself withdrawing from Augusta altogether. My mother and I might not be getting along, but I didn't want to hear someone else pass judgment, especially someone who had affairs with married men. Even the stories Augusta had told me—even the one about Allan and the ham—my mother might have been wrong, but she had done it for Augusta's sake, hadn't she?

"Now I've done it," Augusta said, looking me over. "I knew my mouth would get me in trouble eventually. I'm sorry, okay?"

I could see on her face that she didn't take back a thing she had said, and anger flared up inside me. "How come *you're* so special?" I muttered before I could stop myself.

She turned directly toward me and looked me in the eye like an enemy. "Maybe I'm not. But I'll tell you one thing, I've lived over twice as long as you have. Things are not anywhere near as black and white as you think, you'll find that out someday if you have the nerve to pay attention."

"What do you think I've been doing ever since I got here except listen to you talk?"

"That can be remedied easily enough," she said, staring at me in a way that made the back of my neck prickle.

"You bitch," I said, and ran. In a second I was up the stairs. I barely restrained the urge to run into my room and slam the door hard enough to knock the pictures off the walls. Instead I stood in the dark upstairs living room, leaning on the big table and panting—furious and scared at what I had done. You bitch, I thought (it was a word I had never used out loud before in my life), I . . . but I didn't hate her, and what was worst was that what she had said was maybe nothing more than the truth.

At least it was the truth about how much I didn't know. I stood there in the dimness, surrounded by the sound of rain, and asked myself if my mother was a selfish person, if Augusta was, if I was. Just posing the question made me feel guilty. God knew that I was full of faults. I had made my confession to Him often enough, along with the rest of the congregation, in a half-hearted Episcopalian way that I wasn't sure I believed in. I wasn't even sure who we were telling our shortcomings to, God or the rector, Mr. Mellender, a nice man who, when he wasn't in his robes, sometimes came over and had a drink with my parents. But I was convinced of one thing: it took more than Mr. Mellender's absolution to make my imperfections go away. Whoever else might be selfish, I certainly was; the only person whose happiness I ever thought about was me, or so it seemed at that moment. Even Augusta, who talked as if she was proud of being selfish, had put herself out for me, and now I wondered what I had done to deserve such treatment. When things got too serious, I called her a name and stormed up the stairs. The worst thing in the world was catching myself acting juvenile, and here I was doing it.

To calm myself down I went into the bathroom and brushed my hair, which was too long and incorrigibly kinked. Sun had lightened it in a way that only made it look more brassy than ever, and my freckles were so brown they almost seemed to bulge out from my face. I looked about twelve years old. At least it would keep me from feeling high and mighty.

I took a deep breath and descended the back stairs, much more slowly than I had come up. There was no sound from below. I tried in vain to think what I would say. But when I reached the bottom of the stairs I saw that the kitchen was empty. Perhaps she wanted nothing more to do with me. I turned the other way and opened the door to the dining room, which was dark; past it, in the parlor, Augusta sat with her back to me in the heavy armchair that had always been her father's special privilege. She did not seem to be reading, or doing anything, and I was afraid to disturb her. I closed the door again. Back in the kitchen, I put away the leftovers (my leftovers, though cooking them seemed a long time ago), stacked the dirty dishes in the dishpan, ran water to get it hot. Impulsively, before I squeezed the detergent in, I reached over and turned the radio on as Augusta would have done, knowing it would be tuned to the ball game. It was the only apology I could think of.

After what Augusta had told me that evening I could understand at least one of the charms of baseball: it wasn't personal. To my surprise I found myself paying attention, hoping that the Cardinals would get a hit; I had never cared about baseball in Chicago. I wiped all the dishes dry—something we never did—and kept on listening until I had put them all away and wiped off the table and the stove. Then there was nothing left to do. I had heard nothing from Augusta. I turned the radio off, and the house was perfectly quiet. Once again I opened the door to the dining room, but she was not there.

I wandered upstairs, afraid of finding her but unable not to look, and then came down, through the study and the back sitting room that no one ever used. It appeared that I had the house to myself. I struck a sour note on the old piano that no one had played since my grandmother died. Idly I opened the door to the tiny conservatory and turned on its one unshaded light bulb.

What was in those boxes, anyway? The first one I opened was nothing but the Christmas ornaments I had expected. I remembered some of them, especially the wooden figures of deer and the Magi that I had always wanted to take home with me as a child. I wondered if Augusta bothered to decorate, all alone in this house. Sometimes any departure from tradition seemed to her a kind of treason, and at other times . . . but I didn't want to think about what she had told me if I could help it.

I opened another box, heavier than the first. It was filled with letters, jam-packed with torn-open envelopes wedged so tight it would have been hard to stuff another one in. I pulled one up at random and saw my mother's handwriting. "Dear Guster," the letter began, but I couldn't go on, didn't want to know whatever I might find out. Yet if that was so, why couldn't I stop prying? I sat down on the dusty floor and pulled out handfuls of letters, all addressed to Augusta in handwritings I did and didn't know. They seemed to be in no special order; the postmarks, when I could read them, leapt from year to year and even from decade to decade: some of the letters had come from the very house they were now in and been mailed to Augusta in college. The sight and feel of all those letters was oppressive when I thought of how many live moments were trapped there where probably no one, not even Augusta, would ever read them again. How complicated she must be after all of this, and all that it represented, had gone into making her. I couldn't see how anyone else could ever know all that or understand it, and the thought made her seem terribly alone.

Suddenly I saw myself surrounded by Augusta's letters on the conservatory floor and panicked, remembering that I didn't know where she was or when she might come in. It was incredible what childish things I did as soon as I was left alone. As fast as I could, I jammed the letters back in their box, dusted myself off, turned out the light, and closed the door. Only when everything was as usual could I breathe.

To keep myself out of trouble I went out on the front porch and sat in the swing. It was still raining lightly, a fine filtering down that Augusta or my father would be sure to say was ideal for the garden. An evening to sit under the porch's broad roof, where one could last out a thunderstorm if the wind didn't blow the wrong way, and swing creaking toward the world out front and then away again, over and over. Perhaps she had sat there with her lover. But not if it had to be kept a secret. Though it was dark on the porch, and possibly on a night such as this . . . I wondered what it would be like to sit kissing someone on that swing with that whole empty house behind me, and then eventually go in with him and—go upstairs.

A couple of years before, I had spent several weeks, or so I seemed to recall, lying on my bed one summer trying to figure out sex, trying to put falling in love with someone into the same category as taking my clothes off and letting him see me naked, or, worse yet, seeing him—and whatever happened then. The pictures wouldn't fit, and thinking wouldn't make them fit or take the embarrassment away, and yet somehow I got used to the idea, if only in theory. It was a good deal closer now, but I remembered the discomfort of first imagining it. This can't be what *I* am going to do, not *me*. But somehow it had taken hold of Augusta and made her do something she knew was wrong. I could halfway understand that, so far and then no farther, as if I were reading a book and turned a page only to find the rest of the volume blank.

A woman without an umbrella, wearing a floppy wide-brimmed hat, was coming down the street, and when she walked under the streetlight I saw it was Augusta. I thought of escape, but it was too late. She turned up the front walk and didn't seem surprised to see me sitting in the swing. Without speaking, she took off her hat and sat down next to me, and we swung. The swinging seemed to take the place of what I didn't know how to say.

Her sneakers and the cuffs of her pants were soaked; she must have been walking for a long time. I didn't know how to feel about her; the day seemed to have made me closer to her than I wanted to be. I couldn't get out the words "I'm sorry."

After a while she said quietly, "How are you?"

"I'm okay." We didn't look at each other. The Buick was parked in front of the house, and perhaps our gazes met there.

"I didn't really intend to tell you all that, earlier."

We swung forward, and I stretched out my toe to touch the porch railing. "You didn't?"

Augusta pushed off, her sneaker squeaking against the floorboards, and we swung slightly crooked. I tried to compensate by giving a push on my side.

"Well. Maybe I shouldn't have."

"It's all right."

In the distance I could hear a train just beginning to come our way. "I'm sorry I blew up," I said.

Augusta stretched her arms up over her head and with a sigh let them down onto the back of the swing, her left arm behind me and resting lightly against the back of my neck. To my left her strong hand gripped the chain. "Maybe we should stop apologizing," she said, and we sat that way while the train blew its whistle for the first time, and the dinging of the crossing signals started, and through the whole long rise and fall of its going by.

I slept late the next morning; it was almost ten o'clock when I opened my eyes. I pulled on my cutoffs and an old shirt of Augusta's I had been gardening in, grabbed my sneakers, and hurried downstairs, hearing hammering coming from outside. From the kitchen I could see Augusta prowling around the ancient gazebo with a hammer in her hand and nails protruding from between her lips, trying to tack together its latticework of old slats. It seemed a futile undertaking, and as I sat lacing up my shoes, I realized I didn't feel obliged to join her in it. Whatever else might come of the night before, it had left the terms of our summer permanently changed. I sat down at the kitchen table with a cup of coffee and a piece of toast, and slid off into the world of Lord Peter, but after a couple of chapters I was afraid that I might read the whole book and use it up right then if I didn't stop, so I made myself close it and get up. It was nearly eleven. I didn't care if I had been brought up to go out in the back yard and help Augusta; I gave my hair a couple of swipes with a brush and left the house by the front, turning away from the side of the yard that she was on.

A perfectly innocent occupation, wasn't it, taking a walk?

A couple of blocks from the house I saw that two girls and a boy, about my age, were coming down the street toward me, watching me in a way that pulled me out of my reverie. I had been watched that way while I read magazines in the drugstore. And several times a boy about eighteen, with the muscles of someone who did serious labor, had stared at me as he passed me in his car. I had hardly spoken to a soul except Augusta since I had come down, and I hoped I hadn't forgotten how, because I could see that these three were getting ready to talk to me.

"Hi," one of the girls said when they got within range.

"Hi," I said. We stopped about six feet apart.

"Who are you, anyway?" she said. I could see her turn a little pink at her own rudeness.

"I'm Karen Moss, I'm Augusta—Miss Streeter's—niece. You know, she lives on Washington?"

They gave each other meaningful looks whose meaning I didn't know. "Where are you from?"

"Evanston."

"Where's that?"

"Near Chicago."

"Oh."

The two girls were wearing proper blouses with page-boy collars, and their hair was wavy and short—shorter than mine and much less frizzy. The more I thought about what I was wearing, the more uncomfortable their inspection made me, and I couldn't think of anything to say.

"What church are you?" the other girl said. I'd been taught never to ask that straight out, but she didn't sound as if she thought it was impolite.

"Episcopal, actually."

She looked disappointed. "If you were Methodist you could go to youth group," she said. "If you're going to be visiting for a while."

"I don't know how long I'm going to stay, but . . ." I couldn't thank them for inviting me, since after all they hadn't.

"I'm Jeannie Holzman," the first girl said, "and that's Doreen Schatz, and that's my brother Joe." She said the last with a kind of he-can't-help-it look on her face that made me feel for a second she was actually trying to be friendly. Joe, who had been staring at me the entire time, looked up at the sky glumly. "Tell your aunt my mom said hello," she added. "Mrs. Holzman, okay?"

"Okay." She hadn't given me a chance to say How do you do, and now I felt rude myself. There was an intensely awkward moment.

"Well, see you later," she said, with a gesture of her head that would have been tossing her hair back except it was too short to toss.

"See you later," I mumbled, relieved. Then they were behind

me and I was continuing down the sidewalk, but I heard one word from Jeannie Holzman, pronounced just loud enough for me to hear: "snob."

That hurt, and it was wrong—I was no snob—was I? I didn't know what to *say*, I protested inwardly, but nothing could cure the sinking feeling that I had been tested and failed. I withered under the memory of their eyes, realizing that to them I was probably outrageous, with my weird hair and my cutoffs and my paint-spattered work shirt tied in a knot around my waist. Suddenly I knew what the boys thought, why the older one in the car stared at me: they thought I was loose. Jeannie Holzman and her little friend would boast that they had talked to me as if it were a racy encounter with someone outside the law. Now I remembered things I had almost managed to ignore—a suspicion that one day when I left the drugstore with an Eskimo Pie, what the girl behind the counter muttered to a boy, what he snickered at lewdly, was a remark about me. Things I should have realized you could ignore only at your own risk. Too late. To think that I had believed I was invisible, that the advantage was mine. Maybe that was what came of being an only child, or of being alone with Augusta, or maybe I really was a snob and didn't know it. And instead of being invisible I had been exposed all along, with no place to hide.

All the New Franklin women I had seen finally registered, and I could see not only how I looked next to them but how Augusta did: her hair was too long and too straight, and no woman of her age, even if she had that gorgeous hair, would ever wear it down, or be seen in town in blue jeans and mannish shirts, or wear socks instead of nylons. And that was the least of it; what was really wrong was the look in her eye, lonely and defiant. Fierce—but with no one to back her up, and she knew it.

"People find out everything eventually"—that was what she had said, and I could only suppose she knew. A losing battle, or maybe a battle already lost, if the town knew about her and Jim. The thought made me writhe.

chapter 8

All I wanted to to do now was get home and stay there, and I thought I understood why Augusta hadn't made any effort to help me meet the kids my age in the town. Perhaps she wouldn't even have been able to. She belonged to the Presbyterian church, I knew that, but I hadn't seen her go to it, and as far as I could tell, there was no other way into the life of the town. My name had appeared in the *Advertiser* as Augusta's visitor, and everyone knew whose relative I was, but that was all the notice New Franklin seemed inclined to take of me—except for stopping me on the street and calling me a snob because I didn't know anyone.

I cut across the yard instead of going through the house, past the weedy, overgrown grape arbor, which needed more than a little tending, and sat down on the steps of the back porch. Augusta was still hammering, now from the inside of the gazebo. New nail heads sparkled in the sun against the peeling yellow paint like random improbable sequins; each time the gazebo shook under the blows of Augusta's hammer, they glinted especially brightly.

After a while she came out, mopping sweat from her forehead. "What's up with you?" she said. Something about her tone

confirmed that there had been a change between us, some cere-
mony stripped away.

"Nothing. I went out and took a walk."

"Anything interesting going on out there?"

"No."

She examined me: uncooperative teenager. "Hmh. Well." She
pulled a few finishing nails out of the back pocket of her jeans
and put them back in the box. "Want to eat some lunch?"

"In a little while."

"Suit yourself," she said. To my surprise she ran a hand
through my hair as she passed me; I looked around, but Augusta
didn't. She put her hat and the hammer and nails on top of the
old chest of drawers on the back porch where she kept all the
tools, and went inside. The back of her neck looked as regal as
ever. I wanted something from her but I wasn't sure what.

"Hey, Karen? Your father called," she said from inside. "I just
remembered. I told him you were asleep, but I guess you weren't."

"He did? Is anything the matter?"

"I don't think so. He didn't say, if there was. I wrote down a
number he gave me, said he'd be there all day."

That was not like my father. Why bother to call me up while
he was working? And leave a number for me to call him back?

"Well, it must be something," I said, coming into the shade
and relative cool of the kitchen. "I guess I'd better call him up."

"Here." She handed me an old gas-bill envelope with a number
written on it. "Sure you don't want some lunch first?" She was
making a sardine sandwich.

"No, thanks."

"You can use the phone in my room, if you want."

I had not set foot in Augusta's bedroom all summer, and now
entering it was almost spooky. I knew too much about what had

gone on there, when the door was locked concealing her and Jim—knew too much and not enough, some words for what had happened, polite and impolite, but when I looked at the carefully made bed with my grandmother's old spread pulled taut at all four corners, I couldn't imagine it after all. What came to mind was a steamy paperback that M.J. passed me in school one day with a page folded down about "tender pressures" and "glowing oblivion," but that didn't help much. What had happened to Augusta sounded stranger and harsher than that, almost ruthless.

The shades were drawn and the shutters outside them closed; even midday sun hardly penetrated. In the dimness and quiet I sat down on the bed and dialed the phone on the night table.

"Hello?" a strange man's voice said impatiently over some noise in the background.

"Hello, is Mr. Moss there?"

"Hold on." It sounded like saws; I could hear some faint yells, unintelligible, then footsteps.

"Hello, this is Steve Moss," my father said.

"Hi, Daddy, it's Karen."

"Hi, sweetie—hold on, let me close the door." He put down the phone with a clank; quickly I got up, too, and closed the door of Augusta's room. I lay back on the bed, phone against my ear. The background noise had subsided. "Hello, Miss Moss," he said.

"Please." I tried to sound disgusted.

"How are you?"

"Hot. I'm fine, I guess. How are you?"

"Oh, I'm okay. We're painting a big apartment building, and they're putting up another one next door, so everything's a little crazy. How's your visit going?"

What was I supposed to say? "Fine." There was an unsatisfied silence from the other end. "We've been very busy; you'd be proud of me, I've been scraping paint off shutters ever since I got here."

"Is that what Augusta calls a vacation?"

"I don't know, maybe."

"Sounds just like work to me."

"When Mom called she said she was making you cook."

"Yeah—I guess she doesn't care what she eats. I think she's trying to sell every house in Evanston before the summer's over."

"And then what?"

"I don't know—maybe she'll start on Winnetka."

"Is everything okay? I've been meaning to call, really."

"Yeah, I just wanted to talk to you. You didn't seem overly happy when you left, you know; I've been a little worried about you, that's all. I know it's none of my business," he said. That made me want to hug him, though I wouldn't have if he had been right there.

"I'm all right, Daddy, I just—" What to say?

"Miss your friends, I bet."

"Yeah." That was an easy out.

"They're still here. I'll bet Jeanette has called every other day. Even Rodge called, according to your mom." I wasn't sure whether to be grateful to him for using Rodge's name or to resent the word "even."

"Yeah, she told me." If it was true, then . . .

"Absence makes the heart, you know."

"Oh, Daddy," I groaned, embarrassed. Was he encouraging me or what?

"All right, all right. Well. Anyway. Miss Moss is missed here in Evanston. It's in all the papers."

"I'm sure."

"Does she just make you scrape paint all the time, or what?"

"Well, we do a lot of yard work, too. You'd love it. Her garden's almost as big as yours. That and the house is all she ever thinks about," I said, calling myself a liar. "It's not so bad. I read a lot of books."

"Hmm." There was a silence while we both thought, tired of beating around the bush.

"Is Mom still mad at me?" I said, surprised at my own directness.

He thought it over. "No—I don't believe she is." He spoke after a moment in a hesitant tone that said more than his words. "It's—I'm not even sure she was. I'm not mad, I know that."

"Were you?"

"No." He sounded almost offended. "Of course not. It was just . . . friction, you know." I could picture him waving his hand at the word "friction," waving it away to insignificance. "Everybody's got to grow up somehow," he said—sadly, I thought.

"What's wrong with that?" Augusta's bed was soft, to my surprise—too yielding for someone like her.

"Nothing." The room's dimness, its closed-up air, even the comfort of the bed, seemed to bespeak secrecy and melancholy and something wrong with growing up. I looked around for one thing truly personal, a clue perhaps, but everything in the room had belonged to my grandparents. Finally in one corner of the mirror I noticed a tiny snapshot. It was a child of five or six, and after squinting at it from the bed for a few seconds I realized it was me. "Are you still there?" my father said.

"Yes." Me—over Augusta's dresser. What was I doing there?

"What's on your mind, kid?" He said it cautiously, even tenderly, so that I hardly minded him calling me "kid."

"I'm not sure." Only my father would take that for an answer. "A lot of things. I can't really tell you right now."

"Well, you don't have to." Why was he being so careful? I could almost hear him weighing his words; it made me tense.

"Am I keeping you from working?"

"Oh—the boss only works when he feels like it."

"Ha ha. You must love it, then."

"Have you got enough money? You do have your return ticket, don't you?"

"Of course I do, you only told me not to lose it about ten times before I left."

"Touchy Miss. Very touchy. Well, whenever you feel like using it, we'll be glad to see you, okay?"

Did I have to be told that? "Okay."

"I love you," he said, and for some reason those words put a weight on my heart.

"You too, Daddy."

"Call sometime, okay?"

"I will."

"Bye."

"Bye," I said, taking the phone away from my ear. I held it with both hands on my stomach, gazing at the ceiling, and listened to it buzz. After a while it began to beep, telling me it was off the hook. I rolled over and hung it up and rolled back. If only I were at home and my father would take me on one of his dumb expeditions and not let me come home until I'd had a chance to talk. Then maybe I would know what was on my mind.

I lay there thinking about calling him back, wishing, among other things, that I could tell him I loved him straight out. Why did thinking about saying those words make me, of all things, angry? A few years ago they had been easy. But if I called him back . . . well, it would be too late, anyway. You have to do things at the moment when they matter or they don't count. And that man would probably answer again and yell at me for interrupting them at work.

It was neither day nor night in Augusta's room, neither cool nor hot, and I lay suspended, trying to picture my father leaving some office trailer at a construction site, out of its air conditioning and relative quiet into the heat and dust and the roar of power tools, men shouting at each other over the noise—I would never be able to hear a thing with all that racket, I was sure of it—and my father among them, doing what? Was he shouting, too, telling expectant or sullen faces what to do? That was hard to imagine. At home he almost never raised his voice, except to tell the cat to get down off something, or occasionally when a mechanical device absolutely refused to work. I couldn't quite put myself in his place; when I tried, it was more as though I was riding inside him, looking out through his eyes as if they were windows, a way I felt inside myself sometimes, as if I were a little smaller than my body and there was kind of a gap between me and me. The difference was much greater when I tried to imagine being my father, and even in my mind I couldn't be the one giving the commands.

What a softie you are, I thought. A tenderfoot.

The sound of the doorknob broke into my reverie; the door opened, and Augusta said, "I just wanted to see if you were still alive."

Feeling caught, I sat up as fast as I could, but the bed was soft and that made it awkward. "I'm okay," I said, pushing my hair back and trying to think of a way to show some initiative. "How about—" I scrambled for a way to finish the sentence. "How about if we try the driving lesson again?" I half regretted the words as soon as they were out.

"Good idea," she said. "I left the lunch stuff out if you feel like eating something, okay?"

Boy, now I've done it, I thought. At least I owe myself a fat sandwich for that.

The second time, however, was not as close to disaster as the first. Something seemed to have sunk in from my original effort, and I found that I could go in a circle with almost no trouble, though for a while I thought that I might have to confine myself entirely to left turns. At five miles an hour, the Buick, with me at the helm, described stately circles on the high-school parking lot, while the people of New Franklin added one more story to the tally of Augusta's eccentricities. Or perhaps I was starting an account of my own. Going straight was still harder than it looked, and stopping without a jolt and a screech took thought that I couldn't always spare from the task of steering. I wasn't quite fit to be let out on the streets, but Augusta seemed pleased, and if anyone gave us a funny look, she gave it back in spades.

"While I was out taking a walk," I said when we got home, "I ran into a girl who told me to tell you Mrs. Holzman says hello."

Augusta looked at me, then away, almost dangerously. "Jeannie Holzman," she said to herself. "What else did she say?"

I thought Jeannie Holzman had better leave Augusta alone, if she knew what was good for her. "She wanted to know who I was and what I was doing here."

"Hmh," Augusta snorted.

"How does she know you, anyway?"

"She was in my class once. Her mother just happened to be on the Collinsville school board, which generally meant that Jeannie got all A's, even though she's just about smart enough to pop bubble gum. I didn't give them to her."

"And?"

"Aah—I had a run-in with her almighty mother. Fortunately they moved, and she had to quit the school board, so she didn't get a chance to have me fired. Unfortunately she moved here."

"Geez—this is a nice, peaceful little place, isn't it?"

"You said it," Augusta muttered. She didn't sound as though she had any idea that she went around asking for trouble. Was that why she lived in New Franklin? So that when she asked she'd be sure to get it?

After dinner I thought I might as well ask. "What made you move back here?" I said.

"What I told you—I wanted to be at home."

"Is that enough all by itself?"

"I never said it was *enough*." She seemed impatient. "It beats a lot of other things."

"Like what?"

"Like not being at home."

Thanks a million, I thought. "I still don't see what's so wonderful about having to put up with Jeannie Holzman and her mother."

"Believe me, I didn't come back here for that."

"But why do it at all?" Today I could insist on an answer.

"Why? Don't you ever get homesick? Don't you want to go back to Evanston?"

"Do you want me to?"

"No, damn it."

I smirked at her, pushing up the corners of my mouth in a way that I knew was irritating.

"You're a difficult child."

"I'll bet you could find someone in Evanston to agree with that," I said, but my mind was on M.J. and Jeanette, and the thought of them did make me homesick. What was I doing in New Franklin hearing about Augusta's private wars when I could be lying on the beach with them talking about last night but never quite telling it all? I wondered again if Rodge really had called, if he had given up when he heard I was out of town or stayed interested—if my father was right. It wasn't him, a mean, factual voice said inside me, Mom doesn't know his voice over the phone. He didn't call. But even if I could forget about that, I was still afraid that Jeanette and M.J. might be meeting boys I didn't know, making new girlfriends, slipping away from me . . . but they weren't learning how to drive, I thought. Besides, they were probably going away on vacation any day now.

"Feel like sitting on the porch?" Augusta said.

"Okay."

The slow back-and-forth of the old swing was hypnotic; we swung without needing to speak. After a while Augusta went inside and came back with two pieces of watermelon on plates. "Try this," she said, and picked up a seed. She held it between thumb and forefinger, squeezed, and it shot away invisibly into the front yard. A few late fireflies were blinking around out there, and I thought about the impossibility of hitting one of them. Mine wouldn't shoot like hers, anyway.

"How do you make them go so far?"

"Squeeze as hard as you can."

I tried, but mine shot to the side and hit her on the arm. "Cut," she said, handing it back to me.

I squeezed again and the seed bounced off the porch railing. "Now I'm getting it." Augusta plinked one off my bare leg; another hit my neck and stuck. I tried to shoot one right at her, but it flew over her head.

"It's easy to see you weren't brought up right," she said, causing a seed to hit my face. It dropped down my shirt front.

"You better watch it." I scooped up seeds on my spoon and threatened to catapult them at her point-blank.

"That's cheating!"

"Tough." I let fly, and she ducked; the seeds stuck in her hair. She swatted them out with one hand and grabbed for my spoon.

"No you don't." But she was too fast for me; she got my wrist in one hand and the spoon in the other. The plate on her lap tilted, juice and seeds and watermelon poured onto the swing; I grabbed Augusta's spoon. "Ha, ha." I aimed at her again, but she ignored me.

"What a mess," she said, picking up her piece of watermelon and moving away from the juice that was dripping onto the porch. Smiling, she took a bite. "You're fun sometimes," she said, "when you're not so damn serious."

"Me? What about you? I've never heard so many depressing stories in my life."

"Oh, go get a dishcloth, why don't you, and clean this up."

"Why? It's your mess."

"Go on, we'll be stuck to the swing forever if you don't."

Back in the kitchen, I ran cold water on a sponge, then got an ice cube out of the freezer and held it inside the sponge as I stepped out onto the porch. Barely holding back laughter, I mopped at the juice from behind the swing and then with one simple motion released the ice cube down Augusta's back.

"Aiee, God! You little fiend," she exclaimed, jumping up. I was too fast for her this time, and kept the swing between us; we were both giggling. When she realized she wouldn't catch me, she sat down on the porch railing and removed the ice cube from her shirttail. "Feels good, actually, after you get over the shock."

She popped the ice cube into her mouth and chewed it up. "Are you going to clean that up or not?"

I mopped up most of the pink juice and pushed the seeds over the edge of the porch so that they fell down behind the evergreen bushes along the front. "Still think I'm too serious?"

"Everybody makes mistakes." Augusta gathered up the plates and rinds. "Give me that." I handed her the sponge. "You're dangerous with this thing."

While she took the plates in, I started swinging again, thinking how seldom Augusta seemed thoroughly happy, and how delightful she was at those times. I wondered what she was like with someone her age who wasn't family—what she had been like with Jim. Those were the things that I would never know. Maybe a whole different person. But I couldn't forget about my tiny picture stuck in the mirror over her bureau.

"Do you like having me down here, really and truly?" I asked, when she had come back out.

"Of course."

"Don't just say 'of course.' That's what my parents always say to me." Meaning my mother—Of course we want you to be happy . . .

Augusta messed up my hair and let her hand rest on top of my head. "I love you," she said in a diffident way, almost as if she wasn't sure she wanted me to hear. What she had said didn't register for a moment; I wasn't used to her touching me, and the gentle presence of her hand on my head almost blanked it out. I tried to look at her and couldn't.

I love you too. I thought the words to her, but I knew my mouth could not speak them.

Augusta cleared her throat and took her hand away. "You know that, don't you?" she said.

A tightness in my chest made me seem to hesitate. "I know," I said, but I thought that tiny pause had made her sad. "I really do."

"Okay."

We swung, toward and away.

"Do me a favor?" I said after a minute.

"Sure."

"Tell me a story with a happy ending."

chapter 9

Augusta thought for a moment. "Well, I could tell you how the Cardinals won the World Series in 1946," she said.

"No, come on."

"It's a tall order, I have to think for a while."

"I can wait." I had enough to think about for myself. Hearing Augusta say she loved me made me aware for some reason that I couldn't take her for granted as I always had. Especially after some of the stories she'd told; most of them seemed to be about people not forgiving each other. Yet having her family make her unhappy didn't stop her from wanting to go home. How did that work? I thought of my friend M.J., whose mother was a chronic invalid, or said she was, and whose father was a crazy college professor who would yell from above, as we were about to go out to a movie, "Mary Jo, come to the foot of the stairs! I want a complete itinerary!" Yet one day she said to me, "You know, my family may be nuts, but you don't even *have* one really." I was too surprised to be insulted; for a minute I could imagine how it looked through her eyes, when she came over and found all three of us with our noses in books or newspapers, not talking. "Your house reminds me of a study hall or something."

"Me too" was all I could say. Moments like that always made me wonder what it would be like to have a sister, and thinking about Augusta and my mother made me wonder even more. Nothing sentimental there. But was it as hard to be a family as Augusta made it sound, or did she just love fights? She would be embarrassed, I was sure, if she knew that I had read the nickname my mother called her, and it was dangerous to embarrass Augusta.

It seemed that Augusta had an answer for everything but a happy ending; she was still pondering, while the cicadas whirred around us. I licked watermelon taste off my fingers.

"Well," she said, "I could tell you about what happened finally with Allan."

"I thought you broke up after that time he came for Thanksgiving." When were the stories over, anyway?

"Ah, you *thought*—well, we did, more or less. We did break up, but it wasn't as though we hated each other or anything. Seeing each other was too sad to put up with, that's all. But right before we both graduated he sent me a card with his family's address on it and said he'd write to me if I wrote to him. I waited about six months and then I did write. It was hard to know what to say; I suppose I wasn't very inspired, but I tried to tell him how I had felt, especially that night on the bus. It took me a week to write the letter, because I kept tearing it up and starting over again, and even when I sent it I felt foolish about it, but I sent it because I didn't have anything to lose. After a couple of weeks I got one from him that must have taken just as long. I'll never forget one thing he said. 'I hope push comes to shove for you sometime,' he said. 'You think it has already, but you're wrong.' "

She paused so long I wondered if that was it.

"Every time I think about that, I change my mind about what

he really meant. But that's not the story. The story is, we kept writing, every few months, maybe four or five times a year at the most, but we didn't quit. I went to Harris Teacher's College, he went to law school at NYU, we wrote each other about our love affairs and the meaning of life and so forth. I used to call him my pen pal. The letter writing went on so long it was more real to me than the idea that I had actually gone out with him in college. He almost got married once, and I said I was going to send his fiancée a time bomb in the mail. He just thanked me and said he'd pass on my congratulations. She was Jewish, by the way, but they didn't get married, don't ask me why. He never said. After that he didn't write for almost a year, and then I just got a postcard saying he'd write me later. But here's what happened. Eventually I got a letter saying he was coming through St. Louis on business and inviting me out to dinner.

"I hadn't seen him in seven years, and I wasn't even sure I'd know what he looked like. When he got to town he called me on the phone to make sure it was okay, and I asked him if I would recognize him, and he just laughed. The truth is, he was exactly the same. I was supposed to meet him in the lobby of his hotel, and while I was waiting I got so nervous I almost ran away, but as soon as I saw him it vanished. He didn't see me, but I saw him, in his gray suit and striped tie and the works, coming through the lobby looking for me—and he was nervous, too, I saw it—and I was so proud of him I forgot about everything else. I even forgot there was no reason for *me* to be proud.

"Well. Anyway, he found me, and we went out to dinner and had a fine time, and while we were having dinner he said he was taking the train back to New York the next day and why didn't I come with him? Because it was summer and school was out and there was nothing stopping me. So I did. I met him at the station the next day and he had booked a room for us on the sleeping car. Some situation. I guess we made a spectacle of ourselves, because after dinner we were sitting in the club car having a drink and holding hands, and the Pullman-car porter came in and said, 'Your bedroom is ready whenever you like, sir,' and everyone stared at us. But who cares. It was a fine night."

She put her hands behind her head and arched her back, stretching reflectively. "Now there's a happy ending for you."

Ending? "What happened after that?"

"Well, we got to New York and I stayed about a week. It was what's known as a fling, I guess. Very romantic. Well, maybe fling's not the right word, that makes it sound as if I didn't really care about him. Anyway, after a week or so, I came back."

"Just came back?"

"Well—he had a whole life there already, I could see that easily enough. It was great for a week."

But since when was a week of happiness enough? "I thought this story had a happy ending."

"We still write, we're still friends, we always will be, how much more do you want? You're greedy, that's all. Too young to know better."

"At least I've got an excuse."

"Don't you sass me, young lady," she said, without bothering to pretend that she was mad.

"But didn't you want more?"

"Everyone always does," she said. "Especially me."

I waited. "But what?" I said finally, when it seemed she wouldn't go on.

"There is no but. That's the way it works."

I tried to puzzle that out, but there weren't enough lines to read between. "I really don't understand," I admitted after a minute.

Augusta seemed in no hurry to enlighten me; perhaps this fell into the category of the advice she had once said she wouldn't give me. She stretched out her long legs and perched her feet on the porch railing, stopping us from swinging, and thought. My attention wandered. I tried to imagine Augusta having a romantic tryst on board a train, but all I could think of was Cary Grant and Eva Marie Saint in *North by Northwest*. Augusta was a lot bigger; it wouldn't be that easy to pull her up into a berth. I wondered what Allan looked like. He was Jewish; would that prevent him from having a gorgeous Cary Grant chin?

"Well, look," she said when I had almost forgotten what she had been talking about. "Do you want to hear my theory? In my opinion, it's very simple. People want something they can't have."

"I thought you told me that was baloney—that grass-is-greener business."

"Oh, that's not what I'm talking about." She thought again. "I mean people have desires that can't be fulfilled, period. Think about this: think about the word 'freedom.' We always talk about it, we say we have it, but the fact is, you can't ever get there. No matter how free you are, there's always one more restriction you could get rid of that would make you a little bit freer. The only way you can get there, really, is to be God."

It shocked me slightly to hear the word "God" from Augusta's mouth; she used it in a familiar way that I never would have expected.

"But we're not God, obviously. We're only halfway there. It's set up so we can imagine something like freedom, and want it, but just by the nature of being who we are, we'll never have it. And freedom's not the only thing that's like that. But at least we know the name of it. See, here's my real theory: there's something we want that we not only can't have, we can't even know what it is. If you talk about the grass being greener on the other side, you're saying that it's just an illusion, it's the same grass that's over here, but what I'm saying is that deep down we're convinced there *is* another side, and the grass really *is* greener there; in fact, it's a whole different thing, it's not even grass anymore, and that's where we really belong."

I had never heard her so vehement; she seemed to make a conscious effort to rein herself in.

"And the things we want on this side," she said more moderately, "it's not that we don't want them, but what we really want is . . . what they represent. That other thing, whatever it is that we can't have."

I felt bombarded by too many unfamiliar thoughts; it was an almost physical sensation, like driving the Buick for the first time.

"So in other words," she said, "you spend a week with the guy you've been in love with for a long time, and you realize that even though you love him he's not the way to get to *that*, and you come home."

I couldn't make that add up. "But I thought you said there was no way to get there anyhow."

"There isn't."

"Then . . ."

"I know. Then why come home. It's a hell of a good question. I don't know why. Maybe we're just made that way. Once you get home you want to turn around and go right back."

Maybe you're made that way, I thought, but that doesn't mean I have to be. "It doesn't make any sense," I said.

"I knew it wouldn't," she said. "When you're my age it might."

"I hope not." We sat staring stubbornly forward, stuck in disagreement. "Weren't you happy when you were there?" I asked, unable to let it go.

"Of course I was. That's not what I'm talking about."

"What *are* you talking about?"

"Look, if you don't get it, maybe I can't explain."

"But it's important. Don't you even want to try?"

"Karen." Her voice was distant and flat. "Maybe I didn't want to be happy. Maybe I can't stand what people call happiness. Think about that." I tried but couldn't; my mind rejected the idea. "Maybe I don't even know how."

Before I could think and stop myself, I put my arms around Augusta's neck as if I could hide from what she was telling me or even pull her out of the dilemma of being herself. For an instant she was rigid as could be, and then she turned toward me and hugged me back.

"You're a good kid," she mumbled, patting me on the head, and released me. I sat up again, feeling helpless and almost rejected; what could I do for a sadness like that?

But she was wrong, I told myself, insisting. About some things Augusta was wrong.

"It's late," Augusta said abruptly, after we had sat without talking for some minutes. "I'm going to bed."

"Okay."

She got up; in the doorway she paused. "Coming in?"

"In a few minutes."

"Well, good night."

"G'night."

Inside, I could hear her wandering around the downstairs. She snapped on the kitchen radio and out of it came the voice of the Cardinals' announcer, muttering, then suddenly excited: "Holy cow! Way back! WAY back! It might be! It could be—it is! —a home run! Number eight of the season for Coleman ties it for the Redbirds in the top of the ninth!" He subsided somewhat, and I could no longer make out what he was saying. Good timing, I thought. The St. Louis Cardinals could probably do more for Augusta than most of the people she actually knew.

Still not sleepy, I stayed where I was while Augusta went upstairs. After a few minutes her bedroom light clicked off; the faint stripes it had cast on the lawn, through the shutters, disappeared. It was odd to imagine her sleeping just above me and slightly to my right, while I sat on the porch in the dark below. Now I was the one to whose footsteps she might awaken, confused, in the middle of the night.

I felt almost like a guardian of sorts, a sentry posted to watch out the night, though against what dangers I couldn't tell. Was this what Augusta did? Maybe, I thought, I should take her part altogether, water the plants, wash the clean dishes, sit on the swing and smoke cigarettes (if she had been the person who left the butts I had once found). But cigarettes were disgusting— M.J. and I had tried to smoke once and hated it—and the rest of her midnight activities sounded dull.

There was action enough anyway, on the inside. How could she believe what she had said—that people didn't really want what they wanted but always something else they couldn't have? It couldn't be that complicated. That would be like saying I hadn't really wanted Rodge to kiss me, which made no sense at all. I knew better than that. What about Jim, for that matter? Where did he fit into her fancy theory?

But thinking about Rodge at midnight made me horribly nostalgic. I did something I would never have let Augusta catch me at, because she'd laugh at me, I was sure: I got the car keys off their hook in the kitchen cabinet, turned out the lights in the kitchen and the front hall, went out to the Buick, and got in. I turned the key to the first notch so I could play the radio, rolled down the windows, and then slowly tuned my way along the dial, trying to get Chicago stations, fantasizing that there was no house, no Augusta, no parents looking over my shoulder, no nothing but me and my life, on the road to somewhere. I got

WGN at last, but it kept fading away, and finally I settled for a St. Louis station playing an old soul song—

> It's *so* good to see you back again
> Just the way it used to be then
> It seems like a mighty long time, my baby, oo.

Slumped down in the Buick's huge seat, I thought about the way it used to be then. Had he called me, really? Had he?

Nothing was happening in New Franklin but me sitting in front of the dark house. When one car passed I noticed it. When it passed again I was mildly surprised; then it pulled over and parked. Had somebody noticed me? Was I doing something wrong? What if it was that boy with the muscles? I turned the radio off and slid down even lower, so that I could just see out. The driver of the other car—a big one, like the Buick, but newer —did not get out at once but looked over his shoulder, not at me, but at our house. Courage, I thought to myself, but I was scared. What if Augusta needed a sentry and she didn't even know it?

I strained to see the dim shape in the other car, but he was too far away to be anything but a silhouette against the faintly lighted backdrop formed by a gray house down the block with a street lamp shining on it. For some reason I wanted it to be Jerry, even though Augusta had told him to go away just the day before. He turned and started to get out, and I thought, The front door's not locked, I know it's not, I've got to do something, and with my left hand I felt along the dashboard as I remembered Augusta doing, pulling at knobs, until I turned on the headlights. It wasn't Jerry but a man his age or older, wearing a checked short-sleeved shirt, who froze there for a second in the act of getting out of his car, panic on his face, as it must have been on mine. But he got control. He straightened up with a peculiar half-friendly look on his face and began to walk toward the Buick. There was something insinuating about his look or his walk that made me sure I knew exactly what he wanted, and now I was the object of his attentions. I could get out and run, but I knew he'd catch me. He was trying to see around the headlights at me when I finally remembered I could start the car. With fumbling fingers I turned the key and the Buick roared to life; his eyes widened and he stopped short as I put the car in Drive and began to inch forward, unable to step on the gas for fear I might hit him.

"Karen!" Augusta's voice shot out of the dark and stopped me cold. She was leaning out her bedroom window in a nightgown, and I didn't know whether to be relieved or terrified. The man in front of me was staring at Augusta as if the car and I didn't exist.

"Turn it off," she said in a voice that meant Immediately. I did. The night seemed doubly quiet. I moved the shift lever back to Park.

"The lights." I fumbled for the knob and pushed it in, reducing the stranger to a dark silhouette again. He stared a second longer, gave Augusta a slight wave, walked deliberately back to his car, got in it, started it up, and drove off. Bewilderment made me forget for a moment to be scared of him or her. As he drove away I saw Augusta watching him out the window; then she disappeared into the darkness inside.

How did I get into this, I asked myself, as I rolled up the windows and got out of the Buick. Something terrible would happen to me when I walked back into the house, and why? I closed the door of the Buick as quietly as I could and started up the front walk, my eyes on the bricks, and heard the sound I dreaded: the front door opening. I looked up and Augusta was standing on the front porch in her bathrobe.

I stopped on the front walk, two steps below her as if her own height wasn't enough. Her arms were crossed on her chest, holding the robe closed, and she seemed unwilling even to look at me. If I could have vanished, I would have.

"Come inside," she said. She turned around and preceded me, holding the front door open as I passed her without being able to meet her eye, and closed it behind me.

"What were you doing out in that car?" she said in a subdued voice of amazement and—I was sure of it—disappointment. Her hand was still on the doorknob, holding on to it hard.

"Listening to the radio."

"The *radio*?" She sounded as if she couldn't believe her ears.

"I was just sitting out there listening to it, for a long time."

"You weren't sitting there when I looked out the window, you were going somewhere."

"It was that man. He scared me to death; I was trying to get away."

Augusta turned away from me and heaved a sigh through her teeth, shaking her head slightly. She leaned her forehead on the front door. "Jesus Christ," she said, quietly and precisely.

"I didn't know what was going on, I thought he was after me—did he know you? Who was that, anyway?"

Without taking her head away from the door, she turned so she could see me over her shoulder, and she examined me with a look that felt as if it denuded me of what defenses I had left and left me naked to the world.

"That was Jim."

I couldn't do anything with that piece of information; all I could do was stare. She turned toward me and put her hand on my shoulder with surprising gentleness, as if to hold me back.

"Don't even ask, okay? You've asked enough questions today. I lied; I'm sorry. I just wanted to protect you. And me, and him. But I guess that wasn't possible." What had she lied about? I still didn't follow. "I suppose I shouldn't have invited you down, but you see? It was selfish. I told you I am. I figured having you here would change everything, and . . . it would be a way out."

I got it. I didn't want to, but I understood, and yet I still didn't want her to say out loud that she was having her affair with Jim right that very summer, that very minute, because if she didn't say it, then perhaps somehow I could still pretend I didn't know.

Augusta put her arms around me, but now I was the one who shrank from contact. "I'm sorry," she said again. "I should never have involved you in all this. I'm supposed to be old enough to understand these things."

I couldn't say anything, not even a mumbled "It's okay," and I couldn't hug her back. She let me go, stepped back and looked at me, her arms limp at her sides; she seemed smaller than I had ever seen her, as if some of the life had been knocked out of her by the events of the night. I handed her the keys; she took them indifferently. "I don't know what he was doing here," she said in a lost voice. "I told him never to come over. It isn't safe, anyway. Not for anyone. People are starting to find out. That's what Jerry wanted to tell me yesterday. And if the neighbors didn't know something was up before tonight, I'm sure they do now."

I couldn't look at her; the word "terrible" came back to me from when we had met at the station, and I wished that I had, in fact, turned around and gone home. Then I would never have had to turn on the headlights and make things, perhaps, a great deal worse.

"If you had told me . . ." I said.

"I know."

"What do you really do at night?" I said, suddenly the interrogator. We were shifting from foot to foot awkwardly in the dim hallway, avoiding each other's eyes.

"Think."

"That's it?"

"He's married, you know; he's supposed to be home at night." It was much worse to hear such a thing said in the present tense.

"Do you drive around? I thought I heard you, once."

"I did. I met him once. Don't ask, I hate telling you all this."

"I thought you said you wanted to corrupt me."

"I was wrong."

"Well, what *did* you want, anyway?"

"Stop it, I already told you. I've apologized to you more tonight than I ever apologize to anybody. You've got to let up."

"Why?" I looked at her, and Augusta stared back. We defied each other.

"I didn't know you could be cruel," she said.

"Maybe it runs in the family," I said, starting to cry, and bolted up the stairs. I slammed the door of my room and threw myself on the bed, wishing I could lock the door and close out everything that had happened, everything I didn't want to know.

After a minute or two I stopped crying and simply lay there, curled up facing the wall. Above all I felt betrayed, hurt most because I hadn't been asked if I wanted any part in this, or even told that I had one. And beyond that I wanted Augusta to be different, to be a person who would never do such a thing; I wanted adultery to stay unthinkable, I wanted her to be wrong about her selfishness . . .

She opened the door and I gritted my teeth. A couple of boards creaked as she crossed the room and sat down on the edge of the bed.

"Please don't do this," she said. She put a hand on my shoulder, but I stayed put, unable to respond, unable to be reconciled, until she left the room.

chapter 10

I awoke as usual to the conversations of mourning doves and the screech of the blue jay who patrolled our street, but before I could stretch and lie back again and savor the me-ness of my own waking-up self, what had happened came back to me and drained all pleasure out of the morning. I lay and thought about how Augusta had used me for her own purposes, and then, just like anybody else, claimed to be teaching me something; even the excuse was disappointing. I didn't want to know any more about life from her point of view. If she had made a mess out of it, that was her problem. I hadn't come to New Franklin to solve it for her.

What *had* I come for, that was what I had to ask. My mother said Go, so I went—but when was I going to do something because I said so?

I could think of one decision that was mine to make. I got up and checked: on top of the dresser, where it had sat since I arrived, was my return ticket, and the time to use it had come.

Looking at the favorite picture of my grandmother's that hung on my bedroom wall, I felt that Augusta had betrayed the house itself, the way of life that was built into its corners and moldings.

I was almost surprised that the house didn't repel her, force her out, as she now repelled me.

Much as I condemned her, that made me sad. But she had lied to me, and I had to go home, even though I wasn't sure I wanted to be there, either. Jeanette and M.J. seemed more important than ever, and I prayed that they wouldn't be away on vacation.

I didn't want to face Augusta, but once I was dressed, there was no alternative. I went down the front stairs instead of the back, to give myself more time; in the front hall recent events crowded in on me—not just Augusta making her confession the night before, but also seeing Jerry through the front door glass, and walking that way, unwillingly, to be shown how to drive the Buick, and arriving there what seemed a long time ago, awkward, obnoxious, and bored. Oh, I was no prize—I admitted it—but still, that was no reason why I should be deceived, by a member of my family least of all. That was something my mother would never do; you could always credit her at least with that much.

Move on, I told myself. Show some courage.

All the doors off the front hall were closed. I opened one and passed through the back sitting room no one ever used, past the foot of the back stairs, into the kitchen—but no Augusta. There was coffee in the pot. It was nine-thirty by the clock on the top of the refrigerator. Everything was cleaned up, wiped off, put away, except, uncharacteristically, a plate and silver and a coffee cup, neatly set on the kitchen table for my breakfast. Did she think it would be that easy to make me forget?

But I was touched, no matter what I told myself. More than anything, that place setting looked lovely, there by itself in the kitchen of a big old house on the verge of decay, in a small town in the middle of the endless Midwest. The thought of my grandparents spending their entire lives there, among the tiny importances and defeats of such a place, and Augusta coming back—on purpose!—and what had become of her—made me resolve that I would get out, not just out of that town, but out of it all, despite whose granddaughter I was. No wonder my mother hadn't wanted the house. But Evanston wasn't far enough by half; it wasn't Away.

I felt the coffeepot. It was lukewarm; I turned on the gas under it, got the bread and eggs out of the refrigerator, before I saw Augusta bent over in the garden, weeding. I put the food down on the table and marched myself out onto the back porch, down the steps into the yard. She had her back to me and was wearing old, faded work clothes and a beaten-down straw hat that hid her hair; she could have been almost anyone from the back—a farmer's fifty-year-old, graying wife. What she did not look like was my strange and halfway glamorous aunt who had done that which she ought not to have done.

She knew I was there, I was sure of it, but she wouldn't look around. "Good morning," I said to her back, after I had waited for a while.

Then she did turn and straighten up; she had no expression on her face at all. "Good morning," she answered. She stood and looked at me as if to say, I shall carry on this conversation if you wish to do so. At once I felt intensely uncomfortable, already at a disadvantage. She would stand there without speaking for five minutes—an hour—if I didn't speak first.

"I think, um . . ." Saying the words was much harder than I had thought. My certainty had evaporated.

"Yes?" she said politely, correctly, without a trace of warmth, hurting me—but what did I expect?

"I think it's time for me to go home," I said.

Her control was intimidating in itself. "I'm sorry you have to go," she said, without appearing to feel a thing. I *was* sorry, that was the hard part. "Have you checked the train schedule?"

"No."

"If you'll find out, I'll drive you to the station."

Hadn't I known she was tough? Had I somehow forgotten that? It was absurd, I told myself, to feel rejected, but I did. "All right," I said. She was still watching me, waiting. I felt shriveled like an ant that a cruel boy burns with a magnifying glass. She was not going to dismiss me or make it easy to turn away, I could see that, and I knew that in a second I would be helpless, would cave in somehow and babble stupid things that would make me squirm to remember, forever after. At the last moment I did turn, though, and did not look her way again until I was safely inside the house. Then I peered cautiously at her out the kitchen window, trying not to show myself. She had gone back to weeding. I saw her jam the straw hat more firmly on her head.

You bitch, I thought, or tried to think, but another voice, the mocking one I couldn't escape, said, Well, I hope you're satisfied.

Why had I thought that she would argue with me, try to persuade me to stay? If there was anything Augusta had plenty of, it was pride. Like my mother, and even, I would have to admit, like me.

Halfheartedly I made myself some breakfast and ate it without tasting, dreading the day and most of all the ride to St. Louis, hating my dependence on her, the fact that I had to eat her food and ride in her car, become still more obligated to her even in the act of getting away. I washed my few dishes, the frying pan, the coffeepot, dried everything, and put it away, wiped the tabletop and the counter, washed out the sink, trying to erase the marks of my presence. Perhaps that had been Augusta's intention, too.

I draped the dishrag carefully over the spigot and climbed the stairs to pack.

But packing didn't take long enough. In half an hour I was done, even though I stood for a while with a pair of shorts in my hand wondering if I would regret leaving like this. It was too late anyway to change my mind, no matter how hastily I had spoken. Much as I didn't want to, I couldn't help noticing a family resemblance between myself and the people in Augusta's stories—my mother selling the watch back and giving my grandparents the money, or Augusta herself walking out on the uneaten Thanksgiving dinner. We didn't seem like a very forgiving bunch—and thus far, that quality hadn't made any-body's life noticeably easier.

But I couldn't unsay my decision to go. It was midmorning of, like it or not, my last day. I went into Augusta's room and called the train station. There was a train at eleven-thirty which we would not be able to make, three more during the afternoon, and then one at seven; even the first train we could catch seemed an eternity away. My heart sank.

Once again I looked over the room. The picture of me was still there, and I wondered if she would take it down, perhaps put it in one of the boxes that filled the attic and the conservatory, where it would join all the other mementos consigned to heat and dust, saved but already forgotten. Did I deserve anything else? I remembered what she had said the previous night, just before I stormed up the stairs: "I didn't know you could be cruel."

As I was leaving my room, a flash of black handwriting caught my eye, the bottom of a letter sticking out from under the clock: "Yours as ever, Allan." Unable to resist, I lifted it up. "You love who you love," I read. "Such things happen. If we did right all the time we wouldn't be human, and I'd be out of a job. People were born to break the rules. Try not to get hurt. If you do get hurt, try not to let it kill you." I put down the clock and closed the door gently behind me.

It was a few minutes before eleven, and the time until I could leave stretched before me, horrible in its awkwardness, yet I felt as though I had already gone. Standing in the living room, I thought I could see what Augusta's life was like when I wasn't there; for the first time, I felt the oppression of the quiet in her house, and I could halfway imagine the grip she must have on herself in the face of such a solitary existence. I appreciated the importance of the letter in the bedroom, and why it would be read again and again, even after she knew its words by heart. And her projects—they were like fortifications, walls of distraction that kept the monster at bay. Because wasn't loneliness a monster, after all?

I sat down on the top step of the front stairs like Christopher Robin and thought about going home. I'd be a child there once again, for better and worse, no matter what I or anyone else might say otherwise. My parents would be hard at work, and I—what would I do? The whole rhythm of the summer had slipped away from me, the lazy routine of shopping and going to the beach and reading halfway-exciting books; there was no Rodge to talk about with Jeanette and M.J., much less go out with. I wanted to believe that he had called, but I couldn't. Maybe I didn't care enough anymore to convince myself; maybe the visit had served its purpose. Maybe one more of my mother's plans had worked. Let it. Even that I could stand, if only she wouldn't say she had told me so.

Outside, I could hear Augusta hammering again, and I knew she must be back at work on the gazebo. That wouldn't stop whether I went or stayed. It would be easier for her to see Jim, if she really wanted to; if the night before was any indication, she wouldn't be able to keep him away. But about that I would know nothing, and even what I knew I had to keep a secret, unless perhaps one day this summer would become an old story that I could tell to someone as Augusta had told hers to me. Probably she regretted the impulse already, I thought gloomily. Well, in some ways I did, too. But I would never find out how this episode came out.

I got up and trailed down the stairs, wondering if I should join her at work one last time, whether I could bring myself to offer her any help and whether she would accept it. Probably she would just look at me and say nothing, but still, did I owe it to her to try? The idea seemed too much like an apology. I was sure I didn't owe her that, but I had to tell her when the trains left.

She did not seem to have made much progress with the summerhouse when I returned to the garden. Again I stood and waited, but this time she turned around without my having to speak first. "Did you find out the times?" she said, as if asking whether there was any beer in the refrigerator.

"There's a train at one-thirty, and three o'clock, and five-thirty," I said; the later the time I mentioned, the worse it felt.

"Anything after that?"

"There's one at seven, but—"

"Good. I'll drive you to that one. There's a lot of stuff I want to get done today."

For a moment I couldn't get a word out, imagining eight more hours of this impossible situation; before I recovered she had turned around and was ignoring me again. And how could I object? Without Augusta I would never get to the train station at all. Finally I turned my back to her, too, and put one foot in front of the other, back to the house; if there were doors and walls between myself and her, the day might be possible to bear.

I had to search through the entire downstairs to find the book I was reading, and as I did so, I was conscious of trying to stay out of sight, avoiding windows that looked out on the summer-house, where Augusta continued to nail relentlessly. I had a feeling she didn't really know what she was doing, that she was hammering just to do *something*, or that she was pretending the nails were pins stuck in an effigy of me. But I had left myself no choice: I would have to carry out what I had started. I sat down in the parlor, because it was away from the back yard, and because I wouldn't let myself hide in my room, and grimly read my way through the rest of *Murder Must Advertise* without stopping once. The reproachful sound of Augusta's hammer barely penetrated, but I couldn't stop being aware of it, and the silences were equally nerve-racking. It took all my determination to keep reading when she came in the house to eat lunch, because I was sure every time I heard her footsteps that she was about to come find me and deliver a tirade on what an ingrate I had proved to be. When she finally went back out, I was momentarily relieved, but she didn't start hammering again, and I had no idea where she was or what she was up to. My eyes traversed every page of the book, and with part of my mind I knew it was entertaining, but each sentence slipped out of my head as soon as I read it, and I had no more idea of the plot when I reached the last page than if I had turned to the ending after Chapter One.

With a silent apology to Lord Peter, I put down the book and admitted that that hadn't solved a thing. I was starving, and there was nothing to do but brave the kitchen and get something to eat. Before I left the parlor I ordered myself not to sneak out, to show some backbone if I should encounter Augusta, but she wasn't in evidence. Guiltily I took some cold cuts and cheese from the refrigerator and ate them without bread, standing up. I could just picture myself—a wretched little parasite. Something had gone wrong with my high moral tone, but I was still mad at Augusta.

Yet if I wanted to preserve some self-respect I could see that I would have to help her out one last time, whether I liked it or not. While the resolve lasted, I stepped out the back door and looked around. No one. The sun beat down on an empty back yard. Augusta's hammer and a box of nails lay in the grass next to the summerhouse, and the hose was partially uncoiled, but beyond that I couldn't find a clue. It was two o'clock in the afternoon; I felt as though one painful week had passed since the morning, and it would take another to get to night.

After weeks of following Augusta through her labyrinth of chores, I could surely think of something to do. Setting myself in motion with an effort, I picked up the hammer and nails and put them back on the porch with the rest of the tools, rolled up the hose, looked at the shutters for a while but couldn't bring myself to fool with them, and turned to the garden. I hated weeding, but I hated it less than scraping paint.

I was bent over in the garden, sweat running down my face, pulling Bermuda grass from between the bean plants, when I heard Augusta behind me, shifting the wheelbarrow. I didn't turn around until her shadow fell across the dirt under my fingers; then I straightened up and wiped my forehead with my arm.

"Hi," she said. She didn't look very friendly, but somehow she seemed less expressionless than she had in the morning.

I made an effort to show no more emotion than she. "Hi," I answered.

"Weeding?"

I nodded. "Where have you been?" I asked.

"Hardware store." This is really idiotic, I thought. "We'll leave about five-thirty," Augusta said, turning away. "You'd better call home and tell them you're coming."

Some way or other I had managed not to remember that I had to call, and the thought did not do wonders for my outlook on the day. Sooner or later, somehow, I would have to account for what had happened in New Franklin, hand over a narrative of my visit as a kind of payment for permission to go—even though I had been sent in the first place—and that would mean half-truths and things I couldn't explain or even mention. A whole inch-thick book of unwritten rules that I hadn't observed since I had set foot in New Franklin. I felt hemmed in already as I climbed the stairs to wash my hands and call home. I had thrown out the number that my father had called me from a few days before. In the room where I had slept, now stripped of my presence, I opened my suitcase and dug around until I found my mother's office phone number.

The receptionist answered—I could picture her fingernails—and I asked for Mrs. Moss. There was a click.

"Cheryl Moss," my mother said briskly.

"Hi, Mom."

"Hi, sweetie, how are you doing?"

"Okay."

"What's up? How's life in the cornfields?"

"It's all right. I'm going to come back, though."

"Are you okay?"

"Sure."

"Well, when are you coming?"

"Today."

There was a silence. "Oh."

Don't sound so excited, I thought. "There's a train that leaves at seven o'clock, it gets in about twelve." For the first time it occurred to me that this might not fit in with my parents' schedules. And of course I'd be the one to take the blame—cornered between my mother and Augusta.

"Midnight?" my mother said.

I took a deep breath. "Yes."

"Karen, do you have to take this particular train?"

"Well, I decided to come home, and that was the first one Augusta could take me to."

"Are you in a hurry to leave for some reason?"

I knew it, I thought. Here it is already. "I don't know, Mom. Do you mind if I come home?"

"Of course not, Karen. One of us will be there to meet you." She sounded remarkably like Augusta; I felt like a bad penny no one wanted anymore.

"Well, thanks."

"I'll see you later, then, sweetie," she said, but I had a distinct feeling the "sweetie" was an effort.

"Okay, Mom. I'll see you."

"Bye."

I hung up and sat there on the edge of Augusta's bed thinking, I can't win.

Well, you asked for it, a little voice said, and to shut it up I hurried out of Augusta's room, downstairs and back to the garden. Even pulling weeds beat sitting around contemplating my own stupidity.

Probably I pulled more weeds that afternoon than on any other day of the whole visit, because I was trying so hard not to think of anything else. Even the heat wasn't entirely bad, as if I were taking some kind of treatment, sweating something out of myself while the pulled weeds piled up behind me.

At four-thirty Augusta called out to me from inside the house and said that if I wanted to take a shower before we went I'd better do it; I was more than ready to quit, and there was some grudging satisfaction in the thought that I had held up my end of the bargain even at the last minute. But when I emerged from the shower I had the feeling that now the hard part would begin.

Augusta was in the kitchen making sandwiches and drinking a beer; she looked so normal that way that for a moment I wondered if I was really leaving.

"Do you want something to eat before we go?" she said, not looking at me.

"No thanks." I stood wondering what to do with my hands, just as I had on the day I arrived.

"I was thinking you could take one of these on the train."

All right, I'm humiliated, I thought. "Thank you."

Augusta opened the refrigerator, took a tomato out of the vegetable bin, and put it on the breadboard she used for cutting things. With one zip of a serrated knife she took off the stem end of the tomato, and with the next cut half an inch into her left thumb. "God damn it!" she yelled, gritting her teeth in a ferocious grimace. In three long steps she was at the sink, where she hurled the knife viciously in among the dirty dishes (I was sure I heard one break) and turned the cold water on over her hand. I could see the blood welling out dark red and washing away in a steady pink stream. For some reason the sight made me feel guilty; I ran to get the Band-Aids out of the bathroom, and by the time I came back she was sitting at the kitchen table fuming, holding her thumb up in the air wrapped in paper towels.

"That was really brilliant," she growled, more to herself than to me.

"Does it hurt a lot?"

"Aah," she said, disgusted. "It's just dumb, that's all. You'd think I'd never used a tool before in my goddamn life." She unwound the paper towels and examined the cut, fascinated with her own blood. The depth of the cut turned my stomach. "You'll have to finish the sandwiches," she said, strapping Band-Aids around her thumb.

Haphazardly I made use of the ingredients she had gotten out, skipping the rest of the unlucky tomato, and put a sandwich on a plate in front of her. "Those are for you," she said. I wondered if she wasn't rubbing it in, but it was no time for an argument; I put wax paper around the sandwiches and stuck them in a bag. And now, I thought, there's nothing left to do but go.

"Well," said Augusta, in the way that means, It's over. She stood up and took the car keys off the cupboard door. Without speaking we went out of the kitchen, down the front hall. My suitcase was sitting at the bottom of the front stairs. Augusta did not lock the door behind us.

On the front walk she handed me the car keys and said, "Here, you can put that bag in the trunk." I did, and as I slammed down the trunk lid, which was hot to the touch, she got in the passenger's side of the car.

"What's going on?" I said, opening the driver's door.

"You drive," she said, looking straight ahead as if I drove her places every day.

"What?"

"You drive. I'm tired, I've been out there working all day, and my thumb hurts. Anyway, you might as well get another lesson before you go."

"I don't believe this. I've never even been out on the street, let alone on the highway."

She looked at me, maddeningly unimpressed. "Go on. You want to go to the train, you drive."

Oh. So that's what it's all about, I thought belatedly. Nothing comes easy around here, does it? I can't even go away without jumping through another hoop. And yet she had me over a barrel; I couldn't refuse without losing face, I couldn't argue about it for long without missing the train . . . The strategy of it reminded me precisely of my mother, and for a moment I wanted to lock the two of them in a closet together and throw away the key. But I was mad enough to get in the car and drive. If she wanted to risk her neck, fine. I wasn't going to be the one sitting in the suicide seat.

I started the Buick, rolled down all the windows, and put it in Drive. Augusta said nothing. From the house to the corner was easy; there were no other cars on Washington Street except one parked in front of the house next door. Missing that was no problem.

"Which way?" I said at the corner, trying to sound casual.

"Left."

I reminded myself that I knew how to turn, and left was my good direction. The Buick swung out like an ocean liner leaving the dock. It was no time for niceties: I focused all my attention on staying exactly in the middle of the street. We passed the corner store, where Augusta sometimes sent me at the last minute for an ingredient we had forgotten to get at Downtown Market. "Turn right," she said.

I stopped at the corner and thought, I knew it couldn't be that easy. Cars were coming from both directions—only one or two, but they were moving—other cars, huge two-ton machines like the one I was driving under false pretenses, and somehow I had to get out among them and drive without hitting anything.

"Just let them go by," Augusta said. A car and a pickup passed, going the way I wanted to, and she said, "Go."

"What about that guy?"

"He's on the other side of the street. Go."

I was not going to admit that I was terrified of the notion of piloting the Buick down a two-way street while cars came the other way, that I was so nervous my fingers felt as if they were losing their grip on the steering wheel. Gingerly I touched the accelerator and crept out, turning. To me it seemed that I nearly shaved off the rear fender of a car parked on my right, but I made it between that and the oncoming driver without a collision and got myself on course, trying to guide the Buick's left headlight down the street's center line.

"Now all you have to do is go straight until you reach the highway."

That was slim comfort. The thought of the highway churned in my stomach. Though I wanted to shut my eyes every time another car or a pickup truck went by the other way, I managed to keep pointing the Buick straight ahead, and they got past me somehow. I didn't dare look to see if the other drivers knew that something was wrong. The road led quickly out of town; the boundary was the spot where it jogged and crossed the railroad tracks.

Past the tracks were fields, and on a slight rise, maybe a mile away, I could see the highway. A pickup going twice as fast as me loomed up behind in the rearview mirror and passed with an engine roar and a sudden swerve back into the right lane; I could see why Augusta had driven into the ditch. In the mirror another car was overtaking me, not as fast. For a wild second I thought I recognized the car that belonged to the boy with the muscles, but it was an old man and his tiny wife. They, too, passed us. If I was going so much slower than they I must really be crawling. I sped up as much as I could stand, trying not to think about the fact that I was getting closer and closer to the highway. When was Augusta going to give in and say, Okay, enough?

The road from town met Highway 50 at a place where the highway curved—not sharply, but still it curved. To me at that moment it seemed that cars came around the bend and were instantly upon us, going faster than I could imagine doing myself.

"It's to the right," Augusta said, looking both ways. "All you've got to do is get out there and get going and you'll be all right."

"They're going so *fast*."

"Just do about thirty-five or forty and it'll be okay."

That didn't answer the question of how I was going to get out there. "When I say go, just do it," Augusta said. "It's easier than it looks." A couple of cars whizzed past in both directions, and I tried to get some sense of how much time there really was once they came into view.

"Go," Augusta said, and at the same instant that I started I thought, But I'm not ready. "I said go," she repeated, more loudly this time, and I resigned myself to fate and stepped on the gas hard, seeing nothing but the piece of road I was aiming at, hanging on to the wheel with all my might as I charged forward. When I was sure the Buick was actually on the highway, I stole a look at the speedometer and it was close to fifty; scared as I was, a kind of grim exultation gripped me.

"Not bad," Augusta said. "A little rocky, but so what? Now just keep it like this." Just? Did she think I did this every day? Gradually I slowed down until I reached forty; that I could stand. And there I was, driving the Buick to St. Louis. If only M.J. or Jeanette could, for some unknown reason, ride past in another car—which they, of course, would not be driving—and see me and drop dead from shock. I stole a glance at Augusta; she was holding up the roof with her right hand, her hair was blowing out the window, and she had a faint smile on her face. She didn't look at me; she appeared to be sniffing the breeze.

"You know, this could actually get to be fun," I said. "Knock on wood." But there wasn't anything wooden in the Buick to knock. I concentrated on keeping in my lane and trying to ignore the cars behind me, which obviously wanted to go faster; for a couple of minutes we cruised. Then I saw I was coming to a town and a red light.

"Be careful of that brake," Augusta said.

I know what I'm doing, I thought. But the brake did make me nervous. I applied it gingerly in brief spasms until we had come to a stop at the light.

"Congratulations," she said. "You made it to Shiloh. It's only about another fifty miles."

"Yeah, at this rate we might make it by nine o'clock."

"That's okay."

I was just about to say, "But I'll miss my train," and I was finally hoping that we would both be able to admit that was the point, when the car behind me honked. The light had turned green.

"Just keep going straight," Augusta said. The moment was swallowed up in my anxiety to get past the parked cars on my right and reach the next stretch of open road. I could feel the traffic backed up behind me almost as if it was pushing the Buick forward. As soon as we reached real highway again, the car in back of me roared around us. For a moment I was certain that I was about to witness a head-on collision, and then one second later become part of the twisted wreckage. "Ignore them," Augusta said.

"I can't."

"Then go faster."

"I'm trying," I said, but now that I was fully aware of the other drivers' impatience, it was even more difficult to keep up the speed they expected. I kept edging to the right, nearly running my wheels off the roadway in my effort to stay out of the way of any car that might try to pass. It was a relief when we reached the next town, but I knew the respite would be only temporary.

We pulled up at a stop sign and Augusta at last said, "Why don't I take it from here?"

"I think that would be a great idea," I said, not caring if she saw I was grateful.

Augusta got out and came around to the driver's side of the car, giving the drivers behind us a don't-you-dare-honk look as she did so, and I slid back to where I belonged. We drove in silence, me wondering anew at how easy Augusta made it look but proud of myself, too, and no longer mad.

"That was a good job," she said after a few miles.

"Thanks."

We were on the top of a hill, and in the distance I could see smokestacks, the river, and St. Louis, where the train for Chicago would soon enter Union Station and take me away. It made me think of Augusta's trip to New York with Allan. What nerve she had. Hadn't she been embarrassed when everyone stared at them in the club car, knowing exactly what they were going to do? I would have expired on the spot, I was sure of it, but I knew Augusta better than that. Willy-nilly, I knew her better than I had ever expected to, and now I began to wonder when I would ever hear such stories again. If I told them to M.J. and Jeanette, they wouldn't even believe me. Adults didn't talk about things like that.

Augusta turned on the radio and got the Cardinals pre-game show. Someone was interviewing a baseball player in what might as well have been a foreign tongue. We reached the end of the actual highway and passed slowly through East St. Louis, past burned-out brick houses and rib joints sending up sweet-smelling smoke and the De's Is Da Blues Record Shop. Black faces surrounded us, seeming not to notice our passage through their streets. I hadn't seen a black person since I had come to New Franklin, and seeing them now made me realize that I had almost stopped believing in the existence of a world beyond our own.

On an iron bridge whose roadway sang under the tires we crossed over the opaque tan vastness of the Mississippi and, coming down the slope on its Missouri end, were ejected into St. Louis. I started to look for the castle-like tower of Union Station, but I didn't know which way it would be, and my view was blocked by buildings. Augusta seemed to know exactly what she was doing, as we wound our way through streets and past faces like those of East St. Louis but not quite so poor. The traffic seemed extremely heavy, and the streets crowded and tight, but I wasn't sure if I had simply forgotten what cities were like. We turned a corner, and there was a black man waving a red rag, motioning the passing cars to park on what looked like the front yard of an ordinary house. To my amazement, Augusta obeyed him, handing him two dollars and pulling into a space. She took the keys out of the ignition and said, "Come on." She got out; what else was I to do? I was still looking for the train station, and because she seemed ready to walk away with the keys, I said, "Wait a minute, what about my suitcase?"

"You don't need it," she said. "We're going to the ball game."

chapter 11

There was a moment of absolute confusion, a feeling of strangeness and almost of threat being on that street, a sense of "But
you can't do this," of incomprehension, of relief. Augusta was
waiting for me to join her. I didn't have a watch, and I started
looking around as if I might spot a clock somewhere among the
rundown brick houses and find out how many minutes I had to
get to the station; my mind raced ahead—would I have to run
there dragging my suitcase?—would I be able somehow to find a
taxi?—and then unexpectedly and effortlessly I surrendered. It's
not my problem, I thought. It's not up to me. Whatever happens
I'll just say she thought it up. At least I could use that excuse
about why I changed my mind and stayed, and people would
believe it; but I knew that Aunt Augusta and Niece Karen would
just be a show we might put on for other people from now on.

"It's around the corner and a couple of blocks down," she said
as I joined her. Once we turned the corner, I could see the lights
over the ball park shining, even though it wouldn't be completely
dark for a long time yet; the street was filled up with a line of
grumbling city buses flying small red flags that said *Redbird
Express*, cars were trying to squeeze by between buses on one
side and people on the other, hawkers were selling Cardinal

caps, Cardinal pennants, Sno-Kones, peanuts by the bag. The outside of the ball park looked like nothing more than a long blank wall with occasional doors in it; it could have been a warehouse, except that noise and light poured out of its interior into the darkening sky. Augusta was walking faster as we came closer, almost visibly holding herself back so she wouldn't lose me in the crowd.

We lined up at the Reserved Grandstand window, and I found myself hoping we'd get a good seat. At the last moment, as the people ahead of us were leaving the window, she turned to me and said, "You could still make your train," but it didn't matter anymore and all I did was shake my head. Augusta's negotiations with the ticket seller made no sense to me, but she looked satisfied as we merged with the stream of people entering the park. For a couple of minutes it was all I could do to stay with her as somehow our tickets were torn off, we passed through the turnstiles, and she made her way through and across the entering crowds. It was like being in a very crowded basement filled with people on a thousand urgent errands; then almost without warning we were on a ramp, I could see light towers against the sky, faraway buildings, the grandstands on the other side of the field, and we emerged. After the streets and the underworld beneath the stands, the sight of so much space made me almost dizzy, and the green of the grass under the lights dazzled me. On it, standing negligently around playing catch, were actual baseball players. I wanted to stay right where I was, but the crowd swept me on into the aisle and Augusta led me up to our seats. As we sat down, I thought, Why didn't somebody tell me this was what going to ball games was like? Over the chatter of the crowd hawkers were shouting—"Hey, hot dogs!"—"Beer here! Cold beer!" Augusta waved her hand to the beer man and passed money down the row. He put down his case of Stag, flipped the top off a bottle with the opener he wore on a string around his neck, and passed it back. She took a deep swig.

"There is no beer anywhere like the beer you drink at the ball park," Augusta said. "Now. Who's pitching tonight, anyway?"

"You're asking me?"

The game itself didn't mean much to me, and Augusta didn't try very hard to explain. She seemed to feel that any fool would get the point of baseball without an explanation, and I could see now that in a way she was right. I ate hot dogs, there was a home run, somebody pitched well, the Cardinals won the game. It seemed endless and outside of time; it went on for so long after it got boring that it became interesting again. It wasn't until the fifth inning that I finally remembered that we had to call my parents and tell them not to meet me; Augusta called them collect from a pay phone between innings, and when I asked her what they said, she shrugged and gave me a conspiratorial look. "They're all right," she said, as if she could have added, But they're not *here*.

I was half asleep on my feet as Augusta guided me back out through the crowds and the ramps and gates, down to the dark street and the Buick. The several beers she had drunk seemed to have had no effect on her. We got into the car—on the front seat was the bag of sandwiches I had been going to take on the train—and I was asleep for real before we crossed the Mississippi again.

I awoke the next morning back in my bed at Augusta's, barely able to remember getting there. My suitcase stood in the middle of the floor, still packed, and I was sure she must have carried it up. I tried to judge what time it was by the angle of the sun coming in the windows, but it didn't matter.

When *would* I go home, I wondered idly as I padded into the bathroom to take a shower.

As I was drying myself off, I realized that once again I was hearing the sound of Augusta's hammer. I pulled back the curtains of the bathroom window and looked out on the back yard. Augusta had propped a ladder against the gazebo and she was precariously perched on its top rung, nailing down the sheets of rusty metal that formed its pointed roof.

I wondered what my parents had said when she had called them, who she had talked to and whether she had told them she drove me to the ball game instead of the station. My father might understand that; my mother, never. But Augusta would have known better than to tell her that anyway. She could say it was my idea to stay and I could say it was hers, and how would they be able to tell?

If they knew what went on down here . . . I couldn't finish that. What *would* they do? They couldn't very well talk to Augusta the way they might to me—not if they knew what was good for their health. I began to realize what an ally she might be to have. And was I hers?

Well, she had made some kind of an effort to get me to stay, hadn't she?

It was another clear day, but not as hot as usual, and I thought, Now that I'm really here, what shall I do? After the night before, the idea of another ball game sounded like fun, and there was all of St. Louis besides the ball park—we could go to movies . . . I wondered what in the world it would be like to take Augusta shopping.

Below me Augusta shifted her position on the roof of the gazebo. She was almost spread-eagled; one foot was still on the ladder and the toe of the other was precariously jammed against the upturned rim of the roof as she tried to reach some sections that she hadn't nailed down. You *could* get down and move the ladder, I thought, but that would make too much sense. There was a loud crack, almost like the sound of a bat meeting a baseball, and I saw Augusta's hand grab for the point of the roof. For a long moment she seemed frozen there, and I wasn't even sure what I was seeing; then, majestically, the whole summer-house began to slip to one side. "Damn it!" I heard her yell to the sky, and in an explosion of snapping and crunching, the gazebo's thousand individual boards flew apart, and it collapsed with a tremendous *whump!* in a cloud of dust. For a moment I was too amazed to move, then I started to run. I realized I didn't have one piece of clothing on, flew into my room, pulled on the pants I had been wearing the day before, and grabbed the shirt, frantically buttoning it as I ran down the stairs. As I tore through the hall toward the kitchen and the back door, I could see in my mind's eye a picture of Augusta among the wreckage. I couldn't imagine her actually hurt, my mind refused. I banged my way out the door, across the porch and the yard to where she was sitting amid a heap of splintered boards, holding on to her ankle.

"Are you all right?"

"I guess so," she said, wiping her face with one hand and leaving it streaked with sweat and dust. "That was really wild."

"Boy, you're telling me, I saw the whole thing from upstairs."

"What did it look like?"

"Are you sure you're all right?"

"Yeah, I'm okay. I don't know what the hell I'm going to do next. Yesterday I tried to cut my thumb off and now this. Probably I'll set the house on fire tomorrow."

"Please don't, okay? Why are you holding onto your foot like that?"

"Oh, I came down on it funny."

The remains of the gazebo were like a giant game of pick up sticks; the old timbers had snapped and wrenched apart, and nails protruded from them where they had separated; many were the new shiny nails that Augusta had just pounded in. "God, you were pretty lucky," I said, realizing what could have happened. Now I noticed there were rips in her pants. "Did you get cut?"

"I don't know," she said, feeling herself. She rolled up first one pants leg and then the other, exposing a long scratch on one calf, but nothing else. "Help me up," she said. She held out a hand, and I pulled her to her feet; when she tried to put her weight on her left foot, she had to grab for my shoulder. "Uh oh."

"Hurts?"

"Yes." She put one arm around my neck, and like the losers in a three-legged race we hobbled over to the back porch. "I've got a feeling that's sprained," she said. Her ankle was swelling already.

"Don't you think you'd better go to a doctor?"

Augusta looked pained and sighed. "Oh, I suppose so. I don't know what the hell Horstmann can do about this, but I might as well let him look at it. I tell you what, too. You can drive me over there."

After the day before, there was no arguing with that. "Do you think he'll be able to see you right away?"

"Well, I can watch my ankle swell up in his waiting room just as well as I can here."

"Hold on, then." I got the keys from their appointed place and ran upstairs to grab my shoes, thinking to myself, Just look at you, you're being an actual help.

Slowly Augusta and I hobbled from the back porch to the Buick—she got very heavy along the way—and with some difficulty I helped her in. Driving hardly fazed me at all, I was so busy thinking about what might have happened to her. Augusta's jaw was set tight, and I was sure her ankle hurt a lot; she didn't speak except to give directions. It was only a few blocks to the doctor's office; at the last minute I realized I would have to park the car, which I had no idea how to do, but there was a row of empty spaces right where I needed them, and all I had to do was pull up next to the curb. As I got out of the car, who should be coming down the sidewalk, half a block away, but Jeannie Holzman and Doreen Schatz. They watched in fascination as I helped Augusta out the passenger's side and we limped across the sidewalk like a couple of soldiers in a Revolutionary War parade. I realized that I was out in public without a bra—or even underpants, for God's sake—and I felt as if they took that in with X-ray vision, not to mention the fact that Augusta had done one more damn-fool thing that they'd be able to speculate about as soon as they got around the corner. They passed us just as we were going in the door, and Doreen said "Hi." Jeannie just watched; the door closed behind us before I could decide whether to reply.

The doctor's office was air-conditioned, and Dr. Horstmann's nurse took Augusta into a back room at once. To my amazement, it was only nine-thirty in the morning by the clock over the nurse's desk. I sat down to wait. There was a mumble of conversation outside the street door; then it opened and Doreen Schatz looked around it at me. "Is she all right?" she said.

My first thought was to say, None of your business, but I couldn't. "I guess so. She probably just has a sprained ankle."

"I didn't know you could drive," Doreen said, with a respectfulness that I thought was only my due.

"I just learned."

"Oh. Well—do you want to go to the pool some time?" Is there some connection here? I thought. Maybe she was just trying to make up for the last time. I couldn't figure out New Franklin ways.

"Sure, I guess."

"Well, tell your aunt I hope she gets better soon."

"Okay." And you tell your friend I'm not a snob.

"Bye." Doreen disappeared around the door, and it closed again. What had I gotten myself into now?

When Augusta re-emerged, her ankle and foot were wrapped in a huge lump of tan Ace bandage and she was leaning on the nurse. The doctor was behind them, saying, "Augusta, you should be using crutches now for at least a couple of days. You don't want to make that worse. And then if I were you I'd use a cane until it felt just about normal." He paused as if to give her a chance to agree, but she didn't. "Come back in a week and I'll look at it again." He retreated to his inner sanctum, and the nurse said, "Same time a week from today?"

"Sure," Augusta said. "I'll try not to fall off anything else between now and then." She transferred her weight from the nurse to me, and we maneuvered gingerly out the door. "If he were me," she muttered as soon as we were outside, "he wouldn't use a cane for a million bucks."

When I drove up to her house again, the Reese Plumbing and Heating pickup was parked in front and Jerry was standing in the side yard looking at what was left of the gazebo. You could see it from the street, the pointed roof sitting on the back lawn looking like the remains of the Wicked Witch of the West. When we stopped, he turned and waved. I got out. "Looks like you've had some excitement around here," he said.

"I guess you could call it that."

"Come over here and give me a hand," Augusta said, and I

thought, Will wonders never cease. Jerry opened her door and lifted her to her feet with no apparent effort. "What'd you do to it?" he said, with one arm around her waist and the other holding her arm around his neck.

"Sprained. It's not too bad."

"Want to go in?"

"I sure don't want to stay out here and look at that thing." The two of them went up the front walk and inside much faster than she and I would have; Jerry seemed almost to be carrying her. They left the front door open behind them, and I heard her say, "Just take me on up." They climbed the stairs, and I sat down on the front porch swing, feeling left out and relegated to childhood. *I* was the one who took her to the doctor, so there, I thought resentfully.

In a minute he came back out without Augusta. "Well," he said to me awkwardly.

"What's she doing?"

"Gus? She's lying down on the couch upstairs. The doctor gave her some kind of painkiller."

"Oh."

"What did you say your name was?" I could see he was trying to decide what to do with himself; he settled for holding on to one of the posts of the porch.

"Karen."

"And you're Gus's niece." The nickname sounded puny and inadequate. No wonder she hadn't married him, if that was what he called her. I nodded.

"I'm Jerry Reese," he said, brushing his hand off on his pants leg and extending it formally. I shook it; his hand was callused but friendly. "Well, I'm glad you took her over to Horstmann's office," he said.

"How did you find out the summerhouse fell down?"

"I was just driving by and it wasn't there. It's kind of hard to miss something like that."

"I guess you're right."

"It must have been a heck of a crash when it went."

"It was scary—she was all the way up on the roof, and it fell down with her holding on to it. I was really worried."

Jerry traced the seam of a pocket on the outside of his pants leg and then looked up at me as if he hadn't really noticed me before I said that. "Well, it's a good thing somebody was around." He crossed his arms over his chest and stared glumly at the wall behind me. "Why did she have to climb up on that damn thing in the first place?" he said, more to himself than to me. Then he gave me a glance. "Pardon me."

"She was fixing it, that's all," I said, conscious of sounding defensive. "She's been nailing on it for days."

"I told her I'd help her with it a dozen times. Anyway, if she'd taken my advice, she'd have torn it down a long time ago."

He sounded so sad that I had to forgive him for stealing part of my glory. "Sure," I said, "but when does she ever take anybody's advice?"

He gave me a wry look. "You sound like you know her pretty well."

She's my family, I thought. If she had married Jerry, he'd be my uncle.

"Looks like she's been working pretty hard around here," he said.

"Really? Can you tell? I've been helping her; it's about all we ever do."

"Has she got you fixing those shutters? That's a heck of a job."

"I just scrape them. The ones that are broken I don't know what she's going to do with."

"I offered to fix them a long time ago, but she never asked."

I had reckless visions of getting the shutters done once and for all. "She never asks me to do anything, either, I just do it. Maybe you should come over someday and take them away and . . ." Suddenly I felt foolish. He was looking at me tolerantly.

"I don't think that would go over real good."

"But she wants them fixed." Couldn't I keep my mouth shut?

"I'll tell you: your aunt would rather do just about everything the hard way than take anybody's help. Except yours, maybe. But you're related. I don't see anybody else around here giving her a hand. She wouldn't allow it."

"She asked you to help her just now."

Jerry stooped down and picked up a crumb of old brick that had found its way from the front walk onto the porch. "Well," he said, crumbling it between his thumb and forefinger. When it was gone, he looked at his palm. "To tell you the truth, I'm surprised she did. I ought to know better, though. There's no use being surprised at anything she does. If you are, she just looks at you like you're feebleminded."

"I thought she only treated me that way."

He gave me a real smile. "She treats everybody the same. Like she's teaching the dumb class."

I wondered if he said such things to her face; no wonder he made her mad.

"Do you mind if I use the phone? I'd better call the store, find out whose drain I'm supposed to be rooting out."

Do I mind? "It's in the kitchen," I said.

"I know."

Unhurriedly, Jerry went back in the house; I could hear the tread of his boots all the way to the kitchen. I still couldn't imagine Augusta married to him. I wondered what had become of their fight; he didn't seem disgusted anymore. I tried to reconstruct what it had been about—he had come to tell her that other people knew about her and Jim, or maybe just that he knew—and then what? That hadn't gone over real good, as he would say. I could understand that. But think how *he* must feel. And then she had gotten all dressed up and left for her supposed tennis game. Presumably that meant Jim. But who could tell what Augusta was up to if she didn't want you to know?

I was tired of playing Nancy Drew, but at least none of this was my responsibility. Except turning on those headlights. If only she had told me. And yet it would still have happened, most likely; I wouldn't have known what he looked like, wouldn't have known for sure what was going on . . . was there any protection, really? Or only the intention—perhaps it was that you thanked people for.

"That's some kind of a mess out back," Jerry said, stepping out onto the porch.

"I guess maybe I ought to try to get rid of it, since Augusta won't be able to for a while," I said.

"Yeah? Where are you planning to put it?"

"Well, over by the back fence at least, you know, where the brush pile is."

"That's going to be a lot of work for you," he said.

"Well—" This isn't working out right somehow, I thought.

"Maybe I'd better come over and help you. I'd do it now, but I've got to go do something about a flooded basement. I could do it tomorrow morning, though."

"Sure—I mean—are you sure you've got time? We'll get it done eventually."

He gave me that tolerant look again. "Yep, I'm sure," he said, drawing out the word "yep" slightly, and for the first time I had a sinking feeling he might be putting on some sort of act, pretending to be more of a hick than he was. I wondered if I had passed whatever the test had been, or if Jerry was just being himself and I was trying to make a simple thing complicated for no reason.

"Well," he said, interrupting my thoughts, "I guess I'd better push on." He stuck out his hand again, and it took me a second to react and shake it. "I'll come over about nine, okay?"

"Okay," I said. Now I almost didn't want him to leave.

"Don't tell her I'm coming, all right? I wouldn't want her to be overwhelmed with gratitude." He flashed me a sardonic look and turned away.

chapter 12

Upstairs, Augusta was lying on the sofa with all the shades pulled down. She was asleep, one arm dangling onto the floor, still holding a Margery Allingham mystery. The sound of me crossing the room woke her up; she looked a little confused.

"How do you feel?" I said. Her foot was propped up on a cushion.

"Okay, I guess. Whatever Horstmann gave me kind of knocked me out."

"I didn't mean to wake you up."

" 's okay."

"You want anything?"

"No. Well—a glass of water, maybe." I went downstairs for a glass, and by the time I brought it up she was asleep again. I put it down next to her hand as quietly as I could and sneaked downstairs again.

Now I was really in charge of 212 Washington Street. Queen for a Day.

The job of keeping up life's continuity took hold of me and wouldn't let go; the house itself seemed to demand human attention. As if I had no choice I went out on the back porch and surveyed the scene. The presence of that wreckage was unbearable, an affront that I knew Augusta would never tolerate, and despite common sense and Jerry's promise of help, I had to start hauling away the splintered boards. They scratched my hands, stuck me with splinters; a few times I raked myself with protruding nails and thought about tetanus shots. But as if this chore were some kind of crusade, I couldn't quit until I had gotten rid of all the boards that I could extricate from the general heap. It was way past lunch time. Sore-handed and covered with grit, I went inside, washed up, ate a sandwich, but even then I couldn't quit. I felt some obligation to touch all the bases, as if civilization depended on me, and that meant thinking what to have for dinner and going to Downtown Market. Augusta had slept through lunch; she would probably be starving. Only when I got home with my groceries could I finally stop.

I was just going to sit down and do nothing for a while when Augusta called, "Hey, Karen?" from upstairs. The romance of being in charge started to fade. Boy, I thought, as I climbed the stairs, how have my parents done it all these years?

"How are you?" I asked. She was sitting up reading the sports page from the previous day's *Post-Dispatch.*

"Oh, I'm fine. Don't worry about me. What are you up to?"

"Not much."

"You sound pretty busy to me."

"Well, I hauled away some of those boards, and then I went shopping."

"That's what you call not much, huh?"

"I don't know. You do it all the time. I mean—you know what I mean."

"What'd you get?"

"Hamburger."

"The very thing I've been dreaming of. A hamburger and a

bottle of wine, I figure no sprained ankle can hold out against that for long."

"I could even grill it if there's any charcoal."

"Yeah, and afterward you could start a bonfire with that damn summerhouse and we could roast marshmallows."

"I bet the fire department would love that."

"Well, everybody thinks I'm nuts already, they might as well have something else to talk about."

"Jeannie Holzman saw us going into the doctor's office."

"Hmh. I wouldn't hold my breath expecting a get-well card from her."

"Her friend Doreen invited me to go to the pool sometime; I think it had something to do with me being able to drive."

"She probably just thinks she can impress her friends if she rides up in the Buick. Listen: don't take Jeannie anywhere in that car, okay? I don't owe her any favors, that's for sure."

"God, I wasn't even planning on driving it."

"Go ahead. You know how."

She was always one step ahead of me; I couldn't believe how casually she trusted me with the Buick, and I wasn't sure what to say.

"Do me a favor?"

"Sure."

"Go down to the little store and get a paper. I want to read about last night's game."

"You mean being there half the night wasn't enough?"

She sighed and shook her head. "I don't know about you," she said. "Your attitude toward baseball still needs a lot of work."

"Somebody's around here does," I said, heading back down the stairs.

"You know where the wine is?" she called. "Down in the cellar?"

"Yes."

"The corkscrew's in the pantry. And don't drink the whole bottle yourself."

Closing the front door behind me, I twirled my index finger next to my temple as if she could see me and thought how glad I was not to have gone home. Who else would think of saying such a thing to me?

We ate upstairs, sitting on the floor—monumentally thick cheeseburgers and french fries out of a frozen package—and Augusta drank a whole bottle of wine, minus a glass for me. It was like a strange picnic; the ball game, of course, was on; we were at peace.

Promptly at nine the next morning, Jerry knocked at the front door, and I let him in.

"Who is it?" Augusta yelled from upstairs.

"It's me," he said. There was no immediate answer; we both stood in the front hall looking up at the top of the stairs, as though we might see some words floating down.

"I thought I'd help Karen take care of that mess in the back yard," he said. Still silence. "You're welcome."

Oo, I thought, take that. "Thank you, Jerry," Augusta said quietly.

Working with Jerry was something like helping my father build the bookcase. He was so much stronger than I was and so much more certain of what to do that I had a hard time not feeling useless. Not that I didn't work. He gave me a huge pair of work gloves and a claw hammer out of his truck, and the two of us went around prying apart boards that were still nailed together and dragging—or in his case, throwing—them out of the way. The main difference was that he did ten times as many as I did. Once we had detached everything, we carried it by the wheelbarrow load over to his truck and piled it in the back on top of old lengths of pipe and miscellaneous parts I couldn't identify. It was hot, dusty work, and I wondered how he could stand to wear heavy boots and thick green work clothes in such weather. Except for having his shirtsleeves rolled up, he might have looked the same in December. It took only a few minutes to realize that the job would have been impossible without him.

When we were finally down to the octagonal concrete foundation—leaving a few snapped-off posts sticking up—he said "Well?" and I was more than ready to quit. We sat on the back steps and gulped down glasses of ice water, and I was surprised at how easy I felt with him.

"Penny for your thoughts," he said when he had finished his glass.

"Augusta told me you fixed her furnace, too," I said, meaning, See, she does let you help her.

"Yeah. I just charge her for parts. Do it on the weekend."

"That's nice of you."

Jerry seemed to ignore that completely. "What say we take that stuff and dump it?"

Like Augusta, Jerry had left the keys in his truck. I wondered if he always did, or only outside her house. The cab reminded me of my father's truck, except older; it was as crowded as someone's desk in an office, rattling with parts and tools, the glove compartment open and jammed full of receipts, bills, cryptic scrawls on pieces of paper dotted with greasy fingerprints. A wristwatch without its strap was attached to the radio knob by a twist of wire, and I saw that it was eleven o'clock. Fast work.

Jerry took us out of New Franklin by a way I hadn't been,

over a maze of back roads, up and down small hills, dipping down through creek bottoms, bouncing over railroad crossings with loud groans from the truck's frame, past pig farms and cornfields, old houses like Augusta's, and one beat-up house trailer with a Bunny bread sign on the door and a tractor tire painted silver and planted with raggedy, bright blue petunias decorating the front yard. The roads were almost private, and I realized that I hadn't seen the actual country since I had come down. Maybe this was what had drawn Augusta back—some memory or illusion of a memory that the landscape seemed to stir even in me.

Jerry looked like part of it, driving along with his right hand on the wheel and his left resting on the outside rearview mirror. He had grease under his fingernails, as black as shoe polish, packed in by his work with a thoroughness that was almost neat. I wondered if he could ever entirely clean it out. He glanced at me, making me aware that I was staring, and I watched the road instead, jouncing up and down on the lumpy seat.

"Did you know Gus and I were engaged once?" he said.

"She told me," I said, though I wondered if she would have used the word "engaged." I was afraid he could read in my mind the words "How could she?" The roughness of his beard, his graying hair, just the sheer size and weight of him, the fact that he looked so *old*—it was still impossible to imagine. If any one thing reminded me that Augusta was older than I, it was that.

"You remind me of her a little, when she was a kid." I remembered what they had done as "kids," and for a moment I was very scared, out there on some back road where I wouldn't even know how to get home, but a part of me said, Oh, come *on*. You really think he's making a pass at *you*?

I didn't want to look at him for fear I might be right and might seem to encourage him, but the glances I couldn't help taking gradually reassured me; he looked no different from a few minutes before, driving steadily along. Was there really a resemblance? I'd never be as good-looking as Augusta, that was for sure, I thought, looking down my legs, which to me seemed too plump and knobby-kneed to resemble hers in the slightest.

We turned at a sign reading SOLID FILL WANTED, down nothing more than two ruts leading into some scrubby woods. A few yards in, there was a clearing, and beyond it a ravine filled with every kind of junk I could imagine, old auto bodies, radiators out of houses, refrigerators, ancient farm equipment that had been lying there rusting for so long it had congealed into shapeless, flaking, brown-and-orange lumps. Our load of rotten boards was like throwing a bucket of water in the ocean.

As we started back I suddenly felt bold and asked, "What happened about the two of you getting married?"

He looked at me in a way that made me think, Oh no, I've been rude. "You'll have to ask Gus that question," he said; I couldn't tell if he was offended or not. For a few minutes he drove in silence, and I tried to think of some way to take it back.

"Actually," he said, "I think she's known me too long. Since she was your age. It'd be sort of like marrying your brother. At least that's the closest I can figure out."

We rumbled loudly over a set of railroad tracks.

"Besides, I'm not afraid of her," he said with a slight smile. But that can't be what she wants, I thought.

"I guess she wasn't very nice to you this morning."

That made him look sardonic again. "I'm used to it."

I pondered the unfairness of that all the way back to town.

"Looks like lunchtime," Jerry said, when he turned onto St. Clair by the appliance store. "Buy you a hamburger?"

"No—I mean, no, thanks—you've done so much already

today." Inspiration struck, belatedly. "Why don't you come over and have lunch with us?"

He thought it over for a couple of blocks. "Okay."

When we got back to the house, I went upstairs to look for Augusta, but she wasn't there. She was sitting on the back porch steps, looking at the place where the gazebo had been. Jerry, who had found her first, was in the kitchen opening two beers.

"How'd you get down here?" I asked her.

"I limped."

"You better not mess that ankle up worse."

"Okay, Doctor. I hear you dumped everything off."

"It sure is a good thing Jerry came over, I never could have done all that."

"Mm-hm, I get the message. I know. I wasn't overly polite this morning, if that's what you're trying to get across."

"Is she giving you a hard time?" Jerry said, coming out onto the porch with the beers. He handed one to Augusta.

"She's defending you," Augusta said.

"God knows I could use it," he said.

All right then, I wanted to say. Instead I went inside and started making myself a sandwich. They could do whatever they were up to without me.

I had eaten lunch and was standing in front of Augusta's bookshelves upstairs, trying to decide which murder mystery to read next, when there was a knock at the front door. For a minute I forgot about Augusta's ankle and waited for the sound of her answering it; then I remembered and ran downstairs. It was Doreen Schatz, wanting to know if I felt like going to the pool.

"Um—I guess so," I said. "Come on in."

She stepped inside and looked around as though planning how she'd describe Augusta's house to her friends. Out back I could hear Augusta and Jerry still talking.

"Actually, I'm not even sure if I brought my suit with me. I'll have to go up and look."

"Okay," she said, examining the pictures on the wall of the front hall. I got halfway up and thought, She must feel really strange down there. "Come on up."

Inside Augusta's house and away from Jeannie Holzman, Doreen did not look at all formidable. She was shorter than I, I realized, and had less of a figure.

"Is your aunt okay?" she asked, staring at the big oil painting.

"Pretty good. If she's not, she won't admit it. There's a lady in that picture—see, there's her head, and that's the rest of her—see what I mean? One of the other teachers at Augusta's school painted it. I think it's really awful."

"You call her Augusta?"

"It's her name." There you go, being bad, I thought. I went into my room and looked through my suitcase; jammed into one of its pouches was my second-favorite bathing suit. I was surprised that I had thought to bring it down. "Just let me put my suit on, okay?" I said, and closed the door. I pulled my dirty work clothes off, put on the suit, and looked at myself in the mirror. The idea of going to the pool and being stared at by half the kids in New Franklin was beginning to fill me with dread, and I was glad that at least I had a halfway-stylish bathing suit to wear. Over it I pulled on a clean pair of white jeans and a proper-looking shirt with a button-down collar; it was as close as I could get to what I had seen the local kids wearing. I gave my hair a couple of swipes with a hairbrush, but of course it did no good.

"Your aunt sure has a lot of books," Doreen said when I came out. "Do you think she's read all of them?"

"I guess."

"Ooh," Doreen said, looking self-conscious. Her finger was on a book I had never noticed called *Sex Without Fear*. Everything she had imagined about Augusta was confirmed. I was amazed myself, and both of us were too embarrassed to look at each other. If M.J. had been there she'd have said, "Let's read it," but with this stranger from New Franklin I didn't even feel right admitting I knew what the word "sex" meant.

"Let's go," I said, heading for the stairs.

"Don't you want a towel?" said Doreen.

"Oh." In my haste I had forgotten. I grabbed a towel and at the last minute plucked *Lord Peter Views the Body* off the bookshelf; Doreen was back down in the front hall, where there weren't many discoveries to make. I went to tell Augusta where I was going. She was in the kitchen with a pencil and paper, drawing what looked like plans for a new summerhouse. "What happened to Jerry?" I said.

"He had to go to work."

"He's a nice man."

"You sound just like Cheryl," she said. "Who came in, anyway?"

"Doreen Schatz. The girl that was with Jeannie Holzman yesterday. I'm going to go to the pool with her."

"Well, I guess there are worse places to go on a day like this," she said. "Before you leave, what do you think of this?" She held up her drawing; it looked something like a two-car garage.

"Beautiful. We'll build it tomorrow."

"Oh, go on then. Go soak your head."

"Yes, ma'am."

* * *

When we left the house, Doreen looked longingly at the Buick and said, "Does your aunt let you drive whenever you want?"

"No."

She looked disappointed, but it was too late now to uninvite me. "Well, it's not *real* far," she said.

We set off, uncomfortably conscious of having to find something to say. "What grade are you going to be in next year?" Doreen asked.

"Eleventh."

"Oh." That seemed to impress her even more than the driving. "I'm going to be in tenth; Jeannie'll be in eleventh."

"Do you think she'll be at the pool?"

Doreen looked uncomfortable. "I'm not for sure," she said, making me wonder if I had heard right. I began to get the picture, though: Doreen was Jeannie's lieutenant, and she was being disloyal by acting friendly to me. I liked her more than I had expected.

"What's your school like?" I asked, just to say something.

"Awful," she said cheerfully. "We have the grossest boys you ever saw in your life." Great, I thought, and they'll all be hanging around the pool. "What about yours?"

"My school? Oh, it's big, I guess, it's . . . okay."

"Like how big?"

"Couple of thousand."

"You're kidding."

"No."

"You have a couple of thousand kids in your *high* school? Geez—that must be awful."

Wait a minute, I thought, you're supposed to be impressed.

"I'll bet there are some cute boys, though," she said, looking at me slyly. I nodded, able to admit to the cuteness of some boys somewhere. "Have you got a boyfriend?"

"Unh-uh." But I couldn't stop myself. "I had one, but we broke up."

"Did you go steady with him?" Doreen asked. Already I regretted telling her.

"I don't know, not officially." There seemed to be no way out of this but to grill her in return. "Do you have one?" I asked, before she could think of another question.

She rolled her eyes. "Yeah, but . . ."

"But what?"

"Oh, I don't know." Doreen looked coy.

"Don't you like him?"

"Oh, I *like* him okay, but he always wants to go to the quarry and . . . go parking, and stuff."

"Oh." That stuff.

"Why'd you break up with yours?"

"I didn't."

Doreen gave me a frank look, as one woman of the world to another. "Well, you can always say you did. Nobody believes what boys say about girls anyway."

I wondered if this was one of Jeannie's precepts, or if it was just general New Franklin knowledge. Talking to her made me glad to be going back to Evanston Township High. At least instead of going to some quarry to make out we went to Gilson Park on the lakefront in Wilmette, if we couldn't get away with it at home.

We started across the town park toward the swimming pool. It wasn't Lake Michigan, but it looked wonderful in the middle of an afternoon in July. In the ladies' half of a little concrete block building we pulled off our clothes and gave them to a middle-aged woman in a room that opened on the outdoors and the indoors both, with a partition in between. On the dim and clammy inside, she took clothes and parked them in baskets; at the other counter, looking out on the pool, she sold cold sodas and bags of Chee-Tos. She didn't give us tags to pin on our suits, the way the attendant would have at home. We sloshed our feet through a shallow trough of something that smelled like Pine-Sol, set unavoidably across the doorway, and stepped gingerly out into the sun.

I thought that maybe a knot of town kids would all turn to stare at me at once, but nothing happened. "Come on," Doreen said. There was a grassy area at one end of the pool for spreading out towels, and we claimed some space for ourselves. As I threw down my book I wondered if I would get to read it, or if Doreen would go on interrogating me the entire time. "Hi, you guys," Doreen called to someone, but before anybody could ask who I was, I stepped to the edge of the pool and dove in. Being under the water, chlorine and all, was like a dream of impossible coolness. I swam as far as I could beneath the surface and then came up and blew out the air that was bursting my lungs, shaking my head and treading water. I looked around; there about five feet away from me was Jeannie Holzman, hanging on to the side.

"Hi," she said.

"Hi." I didn't want to swim over next to her, so I went on bobbing up and down in the middle of the pool.

"How's your aunt doing?"

"Fine." I went under again, on purpose, dropped straight down till my feet touched the bottom, and propelled myself upward so I popped up like a cork. "Nice down there," I said.

"I guess."

I turned over on my back and lay on the water. "See ya," I

said, backstroking away. When I reached the end of the pool I turned over the other way and did the crawl for a few laps, wondering why I hadn't gone swimming sooner instead of following Augusta around all the time; then I pulled myself out, shook the water out of my ears, and felt like a real human being.

"Hey, Karen," Doreen called. She was standing in front of three boys and a girl who were lounging on towels. "Come here."

I walked over, conscious of all their eyes, resisting the impulse to readjust the straps of my suit. "Hi," I said.

"These are Bobby and Greg Schapenhorst"—anyone could see at a glance they were brothers—"and Lisa"—Lisa waved lazily—"and Benny," she added grudgingly. He smirked at her. "Karen goes to a high school that's got two thousand kids in it."

All four obligingly stared. "Well, I can't help it," I said. "I didn't make them all go there."

"Miss Streeter's your aunt, right?" one of the brothers, the older one, said.

"Yeah."

"I was in her English class in ninth grade. She's tough."

"I know."

"I bet she corrects your grammar all the time, at home."

"No, she—"

"God, I'd go crazy," Benny said.

"You already are," said Doreen. I realized that Benny was her boyfriend.

"You *guys*," Lisa said, in the manner of one whose patience is at an end.

"See you," I said to no one in particular. The two Schapenhorsts watched me, I could feel it; the others were busy bickering. But when I went to pick up my book it wasn't there; instead, a boy on the towel next to mine was reading it.

"That's my book," I said.

He glanced up; he was a small, wiry kid with a dark tan. "It's good," he said, and went on reading. I stared at him until his eyes slid off the page and back up to me. "Are you"—he looked at the flyleaf—"Augusta Streeter?"

"No." It didn't hit me for a second that here was a person who didn't know who Augusta was. "She's my aunt, and I was going to read that today."

"Okay." He handed me the book. "Normally I don't read murder mysteries anyway."

"Oh yeah?" Who was this kid? "Why not?"

"They're boring. Most of them. That one doesn't look too bad."

"Well, I'm sure glad to hear it."

"What's your name, if it's not Augusta?"

"Karen."

He picked up his own book—*All the King's Men*—and searched for his place. "Why don't you sit down?" he said, glancing up. Why is your towel right next to mine, I thought, but there seemed to be nothing I could do about that. "I think I'll go back in," I said, throwing down my book. The sun was hot on my shoulders. He shrugged and continued reading.

I dove back in and immediately got pulled into a splashing contest between Benny and Doreen that somehow escalated into cannonball dives by the two Schapenhorsts and Jeannie Holzman pushing people in the second they got out. I pulled her in with me and discovered that she could barely swim; watching her flounder was sweet. Finally I extracted myself from the melee and flopped on my towel, out of breath and dripping. Next to me the same kid was determinedly reading. When I had gotten the water out of my ears and opened up Dorothy Sayers, he said, with limitless superiority, "That certainly looked like a ton of fun."

Who was he even to talk to me, let alone sneer? I jumped up, mad. The water fight had petered out and the rest of the contestants were standing in the shallow end, insulting each other desultorily and making an occasional splash. I crouched on the edge next to them and said quietly, "Let's throw that kid in."

"Which one?" said Bobby.

"That kid reading over there, next to my spot."

"Who is that?" said Lisa.

"He showed up here about a month ago," Jeannie said. "He never talks to anybody."

"Well, if he did, you'd want to throw him in, too."

"Okay, let's."

All of them got out of the pool, conspicuously casual, and the entire group sauntered in his direction. When we were about ten feet away he looked up. I could see him register what we were up to. He scrambled to his feet; he was no bigger than me, and I thought I could do the job myself.

"Hi, kid," Bobby said, and grabbed for his arm. We had him half surrounded.

"Oh no you don't," he said grimly, twisting away from Bobby, and we all reached for him at once. His brown body slithered and gyrated away from our hands with a frantic energy as if we were trying to kill him; for two seconds of panting silence we struggled, knocking heads and bumping one another trying to get a grip on him, and then he slid between me and Doreen like a fish and got away. He ran halfway down the length of the pool, to the deep water, and dove in cleanly, with hardly a splash; in a second he surfaced facing us, flipped his straight black hair out of his eyes, and watched, treading water. His eyes were deadly serious. I felt like an idiot.

"Was he bothering you?" Bobby said in an I'll-protect-you-little-girl way.

"No."

"He's weird," said Benny.

"Somebody hit me right in the mouth," said Doreen.

"I'm sorry. It was a dumb idea."

"I'm going to get a soda," Lisa said. They wandered in a clump toward the snack counter, pointedly ignoring the head still watching them from the deep end. I could hear Jeannie over the rest telling a story about how a bunch of her brother's friends once threw her in the pool and wouldn't let her out for two hours. How could I have started that? The boy in the pool kept watching Bobby and drifting slowly away from that group until he reached the opposite side. Once they were busy drinking sodas, he got out and walked back toward his towel, not hurrying and not looking over his shoulder. I was standing right in front of his spot; he gave me a black look as he bent over to collect his towel and book.

"I'm sorry," I said. He straightened up with a look of profound gloom on his face and marched by me. He paid no attention to the others either as he passed them on the way into the dressing room.

I tried to pick up Lord Peter again, but I seemed to have ruined my own afternoon. When the others returned to their chosen territory, Doreen rejoined me and couldn't wait to mutter dramatically that Bobby *liked* me; that did nothing for my mood. I told her I had to go home.

"Want to come to the pool again? We do it all the time."

"Sure," I said, to be polite.

"You want to go to Belleville sometime and go shopping? My mom goes there a lot. Or maybe to the movies? Bobby could drive," she said, giving me an insinuating look.

"Maybe," I said. "I better go right now, though."

"I guess I'll stick around." And discuss me with your friends, I thought.

"Well, thanks a lot."

"You want to come back tomorrow?"

"Um . . . okay. Sure."

"I'll call you up."

"All right." Before Doreen could get me signed up for anything else, I hurried across the hot concrete and back through the Pine-Sol into the dressing room; I pulled on my clothes and got away. As I retraced my steps to Augusta's house, I thought glumly that I seemed to fit right in with Jeannie and Doreen.

chapter 13

As soon as I stepped in the door I remembered that for the moment it was my responsibility to keep Augusta's household running, and instantly I was afraid that I had stayed out too long and let her down somehow.

To my relief, though, I found her upstairs and asleep on the couch; she didn't look as though my absence had deprived her of anything. I went back down and read the *Joy of Cooking* for a while, resolving that this time I would buy more than one day's groceries at the store. I even toyed with the idea of driving the Buick to Downtown Market, as Augusta would have done, thinking how impressive I'd be if one of the kids from the pool should happen to see me, but I couldn't bring myself to do that. I wished I had when I picked up the bags I bought.

I was in the middle of making spaghetti sauce when Augusta limped into the kitchen, opened a beer, and sat down. "Did you have a good time with Jeannie and her pals?" she said. I wondered if she was offended.

"One of them said he had you for a teacher."

"Yeah?"

"His name's Bobby Schapenhorst; he said you were tough."

"He did, eh? What did you say?"

"I agreed, of course."

She smiled to herself. "Bobby Schapenhorst's only claim to fame is that he won a Sloppy-Joe-eating contest in the eighth grade. He sure didn't cover himself with glory in my class."

"I have a feeling he thinks he's good-looking."

"Do you?"

"Unh-uh. He's just big. His little brother was there, too, and a kid named Benny, who's Doreen's boyfriend. And Lisa something." Reporting everything was a reflex action; I reminded myself that I wasn't at home.

"That's Benny Alvis. I know his mother, she was in my class in high school." I had to think about that for a moment. Of course Augusta was old enough to be my mother, but the idea was strange and out of place.

"What did you and Jerry talk about all that time?" I asked, so I wouldn't have to admit what I had done at the pool.

"Oh—it wasn't all *that* long," she said, and seemed disposed to add nothing more. I stirred for a while.

"I hope you like spaghetti."

"He said he'd come over and give us a hand with the shutters. In fact, he said he got the idea from you."

"What? He told me he offered to fix them and you refused."

"Now why would I do that?"

I turned around to look at her; yes, there was an ironic gleam in her eye. "Beats me," I said. "I've stopped trying to figure out things like that about you."

Augusta took a drink out of her beer bottle. "Spaghetti's fine with me," she said.

All evening, as I tried to forget it, I kept on returning to what a creep I had been. I had acted as if I wanted nothing more in the world than to ingratiate myself with those kids I didn't even know or especially like. I had a nasty feeling that I might get more and more like them if I kept hanging around with Doreen, and she acted ready to adopt me.

Augusta sat in the kitchen most of the evening listening to the Cardinals and perfecting her design for a new summerhouse; when she finally showed it to me again, it looked less like a garage and more like a figment of some Arabian imagination. It was nice to know that there was at least one thing she couldn't do. We sat on the porch for a while, drinking iced tea; eventually I couldn't keep my eyes open anymore, but she said she was going to stay out on the porch a little longer, and as I climbed the stairs I was sure she had to think about Jim.

The next day Doreen called about noon, and I had to admit that I was waiting for the phone to ring, not because I couldn't wait to see those kids again, but because I wanted another chance to behave in some way I wouldn't be ashamed of. Augusta had started gardening again, since, as she said, she could weed sitting down just as well as standing up. From among the squash plants she gave me a wave and said, "Have fun."

The previous day had taken the strangeness off the experience of going to the pool or making conversation with Doreen, and as we walked along I began to feel as though I actually lived in the town—as though my slowly weakening ties to Evanston could gradually dissolve and leave me a native of this very small place.

But on the way to the pool we stopped at Benny's house to pick him up, and he and Doreen held hands as they walked along. I envied her, though Benny seemed like no great prize to me; at least he was someone to hold hands with. They talked about New Franklin gossip that meant nothing to me and squelched my fantasies of belonging there. Face it, I thought, what you're really doing is called tagging along.

When we emerged from the dressing room into the glare of one o'clock, I dropped my towel and book on the concrete and dove straight into the pool. I couldn't worry about social life underwater; I concentrated instead on holding my breath as long as I could, trying to swim across the pool and back without coming up for air, and didn't stop until I was completely out of breath. Then I hung on to the side and looked around, panting. Lisa waved to me; she was shiny with suntan oil, and looked dazed, as if she had been lying there for hours. Benny and Doreen were two heads close together sticking out of one corner of the shallow end. A couple of children were chasing each other around the edge of the pool, and their mother was yelling at them to stop running and be quiet and not fall in. Some boys about twelve were going off the diving board trying to do jackknives. On the grass, sitting cross-legged on a towel and intently reading, was the boy I had persecuted the day before.

Well, I thought, here's your big chance to act mature. I got out, picked up my towel and book, and approached him uncertainly. He was bent over his book; his black hair shone and made me think he must be hot, sitting there like that, but he seemed oblivious to everything but *All the King's Men*. He wasn't muscular, exactly, but he had a lean, economical body; his back was more flexible than mine—it made almost a perfect quarter-circle as he sat reading. I remembered how we had failed to corner him, even though we had him surrounded. Did he sit there like that every day? Was that how he had gotten so tan? He didn't look up until I was right in front of him.

At first he looked lost, the way people do when they're interrupted in the middle of something totally absorbing, and then I could see him remember who I was. He looked wary.

"Hi," I said, uncomfortable. "I just wanted to say that I . . . um . . . I'm sorry about yesterday. I mean, it was really creepy of me to . . ." He watched me without any change in his expression, and I ran down.

"It's Karen, right?" he said, after a moment.

"Right."

"Did you start that?"

"Uh-huh."

"I hate it when people try to make me do things."

"Me too," I said. Now I felt even guiltier.

"My name's George," he said.

"How do you do?" I said, determined to act civilized.

"Short."

"What?"

"My name's George Short. And I am short. Ha ha." He watched my face, and I had no idea how to respond. He sighed. "I kind of like to get that out of the way as quickly as possible."

"But you're not so short, not really."

That seemed to embarrass him. "Did you read that book yet?"

"Most of it."

"How come you read murder mysteries, anyway?"

I was still standing awkwardly in front of him, clutching my book and towel. It's a free country, I thought, I'm allowed to sit down. "Because I feel like it," I said, spreading the towel out.

"Don't you think it's weird to read about people getting killed?"

I stretched out on my back and propped myself up on my elbows. "I don't know. I don't think about it that way, exactly."

"Well, you wouldn't want to *see* them get killed, would you?"

"No."

"So?"

"Well, it's just a story," I said, beginning to see that talking to George was no pushover. "What goes on in that book of yours, anyway?"

"Oh, everything. It's a great book. Somebody does get shot in it, actually. I've read it before. It's awful when he gets killed, every time."

"Every time?"

"Well, actually, this is the fourth time I've read it. It's my favorite book."

Boy, if Benny thought he was weird yesterday, I thought, just imagine if he heard this. "Do you just sit there and read it over and over?"

"No, of course not. I wait a few months between times. Well, now I do. I did read it the first two times right in a row. An English teacher told me about it."

"My aunt's an English teacher."

"She reads stuff like that?" he said, pointing to *Lord Peter Views the Body*.

"All the time."

"Hm," he grunted to himself, as if he would have to think about that.

"See, I'll tell you what it is," I said. "They're not really about murder, they're about secrets. She has zillions of secrets, that's probably why she likes them."

"Yeah? Do you?"

"What, have secrets?" Since when is this any of your business?

"Well, you like them, too, don't you?"

I had been watching the boys diving off the board while we talked, but now I turned to look at him. He was studying me intently, as if this were some kind of contest. "Tell me one," he said.

"One what?" I was sure he couldn't mean it.

"A secret."

We looked at each other for a few seconds, and when he

showed no signs of giving in, I went back to watching the diving board. Maybe I had had the right idea the day before. I lay back and closed my eyes against the brightness of the sky, but I could still feel his insistent presence next to me. What was it with him?

"George," I said, "you don't just ask people to tell you their secrets. I mean, how would you feel?" I sneaked a look at him; he had turned over on his stomach and was propping his chin on his folded arms, staring off into space away from the pool. His backbone was a series of countable tan bumps. I didn't even know him and here he was demanding one of my secrets. Did this beat water fights or not? At least it was different.

"All right," he said. "Here's one: I can't stand my grandfather."

"Is that a secret?"

"Yes."

"Who from?"

"My mother and my grandmother."

"But your father knows about it?"

"My father's dead."

"God," I said. The size of that calamity struck me with awe and gave George a kind of rank that no one else I knew possessed. No wonder he didn't act like other people. "I'm sorry," I mumbled.

"Me too," he said. He was looking out across the park, through the chain-link fence that surrounded the pool. Past him, in the driveway in front of the pool, I saw, leaning on his car, that boy with the slicked-back hair and the cigarette pack rolled up in his sleeve who had looked me over on some of my walks around town. He was openly checking out the girls at the pool, and as I looked at him, his eye fell on me. Hastily I turned away. "Anyway," George said, "it's a secret because I'm staying with my grand-parents all summer."

It took me a second to remember what the secret was. "Why can't you stand him?"

"Oh, he's an old farmer who made a whole lot of money in the farm equipment business, and now he thinks he's better than everybody else and orders people around all the time. Especially me and my grandmother."

"What about your mom?"

"She's back in St. Louis working." He said it so glumly that I knew I'd better not ask any more about that.

"My grandparents lived here," I said.

"Yeah?"

"Yeah, my aunt lives in their house. I'm visiting her."

"I *thought* you didn't live here," he said. "You don't sound like everybody else. Where are you from?"

"Chicago."

"You come here for fun?" he said, as if that was a truly far-fetched idea.

"Um . . . sort of. For one thing, my aunt's really wild. Everybody in town knows her."

"Everybody in this place knows everybody. All they ever talk about is each other. You wouldn't believe the stuff I overhear at this pool. They think I'm strange, don't they?"

"Yeah."

"Why?"

"I don't know," I said, though it wasn't exactly true.

"Well, *I* know," he said. "They think I'm strange because I am. Don't you think so?"

"You really like to put people on the spot, don't you?"

That made him look at me. "Sorry." He picked at his towel self-consciously. "I think I'd better go for a swim." He stood up, dove in at the shallow end in the same neat way he had done the day before, and began methodically swimming laps, up and down, in an effortless crawl. He swam very well, so well that I finally thought he might be showing off for me, unlikely as that seemed. I had had enough lessons back at the Y at home to know a trained swimmer when I saw one.

Doreen and Benny had joined Lisa, who was still broiling slowly at her spot about twenty feet away, and when Doreen saw me alone she mouthed the words "What's he like?" with elaborate clarity.

"He's okay," I said. She looked slightly disappointed.

"Come over here," she said, beckoning.

"I'm too hot right now, I've got to get in."

"Okay, but bring him over, all right?" She reminded me of a collector; maybe that was what had made her take up with me. I jumped in and started doing some laps of my own—not as smoothly or efficiently as George, who was still going on as if he could continue all afternoon. We passed a couple of times, and then I noticed we didn't and thought he must have gotten out. I stopped at the deep end and George was there, too, hanging on to the side.

"You really know how to do that, don't you?" I said.

He smiled. "I used to be good when I was in the eighth grade. You do all right yourself. But you don't have to slam your arm down like that, you know. You just let it drop and it saves your energy."

"Thanks, I've been told that before."

"All right," he said in a don't-mind-me sort of way. He ducked his head under the surface and flipped his wet hair off his forehead as he brought it up again, all in one motion. He reminded me of a seal. "Want to go on a date?" he asked. Then he sank. I stared as he drifted toward the bottom, crossing his legs and arms so that he was floating downward like a seated underwater

Indian. He bumped gently to a stop, tilting slightly to one side, and stayed there, emitting a bubble now and then; I watched in fascination, wondering how long this could go on and almost forgetting what he had said. No one had ever asked me out like that. Finally—long after my lungs would have given out—he shot back up and let out a huge breath, then clung to the side, panting. It took some time for him to get his breath back; then he looked at me and said, "Well?"

I was almost afraid of what might happen if I refused. "Okay," I said. "I mean—sure, I'd love to." That was the phrase my mother had trained me to use for accepting invitations, but as I said it I was thinking, What am I getting myself into now?

He looked almost surprised that I had said yes, but pleased; then a look of puzzlement crossed his face. "What do people do when they go out around here?" he said.

You asked me out, that's your problem, I thought. But remembering what Doreen had said, I relented. "Well, you can go to the movies in Belleville—if you've got a car." Or to the quarry and make out, but I wasn't about to suggest that.

"Boy," he muttered, "I'll bet it's going to be fun getting the car keys away from my grandfather."

I was on the point of saying, "I've got a car," just for the fun of saying it, when I remembered that it wasn't mine and I wasn't even sure I wanted to go out with George that much.

"Well, when do you want to go out?" he said, as if already planning his struggle for the car.

"Aren't you supposed to tell *me* a time?" He didn't seem to understand that there was a way to do this.

"Okay . . . tonight."

"Tonight?"

"Sure, are you doing something else?"

"I don't know. What's the big hurry, anyway?"

"Well, I've been here all summer waiting for something to happen, and you're the first thing that has."

Since when am I a thing that happens, I thought, half pleased. "I'll have to talk to my aunt first," I said. "You can call me up around dinnertime."

"Okay." I could almost see him thinking, and it occurred to me that he might be one of those boys who have every minute of a date planned out and are always looking at their watch trying to stay on schedule.

"I'd better go see what Doreen's up to," I said. "After all, I came over here with her." I wanted to get away from George; our negotiations had exhausted me, and I'd had plenty of him for a while.

"All right."

I pushed off the side and started to swim away. "Hey, Karen!" he called. I had to stop and tread water.

"What's your phone number?"

"Look my aunt up in the phone book," I said, suddenly exasperated, and swam away. I got out the other end, picked up my towel and book, and joined Doreen, Benny, and Lisa, all without looking in George's direction. Only when I had sat down did I glance back at the pool. He was swimming laps again.

"What were you talking about all that time?" Doreen asked at once.

"Oh—he asked me out."

Her face lit up with the joy of a new piece of gossip. "He *did?*"

"What's his name?" asked Lisa.

"George."

"George? Gawd—George," said Benny, as if no one had had such an absurd name since the world began.

"You aren't going to go out with him, are you?" Doreen said.

"Why not?" said Lisa.

"Well, actually, I said I would."

"Do you know you're practically the only person he's talked to ever since he got here?" said Doreen.

"All he ever does is sit there and read and swim about two hundred laps a day," Benny said indignantly. "I asked him once if he wanted to have a race, and he just *looked* at me."

"He would have beat you anyway," Doreen said. Benny rolled his eyes and lay back disgusted. "What's he want to do on this date?" she said as if she had to give it some kind of seal of approval.

"Go to the library and read books," Benny muttered, his eyes closed against the glare.

"I'm not sure, really."

"I think he's cute," Lisa said. "I don't know what you've all got against him."

"Cute," said Benny witheringly. I had a feeling that a sarcastic delivery was his best trick and he couldn't resist overusing it.

"Really?" Doreen said, turning her attention to Lisa. Lisa's hair was so blond it looked creamy, like butter, and her tan, for very good reason, was just about perfect. So she thought George was cute, did she? Well, I thought, maybe I'll tell him that. But I get to go out with him first.

Just as I feared, Augusta was highly entertained by the news that I had made a conquest at the pool, but after teasing me for a minute she let up. I told her George's grandparents lived in New Franklin, and she tried to figure out if she knew them, but couldn't. "Must be his mother's people," she said. "I don't think there's anybody around here named Short. Anyway, if you want to go out tonight, go ahead. I'm not completely helpless, you know."

"Good grief. Who ever thought that?"

Augusta pointed in the general direction of the sound of drilling, which was coming from where Jerry was repairing the broken shutters. Somehow I hadn't actually expected her to let him do it, but the Reese Plumbing and Heating truck was parked in front of the house and he was hard at work. I wandered out to watch him, figuring that I owed him that much at least if I had started this. He was making new louvers by cutting pieces the right length out of long strips of wood and drilling holes in their ends so he could attach them with dowels, the way the originals had been put in. He even put a staple in the middle of each one so it could be attached to the stick that made the louvers open and shut. Did he know how to fix everything? His new louvers didn't look exactly like the old ones, which dissatisfied him somewhat. "They're the best I could do down at the lumberyard in Collinsville. Door molding. Think she'll notice?"

"I think if she complains about that, you ought to wring her neck."

Jerry gave me a grin; from inside the house, Augusta called my name. "Uh-oh," he said. "She heard you."

Could she have? I hurried around to the kitchen door. "There's a phone call for you," she said. "I have a feeling it's your friend."

It took a second to realize she must mean George. "Hello?"

"Hi," he said, "it's George Short."

"You mean Short George?" I said on some devilish impulse. Augusta, on her way out of the kitchen, looked at me incredulously, and there was a brief silence on the other end of the line, during which I felt contrite.

"Yes. Short George, for short."

Stop being a little snip, I ordered myself. "My aunt says it's fine if I go out tonight."

"Well, I can't get the car."

"Oh."

From the back stairs, Augusta called, "Or if you want to ask him over here, it's okay with me."

"Well, when can you?"

"I don't know. Maybe never." He sounded plunged in gloom. "I told you I couldn't stand him," he muttered desperately but furtively, as if in danger of being overheard. "He thinks I'm a goddamn baby."

"Want to come over?" I had a feeling that if he didn't leave their house, he'd explode.

"Where, your aunt's place?"

"Yes. It's okay, she doesn't bite." At least she won't bite you, I thought.

There was a dubious silence while both of us, in all probability, thought the same thought: If he does come over, what are we going to *do*? "All right," he said. "What time?"

"After dinner. Say eight o'clock."

"Okay, see ya."

"Bye."

What is this? I thought, hanging up the phone. Yesterday I didn't even know this guy, and today I'm practically asking him out.

By the time the doorbell rang, almost at eight on the dot, I was sorry I opened my mouth. I had done nothing but get more and more jumpy from the moment I hung up the phone; my usually mediocre cooking had been more discouraging than usual, I had gone through my one-suitcase wardrobe ten times trying to figure out what to wear, I had taken a bath and had even stolen some of Augusta's perfume, and all the time I had told myself that he wasn't worth the trouble.

I opened the door and realized that up till then I had only

seen George in a bathing suit. He was wearing khaki pants and
loafers and a crisply ironed, blue short-sleeved shirt that made
his tan doubly impressive; for the first time I realized he was
probably older than I was.

"Hi," he said, surveying me up and down. "You look different."

"I was just thinking the same thing." I was wearing one of
the two dresses I had brought with me; it was too formal, but
everything else seemed too sloppy to wear on an official date.
"Come in."

"This is some house," he said, stepping into the front hall.
"My grandmother told me all about it."

"Really?"

"They built it when she was a little girl, she remembers it.
And she went to school with your grandmother, too."

"Wow—were they friends?"

"No, yours was older than mine; they didn't know each other
real well."

"Come on up and meet my aunt." I led the way up the front
stairs.

"You look nice," George said from over my shoulder.

"Thanks," I mumbled, but didn't look around. Maybe there
had been some point to my efforts, after all.

Augusta was upstairs sitting at the big table, studying something; in the background the Cardinals game was on TV. "Hi,"
she said, glancing up as casually as if I brought strange boys up
the stairs every day.

"This is Augusta, she's my aunt; and this is George Short, he
says his grandmother remembers when this house was built."

"How do you do?" Augusta said, extending her hand. George
shook it in a businesslike way. "What does she remember about
it?"

"Mostly everybody was amazed at how big it was—that's what she says, anyway. And there was an iron fence out front."

"That's right." A smile spread over Augusta's face. "There was, of course. I haven't thought of that in a hundred years. I wonder what the hell happened to it."

I was used to Augusta saying "hell" and "damn" in front of me, but still it shocked me that she would do it to a kid she had just met. George maintained a perfect deadpan. "Maybe it got rusty," he said.

"Maybe," said Augusta noncommittally. "What is your grand-parents' name, George?" Now she sounded like a parent dutifully interviewing the kid's new friend.

"Easom," he said uncomfortably, as if he didn't want to get even that close to mentioning his grandfather.

"Oh, the Easoms, of course—he used to run that implement store on the Troy road, didn't he?"

"Yeah."

"I haven't seen them in years, I wonder why."

"Because they hardly ever leave the house," George muttered darkly.

"Oh," said Augusta. I could see her thinking. What now? "Tell me, what do you think of this?" She handed him what I now saw was the latest version of the new summerhouse, this time set in a landscape that bore little relation to the back yard. George studied the drawing with considerable care, and I felt nervous for him; what could he say?

"It's very interesting," he managed finally. "It's a sort of pagoda, right?"

Augusta looked at him and sighed. "It's a gazebo," she said, as if that explained it perfectly.

"Where is it?"

"What do you mean, where? It's up here." She pointed to her forehead. "It's for the back yard. The old one fell down. That's how I got this ankle."

"You mean somebody's going to build this?"

"Yes, me."

George looked at her with frank disbelief. "Well, what's going to hold up this part?" he said, pointing to the sketch.

"Where?" she said. "Give me that."

He put the drawing down in front of her and pointed to it. "This—this roof right here—you can't just make it stick out like that, it'll fall off."

"Says who? I don't see anything wrong with it."

"If you really want that much overhang, you've got to have posts or something to hold it up."

Augusta crossed her arms and leaned back to look George up and down. "How many buildings have *you* built?" she said.

"Lots," said George. I stared; so did Augusta. "Well, they're scale models, but they're just like regular buildings. I build them from scratch. At first I built model trains, but then when I started making the buildings for my layout, I just never stopped." He looked sheepish, as if he didn't want to admit to such a pastime.

"How terrific," Augusta said, half to herself, in a tone that meant she was having an idea. "Could you build a model of this?"

George bent over the drawing. "Sure. If you got it drawn to scale, I could. And change the roof."

"You're pretty sure about that, aren't you?"

"Give me a piece of paper and I'll show you what I mean." She slid one over to him and handed him the pencil. "Now look, if you imagine a cross-section of this thing . . ." I think I'll go downstairs and read a book, I told myself. These two don't even know I exist.

"Does anybody want anything to drink?" I said, starting for the stairs.

"Sure, whatever there is," Augusta said. "Iced tea. How about you, George?"

"That sounds fine." He barely looked around. Seething, I descended and took my time in the kitchen, feeling left out and young. At first I was equally mad at both of them, but then I decided that it wasn't George's fault, because he was trying to be polite and go along with Augusta. She was the one who was monopolizing him when she ought to know better. When I got back upstairs with the iced tea, they were watching the baseball game, and I almost did go and find my book. Augusta had finally found another fan to talk to, and they were arguing about the performance of one of the pitchers, as if they were having a date and I just happened to be in the house. I sat silently through a couple of innings, watching the TV along with them and gradually absorbing, against my will, what some of their comments on the game meant. The next time somebody asks me out, I thought, I'm going to make sure we go somewhere else.

chapter 14

Perhaps it was just good luck that the Cardinals started losing badly, or perhaps Augusta finally figured out how I felt; whichever it was, around the middle of the ball game she said she'd had enough and hobbled off down the stairs. By then she had decided she wanted to hire George to build a scale model of her impossible summerhouse, and I was sure that if he really did it she planned to talk baseball with him for an hour every time she saw him. As far as I was concerned, she already had Jerry, and that ought to be enough. George was too young for her anyway.

A foul ball flew into the stands and for an instant I thought I saw the exact spot where Augusta and I had sat on that night at the ball park when the rules of my life had seemed exhilaratingly suspended. "Do you think she really means it?" George said.

"What?"

"I mean, does she really want to pay me to build that thing?"

"Sure, why not?"

"I don't know. It's my hobby. I guess getting paid for it sounds too good to be true. And it might make my grandfather shut up about me not having a job this summer. Do you think she's got the tools to do it with? All of my stuff is back in St. Louis."

"There's a million tools in the basement, I don't know what all's down there."

"Let's go look."

Did I put this dress on to go digging around in the basement? I thought. But at least it would get us away from the TV and the ball game. "Okay." I led the way down the back stairs, glancing around for Augusta as we passed through the back hall but not seeing her, and then down into the basement. The stairs were so old that each step was worn down in the middle like a soup bowl, and they creaked dangerously as we went down. The basement seemed not to have changed since I had first seen it as a little girl; I still did not know what half of the things in it were for. My grandfather's workbench was crowded and in places even piled with tools; over it were rows of jars, suspended by their lids from overhanging boards, filled with hardware of every kind. A pegboard covered part of the wall, painted with outlines of tools, but hardly a tool hung from its pegs.

When I looked at George I could see that he was in heaven. He stepped up to the tool bench like a musician about to try out a piano and began to pick up and examine the tools carefully, setting them down without noise as if he had to be polite to them. "This is fantastic," he murmured to himself, finding a box of tiny files and holding them up one by one so he could examine them in the light.

"Glad you like it," I said.

He looked sheepish again, as he had when he started telling Augusta about his hobby, but the basement had a hold on him. He waded deeper into the confusion. "Look at that," he said, pointing at a large piece of machinery on the floor which I couldn't identify, "she's got an air compressor, for painting things, I guess." Privately I was convinced that Augusta wouldn't have known what it was. "And a hydraulic jack. Boy, I'm telling you . . ."

"Fun, huh." I was standing at the foot of the basement stairs, next to the light switch, and on an impulse I reached up and turned it off. Blackness descended.

"Hey!"

"I think I'll go upstairs now," I said, my hand on the railing.

"Hey, wait a minute." I heard some scuffling as if he was bumping into something, and a piece of metal hit the floor with a clang. "Ouch, *damn* it," he said. "Turn that thing on."

"Oh, come on, you can do it. I'm standing right at the bottom of the stairs. All you have to do is follow my voice."

"I don't understand you at all."

The truth was, I didn't understand myself either, but I couldn't seem to stop acting this way with George and I wasn't even sure I wanted to. I could hear him feeling his way along the workbench. "Where are you?" he said.

"Right here."

"Where?" he said, and touched my arm. "Ah." His hand took a grip on my forearm; I turned the lights on, but he didn't let go. He was exactly my height. There was a moment of blankness, a held breath of indeterminate length. Something Augusta had said about Jim flashed through my head: "I looked him in the eye and held still. That's all you have to do, you know"—and another part of me said, But *that's* not the point, and before I was sure what was happening, he kissed me on the lips with a sudden dart of his head, as if to get back at me for what I had just done. My heart pounded with consternation, and he looked at me as if he, too, was more scared than anything.

I broke away—he didn't try to hold me back—and went up the stairs as fast as I could. I could hear his footsteps following me slowly. Without knowing what to do exactly, I went through the kitchen onto the back porch and stood there looking out over the yard and the place where the gazebo had been.

Behind me the screen door closed again; I didn't dare look around. There was a long moment while I leaned on the railing as if stuck in place like the Tin Woodsman with his frozen joints; I didn't hear a sound from behind me, and nothing moved but the brief lights of fireflies.

"I'm sorry," George said in a subdued voice.

I didn't have anything to say.

"I didn't mean to do that . . . I mean—I don't know."

I could move again, and I sat down on the porch railing with my back to George, holding on to a post. For a minute the memory of the first time Rodge had kissed me blotted everything out; it had been after a basketball game, in the cold of the parking lot, as we were about to get in his parents' car. I remembered being held against the fake fur of his coat collar. He was big. Nothing like George.

I heard George sit down on the porch steps and tried to imagine how we were going to get out of this. The silence grew more and more awkward. From upstairs I could barely hear the mutter of the TV. If I had had any sense we would have stayed up there.

"You know, you're really lucky," George said.

"What do you mean?" I said indignantly, looking around. I thought he was congratulating me on being the object of his attentions.

"Your aunt, she's great." He was sitting on the top step with his arms crossed and his elbows resting on his knees. I looked away.

"Oh."

"And this whole place. But especially her. I've never met anybody like her."

"Neither has anyone else." I thought, Can it be that we're just going to carry on a normal conversation?

"I wish I had a relative like that." I knew from the way he said it, it was a heartfelt wish. Still sitting on the railing, I turned to look at him; he continued to stare out across the yard.

"She is great," I said. "She's really difficult, too."

"Yeah?" I still didn't want to talk to him, but when he added, "Like what?" I didn't seem to have a choice.

"Oh . . . she gets crazy ideas and kind of drags you along with her, no matter what."

I wasn't going to make it easy for him. Finally he said, "Tell me one," and I thought of the secrets, which irritated me again, but since I was stuck with him, I talked. "She decided she was going to teach me to drive this huge Buick she owns, even though I'm not sixteen yet—"

"You're not?"

"I'm fifteen. And a half. How old are you?"

"Seventeen."

Oh, I thought. A new perspective began to dawn.

"Well, anyway," I said, "I was going to leave a few days ago, and when we were going to go to the train station in St. Louis she told me to drive; in fact, she made me drive about a third of the way on the highway." Or a quarter, anyway.

"First time?"

"Yeah."

"What happened?"

"I did okay."

"No, I mean, what happened to keep you from leaving?"

"She started driving and took us to the ball park instead of the train station."

George leaned back on his elbows and whistled softly, impressed. He looked up at the night sky and said, "Do you think she really wants me to build that thing?"

"I told you she does. When she says she wants something, she wants it."

"Is it okay with you?"

"With me?"

"Well, I mean, if I come over here and do it?"

I hadn't thought of it like that—George showing up here, in our world, day after day . . .

"I'm sorry about what happened downstairs," he said. "I'm not usually like that at all. Maybe I've just been hanging around by myself too long, I don't know."

Thanks a million, I thought, at least you could say you were overwhelmed by my charms. "Well, it's not my house," I said. "It's not up to me who comes over."

He sighed and slowly stood up. "I've really made you mad, huh? I guess I'd better go." But he stood there indecisive, as if I would have to be the one to make it happen. Discouragement was written in the set of his shoulders, and I noticed for the first time a patch of grease on his pants leg where he must have stumbled against something in the dark of the basement. He would get hell for it when he went home probably, and it was my fault. And what had he done? Kiss me; was it so terrible? I had a feeling Lisa wouldn't have minded. The part of me that had hardened against him from the second we met finally melted away.

"Don't," I said. I stood up, too, casting about for something to do. "Want to see where the summerhouse fell down? It's right there." I pointed, but George only looked puzzled.

I came down off the porch and led him to the spot in the middle of the back yard. Jerry had sawed off the few remaining posts so only a foot or so remained above the ground—"enough to grab on to when we go to pull them out," he said, but I had a feeling that "we" would be him.

"That used to be the foundation, see?"

"Wow," George said. "The whole thing just collapsed, huh? Did she build that one, too?"

"No, are you kidding? It was as old as the house."

"And she was climbing around on the roof of it?" Augusta had told him the story. "That wasn't the smartest idea in the world."

"I was just thinking that when it fell down."

"Was the old one the size of this concrete? It must have been."

"Yeah."

"Well, that plan of hers is about three times as big. I can't believe she really thinks she's going to build that."

"She can think anything, take my word for it."

"Somebody ought to tell her how hard it's going to be."

"If anybody tells her it can't be done, she'll have to try it. That's the way she works. If you want to stop her, what you ought to do is make the model really ugly."

"Do you think she'll notice?"

I had to smile at that. "I don't know."

Where we were standing, away from the house and its lights, the night didn't seem to be a darkness, exactly, but rather a difference in the air. It was nothing like the thick blackness of the basement with the lights out. I stepped up onto the low platform of the foundation and turned around, watching the trees and housetops revolve around me. After a couple of turns I stopped, teetering dizzily for a moment, and then looked for George; he was watching me the way he had at the pool when he had asked me to tell him a secret. His eyes made me feel as if I were on a stage and had forgotten my lines. I stepped off, unsure of what to do with myself. "Let's go for a walk," he said.

Motion seemed to relieve us of the obligation to do or say anything in particular; there was enough to accomplish in acknowledging that we were walking along in what might be companionship. I reflected on how very not nice I had been to George; and now, for some reason, it seemed clear that I couldn't do that anymore—it was like being in a tug-of-war when the other person lets go of the rope: there's no point in keeping on pulling. We walked for blocks and blocks, hardly talking. A plucked string of nervousness vibrated inside me, but beneath its one insistent note I felt that at last, for the first time since I had reached New Franklin, I was doing something entirely my own, even if I wasn't sure what it was.

"Can I tell you another secret?" he said when we had turned uncounted corners.

"Okay."

We went on a few more yards, until I began to think he had changed his mind. "I don't believe in God," he said.

"You don't?"

"Not anymore."

"Is it because"—too late, I thought, you have to say it—"your father died?"

He put his hands in his pockets. "Maybe," he said, watching the sidewalk. "But that's just selfish. That's not a good reason."

I couldn't remember having a serious thought about God in my life. God wasn't an issue; there was just church, and church was something you could get away with missing when you got to be my age.

"What is?" I asked.

"Today I was reading the part where Jack goes to visit his

father—well, you wouldn't know the part, anyway—but his father's all religious and weird, and they have this argument where Jack says that God is perfection, and the only perfection is in nonbeing, so God is nothing."

"Is that what you think?"

"I don't know. But it's scary. Don't you think?"

I didn't know what I thought, but I was ashamed to admit that to George. "I guess so. It seems like I've always taken this stuff for granted."

"You're lucky," he said. He had already told me that once, and I began to ask myself seriously if it was true. It seemed dangerous to say of myself, I am a lucky person, almost as if saying it was the same as defying God—if He existed. And yet it might be so. I thought of George's father and wanted to cling to my good fortune.

The night seemed to me like an argument for God, or for Something, but I didn't know how to say it out loud. We turned another corner, and I realized we were back on Washington Street, a few blocks from the house. I felt myself to be in a kind of a trance that would end when I went back in, and I only half wanted to be pulled out of it, but we couldn't just stop where we were. George and I bumped each other clumsily as we turned to go up the front walk. He didn't seem to know what to say anymore than I did. I stopped, finally, when my foot touched the first step of the front porch. "Wait," I said. George stopped a step above me and looked around, puzzled. I withdrew my foot from the step, knowing and not knowing what I was doing. There was one light on in the hall, none in Augusta's study or the parlor, and it was far enough back from the street that the light from the streetlamp was dim. George stepped back onto the walk, and I could see he still didn't understand what was up. I thought what

I had thought before, but this time I was doing it on purpose, and my heart thumped at the audacity of it. She was right; it took a few seconds, but it worked. George kissed me, and when I didn't resist or turn away, he looked at me and kissed me again. This time, just a little, I kissed him back. Then I was afraid; when he went to kiss me a third time, I held him back. A touch was all it took.

"You're not mad at me anymore," he said. I shook my head.

"Maybe I should go now," he said. He looked as if he wanted to think about this as much as I did. "Tell her I'll come over and build that for her."

"When?"

He watched my eyes, hesitating. "Tomorrow?"

"I'll tell her."

He touched the side of my neck. "Is it okay if—?"

I nodded, and he kissed me a third time.

He turned away; in a couple of steps I was up on the porch and looked back. "Hey, George?"

He stopped halfway down the walk.

"I'm sorry I called you short."

I couldn't see the expression on his face; he seemed to think for a moment. "Try small," he said. "I don't mind that so much."

"Okay."

There was no sound inside the house, and all the lights were out except the front hall and a little lamp in the living room upstairs. I turned them out, brushed my teeth, put on my nightgown, but it was still too soon to go to bed. Instead, I padded downstairs, barefoot, and peered out the door at the silent street. You bold girl, I thought, look what you just did. You didn't just let him kiss you, you made him do it on purpose. As I climbed the stairs again, I wished that M.J. and Jeanette could somehow know about this—without my having to come out and tell them—and be impressed. But would they be? I could imagine them sizing up George. So what if he's seventeen, he's a squirrelly kid who thinks too much, and he's short. Or at the very least, small.

But *I* did it, I kept thinking, holding that thought to me as I fell asleep.

"Did you have a good time last night?" Augusta said the next morning at breakfast. For a second, before I reminded myself that she wasn't my mother, I thought, None of your damn business. "Well, you don't have to look at me like that," she said. "All I did was ask."

"Sorry. Yes. I mean, I did."

"He's okay, that George. You could do worse."

I looked at the ceiling, unwilling to touch that with a pole.

"All right, look. I won't say anything more about him, if you'll just tell me whether he's going to build that model for me."

"Yeah, he's coming over today to work on it."

Augusta raised one eyebrow and nodded—just perceptibly—in an obvious display of keeping her comments to herself. I could feel myself turning pink. "Oh," she said. "Well, I think I'm going to get to work." She put her coffee cup in the sink and hobbled out the back door.

"How's your ankle?" I called, conscience-stricken, as she slowly descended the back porch steps.

"Not bad."

"What are you going to do?"

"I thought I'd sand those shutters Jerry's fixing, so we could paint them."

"Want some help?"

There was a short silence. "Whatever you like." Right, sure, I thought, rolling my eyes for my own benefit. "Say hello to George when he comes over."

What are you planning to do, leave town? I thought. She could say hello to George herself. But I appreciated her making such a point of staying out of the way. Now that I had said out loud that George was coming over, I was already nervous, and I didn't want her seeing that, let alone whatever might happen when he arrived. What would he be thinking, expecting, when he walked in the door? In the light of day, what I had started the night before didn't make half as much sense, and I wondered if I would even like him when I saw him again. He was probably convinced that I was dying for him to try something else, when I wasn't even sure I wanted him to kiss me. The only comfort was that he never talked to the other kids in town; if they knew I had kissed him on the first date, I'd be the hot item of gossip for a week.

Stewing over the awkwardness of seeing George again was more than I could bear; to distract myself, I joined Augusta outside where she was sanding, and in half an hour I was too dusty and sweaty to imagine a romantic moment, let alone worry about one. The only thing that broke the trance of our gradual progress toward bare wood was a phone call from Doreen in the middle of the morning, asking me if I wanted to go to the pool again. That was the last thing I wanted—to take the chance of running into George there, in front of all their watching eyes. It would be hard enough at home. Besides, he would think I was chasing him. I was foolish enough to admit to her that I'd already had my date with George, but I was adamantly vague about what had happened. She had me coming and going; if I didn't want to talk about it, that could always mean I had something juicy to hide.

Talking to Doreen, I kept checking the kitchen clock and remembering that I didn't know when George would come over. I was on edge with the impulse to run upstairs and make myself look presentable, but I couldn't stomach the idea of getting myself all cleaned up and then sitting and waiting for him—even the thought was embarrassing. To get away from that possibility, I went back out and immersed myself in sanding until we were both starving for lunch. While we were eating Jerry showed up, saying he thought he could take some time out to work on the shutters between a couple of plumbing jobs, and Augusta offered him a beer and a sandwich, and I began to think that if George showed up right then, maybe no one would notice. But Augusta and I went back to work, and Jerry came and went, and still no George.

When I went inside in midafternoon to drink a glass of ice water, I saw that it was three o'clock and got mad at him—he could at least call, couldn't he?—and just then the doorbell rang and I knew who it was. I had sawdust on my hands, on my clothes, even in my hair—for all I knew, it was streaked on my face with sweat. I turned on the faucet, threw a double handful of water on my face, madly toweled myself with the dish towel, threw it over the back of a chair, and ran to get the door. In the front hall I made myself slow down and thought, It's probably someone else. The mailman with a package. It's a telegram. But when I opened the door there was small George, looking as nervous as I was.

"Hi," we said simultaneously. He was so clean and neat I wanted to disappear. A look at him showed me all at once that he had been anticipating and dreading this moment exactly as I had been, and now he came to the door and who should open it but a slob with sawdust in her hair. Some romantic scene.

"Come in," I finally managed.

"Are you working on something?" he said. "I mean, am I going to be in the way or anything?"

"No, it doesn't matter, we've been sanding all day. It's the shutters, the ones Augusta's friend Jerry is fixing, she wants to get them ready to paint, did I tell you about that?"

"No."

"Well, there's millions of them, and they're all broken, and—you'll see." At last I remembered what you're supposed to say to a guest. "Would you like anything to drink?"

"Sure."

I led the way to the kitchen and opened the refrigerator, ordering myself to calm down. "There's iced tea, and"—beer, but I can't offer him that—"um, ginger ale, but it looks like it's been open for a while . . ."

"A glass of water would be fine," George said behind me, sounding thoroughly uncomfortable. I remembered that that was what I had come in for, before he rang the bell. Getting out the ice cubes and glasses and running the water to get it cool was such an everyday action that it made me feel halfway normal again. I handed him a glass. "Did anybody notice the grease on your pants?" I said.

"Not yet. I don't know how I'm going to get it off, though."

"I'm sorry. That was really a dumb thing to do."

"I don't know," he said, with a glance at me that might or might not have been a reference to what had happened as a result.

"Is that George?" Augusta called from outside, making me feel both interrupted and relieved.

"Yes."

"Send him out here when you're done with him, okay?"

Did she absolutely have to say things like that? George's eyebrows rose in a knowing way that embarrassed me all over again. He finished his glass of water and said, "Well, are you?"

Before I could think how immature it was, I stuck out my tongue at him. He smiled. "She's out back," I said. "I'm going to go take a shower."

As cool water poured over me, the empty, uncertain feeling in the center of me gradually became bearable. George was somewhere in the vicinity, doing whatever he was doing, and when I saw him next I would be clean, calm, self-possessed; I would stop acting like an eighth-grader. I thought for a while about what to wear and decided that there was no point in pretending I went around dressed for a party whenever we weren't working; I pulled on a clean pair of cutoffs and looked through my shirts. But the only ones that were clean were so totally functional I couldn't stand them. A bold thought entered my mind: Wear one of Augusta's. She might give me a hard time later on, but . . . I opened the door of my room and peered out, making sure that George wouldn't catch me in my bra, and hurried into her room. The thought of wearing one of Augusta's mannish cowboy shirts with the mother-of-pearl snaps filled me with a dizzy sense of power; I didn't take her favorite, but they were all fascinating, all too big for me in a way I found irresistibly casual. I put one on, knotted it around my waist, looked myself over in the mirror above her dresser. Almost, for once, satisfactory. Back in my room I laced up my sneakers, did the best I could with my impossible hair, and sneaked out into the living room and listened. Where was he? There were no sounds from downstairs, no voices drifting in the windows; I could hear the quiet scrape of sandpaper that had been going on all day. With the thought that I might as well go all the way if I was going to get in trouble, I went back into the bathroom and found in a corner of the medicine cabinet Augusta's tiny bottle of Interdit. Then I felt silly. She would smell it and give me an unbearable look— and did I want George to, after all? Here it was four o'clock on a hot day and he had come over to do a job. I put it back.

That left nothing to do but go downstairs and look for him. I found him in the dining room, supplied with a stack of blank paper, a handful of pencils, and a ruler; Augusta's sketch was in front of him, and he was reworking it. He looked as if he had already found his place in the house and settled in.

"Hi," I said.

"Hi." He smiled, preoccupied, and kept drawing.

"What are you doing?" I looked over his shoulder, one hand on the table, one on the back of his chair.

"Trying to make some sense out of this. I've got a feeling she doesn't really want it to look like that, anyway." As he talked, his hand continued to draw with a control that impressed me; he put in a vertical line with the ruler, using just enough pressure on the pencil so that its point gently stroked the surface of the paper. Then he began to draw some gingerbread decorations freehand. As I watched, a piece of wooden scrollwork took recognizable shape before me; I had seen its like repeated a dozen times around Augusta's house but had never actually examined it. When had he had time to commit its form perfectly to memory?

"Mind if I watch?"

"No."

I sat on the table, my knee almost at his elbow, and wondered how long it would take him to look up for more than a glance. "That's really good," I said.

"Thanks." He continued to draw methodically without the

slightest hurry or impatience. I was beginning to consider how long this part might take, when he put down his pencil and ruler, picked up a ball-point pen, and without a pause put his left hand around my kneecap to steady it and wrote on it in tiny capitals, HI KAREN HOW ARE YOU? The hand made me self-conscious, but the writing tickled. I took the pen and his left arm and wrote FINE, becoming tensely aware that because of the way I was holding his arm, his left hand was against my thigh. I had meant to write more than FINE, but I stopped there and let go of his arm so he wouldn't get the wrong idea.

"How long do you think this'll take?"

"Oh, I don't know—I'll just work on it till I get it right, I guess."

"Did you get her to agree with you about the roof?"

"Well . . . I don't know if 'agree' would be the right word," he said, giving me a mischievous smile. "But I'm building it, right?"

"You've got the idea, George." They were made for each other, I thought, but not as jealously this time. I got up and searched through the house for my Lord Peter book, finally finding it sitting with a wrinkled cover on top of my damp bathing suit from the day before; I tucked it under my arm, wandered into the kitchen and got two glasses of iced tea and a bag of potato chips, put everything on the dining-room table, and sat down across from George to read. "Thanks," he said. "Does this come out of my paycheck?"

"Not if you're nice."

He tickled my ankle with his foot. "I'm very nice," he said.

chapter 15

For quite a while I read and George worked. Augusta finally gave up for the day, took a shower, changed her clothes, went out for a paper, and sat down in the dining room to drink beer while she read the editorials and the sports page. By the time we all looked up it was past six o'clock, time to start dinner, and she asked George if he wanted to eat with us. He seemed entirely happy for the first time since I had met him. We ate in the dining room, but somehow I didn't feel suddenly formal, even though Augusta and I had been eating in the kitchen all summer; the addition of George made the change seem appropriate, an added festivity that the two of us couldn't achieve by ourselves.

George was on what I was sure must be his best behavior; he entertained us for some time with the adventures of a girl classmate of his who drove a black Impala convertible with black interior and black sidewall tires and whose mother wanted to be an auto racer. He even volunteered to clean up afterward, but I divided the chores with him. Augusta looked smug and, when George was momentarily in the dining room said, "Nice shirt you've got on there. Irresistible, I'd say."

"I would have asked you but you were outside." I knew she didn't mind.

"Well, it's for a good cause," she said. That made me self-conscious again for a moment, but just then George opened the cupboard doors on the dining-room side—they were open on the pantry side already—and said, "Hey. I could just pass things to you, couldn't I? I've never seen a setup like this."

"Maybe you could put one in the summerhouse," Augusta suggested.

"Why not?" he said. "It's already got everything else."

"Kid's got a lot of nerve," she said to me. "You'd better watch out for him."

"I know."

On the other side of the cupboard shelf, I thought I saw George flush with pleasure, but his tan made it hard to tell.

When everything was cleaned up, we looked over his drawing for a while. Nothing in it was terribly different from Augusta's, yet somehow he had pulled together her odd ideas into a proportion that seemed possible in the real world. He had even drawn it to scale, so that you could measure any part and discover its actual size; all he had to do was make a top view and an end view, and then he could begin. But that would take too long to do in one evening, and no matter how one looked at it, it seemed to be time for him to go home. Only no one wanted him to. I began to feel the singing vibration of that same nervousness. "How about if we just sit on the front porch for a while?" I said.

He looked grateful. "Okay."

I deliberately did not turn on the porch light as we stepped out the door; we sat down on the creaky swing, neither close nor far apart. It glided from side to side slightly until I stopped it with my foot. The early dark had just descended. I watched the front yard, willing a firefly to make its silent streak of light. Without saying anything, George took my hand. I didn't dare look at him, and I don't think he dared look at me, but he slowly turned his palm on mine and just as deliberately interlaced his fingers with mine, taking the chance that can't be taken back, and I returned the pressure. I felt as though I was all touch, all that hand, and innocent as it was, the intimacy of that contact nearly frightened me.

We sat like mannequins, barely breathing, for who knows how long, and I hoped to God I was right in thinking no one could see us. I wanted the next thing to happen so badly I could have fainted from holding my breath, and yet I didn't dare do one thing to bring it about; all my boldness had been used up the night before. Then small George let go of my hand, turned to me and kissed me, all in one motion, and we both could breathe out, and when he did it again, I kissed him back. Something was over, he wasn't small anymore, and I could forget about Augusta or anyone else and be Karen, be fifteen and a half and, whether it made sense or not, beginning to fall in love.

We kissed for an indeterminate time before I was aware of anything else; then I began to be certain that someone was watching us. But when I drew back and looked around, the shadow of the porch roof seemed impenetrable and the lighted windows across the street were blocked by drawn shades. Everyone else's concern for their privacy, it seemed, protected our carelessness.

"Do you think—?" George said, having the same thought.

"No." We fell back into our embrace; he had one hand on the back of my neck, hot and intimate against my skin, and the other was at my waist, on the bare strip of me between my tied-up shirt and my shorts; I knew he wanted to touch my breasts and didn't dare. Even if he thought I would let him, being on the porch would stop him from trying, and for that I was glad; I didn't want him to touch me there, at least not yet. Daring to kiss him on the porch in front of God and everybody was excitement enough and more.

From somewhere in front of us there was a tremendous bang, scaring me so much in my vulnerable state of tenderness that I almost dove off the swing, and the unmistakable smell of firecracker drifted across the lawn. "Holy shit," said George. I expected to hear catcalls or screeching tires, but in the yard and on the street in front of us there was nothing out of the ordinary except a fairly large puff of smoke dissipating slowly in the night air. Across the street someone raised a shade and peered out. George had a hard grip on my right wrist; we were both breathing fast. Everything was quiet. Then, faintly, I heard suppressed giggling; at first I wouldn't believe what I was hearing, and then I knew I was right. I broke away from George. "What—?" he said, but there was no time for explanation. I threw open the front door and ran up the stairs two at a time. There in her room was Augusta, bent over with suppressed laughter, one hand clutching the bedpost and the other over her mouth. When I burst in, she pointed at me and let it out, laughing so that you could have heard her a block away. I stood there, hands on hips, and watched until she finally ran out of breath.

"Very, very funny," I said, taking my time over each syllable.

"Oh," she gasped, "I haven't done that to anyone since high school." She started giggling again. "Your face—" She whooped with laughter. "I only wish I could have seen you when it went off."

"I don't believe this. I just don't—how did you know, anyway —did you spy on me?"

"I was going to come out on the porch, but I saw you guys when I opened the door, and you were too busy even to notice."

"Jesus Christ," I said, which was the worst thing I had ever said out loud. "How would you like it, if you were out there with Jim and I pulled some stunt like that? You acted like you were going to kill me just for turning on the headlights."

"Well . . . that was different."

"Why, just because you're thirty-five? I do have feelings, you know."

"No," she said. "Not because I'm thirty-five." The laughter was gone from her face. "Because you have a perfect right to kiss George."

"If he hasn't decided we're all crazy and left by now," I said, but my anger was undermined by what she had said.

"He's crazy about you," she said with a certainty that I was grateful for. "Neck with him inside, why don't you? You can use my study. There's a nice old loveseat in there; nobody's put it to proper use for years."

I was too embarrassed to answer, too amazed that she would arrange such a thing openly, speak of it out loud. I turned away.

"Hey," she said, "I'm sorry. I just couldn't resist."

"If he's still there I might forgive you," I said and hurried down the stairs. George was still sitting on the swing, gliding back and forth, arms spread out along its back. I sat down on his right, and after a second, to my unspeakable relief, his hand curled around my shoulder. "God," I sighed. "I told you she was impossible."

"Is she trying to tell us something?"

I wondered if George would stop wanting to kiss me because Augusta told him not to. "No, no, I'm sure she's not, that was just her idea of a joke."

"What did she do, throw it out the window?"

"She must have."

"I bet it was a cherry bomb," George said admiringly. "It was sure loud enough."

"Enough? God, if that ever happens again, I think I'll die."

"Do you think she would?"

"What?"

"Do it again."

It was not possible to say, No, she says why don't we neck in her study, and could we please go try it? The "No" was all I managed.

"She's funny," George said happily. "I'll have to think up something to do to her."

I was torn between wanting him to kiss me again and feeling that maybe I owed it to Augusta not to do this on the front porch, but I couldn't bring myself to say the simple words "Let's go inside." There was an awkward spell of inactivity, and I was suddenly afraid that Augusta's little joke had tipped a delicate balance the wrong way.

"Well," George said after a couple of minutes, "I guess I'd better go."

"Okay," I said, thinking that I sounded eager for him to leave when I was just the opposite. He stood up, and I stood up, resolving that I would make her suffer for this somehow.

"I'll come and work on the project tomorrow."

"All right."

We exchanged an uncertain look across a strip of porch one step wide, as if all that touching had been a secret even from each other.

"Do you think she'd drop another one right now?" George asked, with an amused gleam in his eye.

"She better not."

George took the one step toward me and kissed me again; my

arms went around him, and for one second the length of him was against the length of me. The completeness of that sensation was almost too much.

"Good night," he said.

"Good night."

I turned at the door to watch him go down the sidewalk and thought, I am lucky. Then I knocked on wood. When I went into the kitchen for a cold drink, Augusta was in there studying George's drawing.

"So," she said, "did I ruin your evening?"

"No fault of yours if you didn't." I poured myself a glass of iced tea.

"Think of it this way: he has to come over here every day to work on this thing, how much more do you want?"

"Did you ask him to do it just for that?" I can take care of my own social life, thank you.

"No, of course not, but it worked, didn't it? Come on, forgive me. No more firecrackers, I promise. I just did it because I was happy for you."

We regarded each other for a long moment, and I knew she meant it; that was a brand-new thought: my kissing George made her happy. I would have hugged her if I hadn't been so filled up with another kind of touching.

"All right, I forgive you," I said. "But don't press your luck."

George finished the drawings in another day, and Augusta drove him to Belleville to get the materials he needed, and then every afternoon I watched him as he cut balsa wood and cardboard with maddening care, bent wires to form downspouts, cut pieces out of tin cans and patiently flattened them to get metal he could use for the roof. For hours I sat perched on a stool at the end of the workbench, dividing my attention between a book and George, who wasn't good for much conversation when he was hard at work. But he told me how badly he wanted out of St. Louis, where he swore nothing new ever happened or ever could. "What about the stuff they're building on the waterfront?" I said. "That'll be new." He gave me a withering look and rotated one finger in the air in a whoop-te-doo sort of way. "Biiig deal."

In between the hours of concentration were half hours of talk punctuated by bouts of flirting, pestering, teasing, sometimes ending in embraces or kisses, but mostly in desire and thoughts of what might happen later. At unpredictable intervals George blurted out things I could tell he had needed to say for a long time. He didn't like his mother (but I knew that) and he was sure she didn't like him. They couldn't be in the same room together without rubbing each other the wrong way, and it had something to do with his father having died—he couldn't figure out what. She had been angry ever since. His father had drunk too much—George realized it only after his death, and now it was too late to know why.

He hated himself for not getting along with his mother sometimes, when he knew she had a tough time, but she kept reminding him that everything he got came from her, when in fact he knew that it was his father's life insurance that kept them living in the same house, that meant he was going to go to college, where he could not wait to be and where he was sure his mother could not wait to send him. My life seemed superficial next to his, and in place of the secrets I didn't have I told him Augusta's. In a way they were mine, too; my secret was that I knew them at all, that I had been told things I wasn't supposed to know, and the knowledge was doing to me whatever forbidden knowledge did.

I couldn't leave George alone for long, even though I felt I should be helping Augusta, but watching him work and waiting for him to look up made me restless, too; I started ferreting through the basement just to entertain myself. There seemed to be one of everything down there, and nothing less than thirty years old. I found two bicycles that might have belonged to my mother and Augusta as children, a huge wooden radio that stood on the floor, rusting pots and pans that I could not imagine ever having been clean, boxes of empty bottles that made me wonder if they had made liquor down there during Prohibition, curled and cracking snapshots of people I didn't know with impossible hair and clothes, a license plate from 1937 . . . I had a feeling there might really be no end to it. I was stopped finally by something out of place: a shoe box from a department store in St. Louis, incongruously new, stuck into the middle of a shelf of mildewed books. Across the room, oblivious to me, George was holding a needle in a pair of pliers and heating it in a candle flame so that he could make the holes that might someday be bored into the gazebo's old-fashioned trim. He had been doing this until I thought it would make me scream. I pulled down the box and opened it. Letters, a handful of them, the return address in New York; I picked one up and turned it toward the light, squinted at the postmark. It was two weeks old.

I had to look at it. The letter was thick, three sheets of difficult handwriting folded over and over and crammed into an envelope that was too small, and it began with the words "Dearest A."

"Oh," I said out loud.

"What?" said George, still concentrating.

"Nothing."

I knew, but I still had to look at the signature. It was a letter from Allan. They all were, half a dozen of them, all from the summer that was still going on as I stood there and could not stop myself from reading the one I had in my hand.

Dearest A,

Do you think you're the only person in the world who ever had an affair with a married man? Why don't you give yourself a break for once, let yourself be happy for two minutes; we're not going to live forever. We're thirty-five, in case you haven't noticed, and I can tell that I, at least, am not immortal. So you love him. Fine. Love him if he's what you want, and if there's trouble, face it. Or stop now, give him up—I'm not going to tell you how to run your life. That never did work, though at times I've thought you actually listened to me, even if it's out of character for you to listen to anybody. But I don't have any advice. What would it be? "Live like me, then you'll be as perfectly serene as I am"? I don't feel very serene. It's 3:27 A.M., I am not sleeping and have not been for the past hour and a half, my wife hasn't had any sex in a month unless it's been with somebody else, and she's starting to wonder why. I could tell her why, but I won't. I don't even want to tell myself. It's you. After fifteen years, it is still you. I feel like a fool admitting that. I've told myself it was over so many times that it would only be embarrassing to count them up, and every time I've been wrong. For years, whenever I got interested in somebody, I ended up finding out all I was doing was distracting myself from remembering you. I've even begun to think that was why I didn't marry Rachel, though God knows you saved me from a fate worse than death, if that was what stopped it. Now I am married, and guess what? It still goes on. I love my wife. That's what all the unfaithful hus-bands say, and I haven't screwed anybody else, but I'll tell you what, I might as well have. You've got two married men in your life, in case you don't know it. I've got to tell you this; I don't even have anybody I can talk to about it. You're the only thing I have to hide from Amy, and it seems as though that one thing outweighs everything else that we share.

I will never understand why you left New York. Or why I didn't take you to bed the day we came back from the Thanksgiving that wasn't. Life was in my hand and I threw it away. I can't even remember what I told myself; all I know is I was wrong. And then we finally got another chance and you threw that away, which is even worse, because a second chance is more than anyone has a right to expect. What the hell was going through your head when you got on that train to go back? Did you think I'd turn you into some kind of monster, a housewife with four screaming babies in a tiny apartment or something? Or were you just afraid? You're probably mad now, because no one ever dares to tell you you're afraid. Well, let me tell you something else. I am. I'm afraid as hell of dying without having lived. And worse than that—knowing that I knew better, that life was an arm's length away and I didn't dare reach out and touch it. Do you know that another one of the partners who is six years older than I had a heart attack last May and almost died? Think about that. Think about maybe having six years left to live, and don't tell me you believe in that Presbyterian afterlife you were raised on, either. We both knew better than that a long time ago.

Here's what I imagine sometimes: I've got some fatal disease, and the doctor tells me that though I'm okay right now I've got a year to live, and do you know what I do? I go home and tell Amy I love her and I'm dying and goodbye, and I take a cab to the airport, and on the same damn day I'm knocking on your door.

I love you, good night.

Allan.

For several minutes I stood frozen where I was, the last page of the letter in my hand, feeling the way I had once at the seashore after a wave flicked me over carelessly like a matchstick and pounded me for a while and left me on the beach. What I had thought, from reading the end of the letter I'd seen on her dresser, had been so wrong, so tame and proper, that I felt as if I didn't even know the Augusta to whom this letter was addressed. Or her life. Or Life with a capital *L*. And I wasn't sure I wanted to.

"What's wrong?" said George, waking me up. I didn't answer as I folded the letter, put it in its envelope, the envelope back in the box, the box back on the shelf. No more random searches, no more detective work, I promised myself.

"Are you all right?" he said.

"Yeah." I messed up his hair as I passed him, and he caught my wrist and tried to hold me back, but I slipped free and went on up the stairs.

"Well, bye," George said to my back, sounding hurt.

"Don't worry, I'm not going anywhere," I said over my shoulder, and closed the basement door. I looked up and down the back hall. The house felt empty. I stepped cautiously into the dining room and caught a whiff of paint remover; outside the open window I could see the top of Augusta's head as she worked on a shutter. She was whistling "Sentimental Journey." I retreated into the hall and stood there for a while, leaning against the wainscoting, thinking, She lives with that every day. How does she do it? I knew what she did, practically every second, and still I didn't understand. I wanted her happier than that, I wanted everything in that letter not to be so; and to keep from crying, I ran back down the basement stairs and grabbed George from behind and almost made him break what he was working on. By the time we had wrestled with each other and tickled each other and gotten good and dirty bumping into the basement walls and kissed for a while, I had forgotten some of it. But not for long.

It came to seem a matter of course that George would eat dinner with us, and afterward, once the kitchen was cleaned up,

Augusta would pointedly ignore us. The night after the firecracker I could not believe that George would want to kiss me
again, and leading him to the study when I found that he did
embarrassed me so with my own boldness that I almost couldn't
let him kiss me once we got there. But I did, and he did, each
night a little longer, cautiously testing my willingness to be
touched. I kept thinking that if the New Franklin kids thought
I was fast, they must be right; yet what was happening to me and
George, which I did not dare call falling in love, did not seem
to go fast—it was time that went slow.

Like news from another country, George told me his grandparents disapproved of everything they knew and suspected was
going on at our house. But there wasn't much they could do; they
weren't about to throw him out of their house, and I had a
feeling that if they did, Augusta would invite him to stay with
us. She told him he ought to move in, as a joke, after four or
five days had passed, and he looked unnerved in a way that told
me she had read his mind. And mine. But if that happened . . .
where would we stop?

In the study, with the doors and shutters closed—one door
could be hooked from the inside, and I made sure it was—I let
George unbutton my shirt and unhook my bra, and very late one
evening, in total darkness, I allowed him, and perhaps without
words I even invited him, to take them all the way off. The
terrifying and thrilling words "half naked" sounded over and over
in my mind, in my voice, in the voice of my mother, the voices of
my friends, of forbidden books. He caressed me that way for a
long time as I hovered on the threshold between desire and trepi-
dation, but when he began to unbutton his own shirt I was
afraid, and in a second I was covered again. I couldn't explain,
couldn't say a word, even though I knew he thought something

was his fault. That night I lay in bed miserable, in turmoil between my own desire and something else in me that resisted with all its might.

We even had the nerve to go to the pool together and let Doreen and Jeannie and the rest see that the two weirdos from out of town had found each other; Doreen told me, with great circumspection and an air of doing me a tremendous favor, how to get to the quarry "just in case" I wanted to do you-know-what with him, though she wouldn't let Benny take her there, and she didn't have to say that she'd go ten times with Benny before she'd think of George. Bobby Schapenhorst just looked sulky and ignored me; Jeannie seemed stymied by my willingness to admit that I went out with the one kid nobody liked. It had been over a week since Augusta had shown George her crazy sketch and started more than she knew—or so I thought—when one night I was going to bed and she floated out of her room as I passed by, looking like a ghost in her nightgown, and said, "Let's have a talk."

I've gone too far—that was the first thing that entered my mind. She knows. The other shoe has finally dropped. But you as much as *said* it was okay, I protested silently.

"What about?"

"I'm not mad at you, you don't have to sound like that. Come and sit down for a second, okay?"

We perched gingerly on the couch; outside the windows the night was pale-dark, and inside the living room it was black-dark. I could barely read the expression on Augusta's face above the whiteness of her nightgown; I wasn't sure if I was seeing her or what I thought she looked like at that moment. The upholstery of the couch prickled me through the thin cotton of my nightgown.

"Listen, I've got to say something to you, because you're staying with me and you're my responsibility." She grasped my shoulder before I could object. "You are. I'm not going to tell you what to do, okay? I promise. But you're fifteen, and I'm thirty-five."

"So what have I done that's so terrible, I'd like to know?"

"Nothing. Please listen to me, just for a minute. I'm not going to tell you you've done anything wrong."

We both sat with our hands clenched in our laps, staring at each other.

"Karen," she said, "please believe me, I don't want to invade your privacy." Which means you're going to, I thought, my gut tightening. "I know you're having a good time with George, and that's fine. I mean, it's not even any of my business."

"But what?" I said, skipping the fact that what was happening to me with George was nothing as trivial as a "good time."

"It isn't 'but.' I just think that you might want to—make love with him, and—"

"What?"

"You heard me."

I had, but the connection of that with me, as something that might happen any day, shocked me so that I couldn't believe she meant it.

"But—"

"Look, it's what people do. That's why I have to talk to you."

I jumped up from the couch in a confused desire to get away. "But I *wouldn't*." What kind of girl did she think I was? "I know better than that."

"Come here," she said, and there was something in her tone that she must have used on her students, to which was impossible to say no. I sat down and looked at the floor. "Listen to me and don't put words in my mouth." She took a deep breath. "If you want to make love to George, it's up to you. I can tell how you feel about him. Maybe you want to. If you want to take him to your room some night, don't stop because of me. I mean that. Don't sneak off somewhere, and don't do it unless you want to. And if you decide to do it, don't you dare think, and don't you dare tell Cheryl, it was because I encouraged you, you understand? That's one thing. The other is this: don't get pregnant. Make him use one of those things, you know what I'm talking about? Condoms. Rubbers. Maybe he's carrying one around in his wallet all the time, for all I know. That's what boys used to do when I was in college."

Hearing all that at once was as stunning as a slap; it made the steamy books M.J. and I had furtively peeked at seem clean and wholesome. Rubbers, getting pregnant—that was dirty, that had nothing to do with me. And she could be damn sure I would never talk to my mother about anything connected with what she had just said. I hadn't even wanted to hear Augusta talk about it, and I hoped I never would again.

"I have no intention of doing that," I said without looking at her, furious.

Augusta sighed. "Your intentions are none of my business. I'm trying to help you out. Somebody has to say these things. And they have to say them before it actually starts."

"Thanks a million," I muttered.

"Okay, go ahead. Get mad. Act your age, even if it's only fifteen. Maybe you'd prefer it if I told you I'd call your mother and ground you if I ever caught George laying a hand on you, how about that? Then you could pretend to be a child, is that what you want?"

At that instant it was as though I could see myself from

across the room; I knew that I could yell at Augusta, storm into my room and slam the door, and that I probably would have done that any time in the last several years. But I could also decide not to, I could pay attention instead. For a long moment, as we sat in silence, I tried to let what she had said sink in, but it was hard.

"Do I have to know all this right now?" I said.

Augusta gave me a look that could have meant a hundred things and reached out her hand as if to touch my shoulder, but drew it back. "Pretty soon, you do," she said softly. "But you can still wait a little while."

I sat back on the sofa. Before me, between Augusta's room and mine, was a door that led out onto the roof of the front porch; it had a screen door, and we left it open at night for what coolness it could let in. It looked from the couch as though one might open it and walk out onto empty air, as if there were another front yard and another New Franklin a story above the real ones that the builders of our house had wanted to reach through that door.

Could she be right? Could it be as simple and brutal as that?

"I'm not you," I said. I glanced at her, thinking of Allan, thinking of the missed chance; she was sitting staring ahead of her.

"I know."

I thought about her being seventeen, a year and a few months older than me, the same age as George, making love to Jerry in a car. Not much fun, she had said a long time ago, when it had seemed like nothing but a risqué story about a wild kid.

"Maybe I forget sometimes," she said. "Maybe I just wish somebody had said that to me."

"What did they say?"

She didn't answer for a while, and I could feel something

powerful emanating from her, some resentment, defiance, that still after all these years hadn't gone away.

"Nothing. Which meant No."

I sat and pondered, turned over and over like a curious shell the fact that she had just told me Yes and said it was her responsibility. But that was not what a responsible person did. "What did you expect them to say?"

"I've always expected too much, I guess. I've always wanted everything and then some. I just thought if you were the same way, I'd try to help you get it. I know I said people have needs that can't be fulfilled, but you shouldn't listen to me. Maybe that's just the way I am. Maybe it's not so unthinkable for people to get what they want; at least that's what I'd like to believe."

I turned toward her, knowing what that meant, now that I had read Allan's letter, in a way I would never be able to admit, but she didn't look at me. Instead, she stood up, clasped her hands behind her head, and arched her back, groaning tiredly. Her arms dropped. "I'm going to go to bed," she said with her back still turned. Her feet made faint swishes dragging across the rug.

"Hey," I said. She turned in the doorway of her room, one hand on the doorjamb.

"Yes?"

It took me a second to get my courage up. "I love you too."

"Then I expect we'll be all right." She closed the door softly behind her. I stretched out on the couch, lying on my stomach with my cheek against the prickly upholstery, left alone with everything I didn't understand, and wished her words unsaid.

chapter 16

Then, for a couple of days, I stopped flirting with George as he worked on the model that grew steadily more impressive under the bright light of the workbench. I watched, and we still talked, but I couldn't let him touch me. I was afraid that too much would happen, that I might want more than I knew. He went home each evening right after dinner, bewildered and hurt, but I couldn't explain, and Augusta saw what was happening and kept her mouth shut—uncomfortable, I could tell, but sure she had done the right thing.

By the third day after Augusta's little talk the model was almost finished, and George looked as gloomy as he had when I first met him; he came in without knocking and marched straight down to the basement, and I might not even have known he was there if I hadn't been sitting in the kitchen at the time. I was avoiding Augusta and the further talk about me and George that had hung over us unspoken for two days. She wanted to help me out, I understood that; but I didn't know what I wanted, and I didn't want anyone else to tell me.

When George came down the back hall and opened the basement door he mumbled "Hi" and barely looked up at me. Okay, his footsteps seemed to say as they descended the stairs, something's gone wrong, something always goes wrong, why did I expect anything different?

I sat there at the kitchen table for several minutes, hearing George take out his tools and uncover the model, and thought, He'll finish it, and that'll be that. He won't have an excuse to come over anymore, and I'll never see him, and he'll think I don't like him; he'll think I'm a creepy fifteen-year-old who led him on and then dropped him, and I won't be able to stand it.

I wished we could just go on with what we had been doing, but the trouble was, it would never be the same, it wouldn't be just something we happened to be doing under cover of darkness and silence, some wordless game we thought up again each night. I wouldn't be able to take back what I had admitted to myself: I was not as far from Augusta as I had thought, not even in this. If I hadn't passed the boundary yet, the line between me and where she lived—and what she did—sooner or later I inevitably would. My privacy rebelled against that, against being like everyone else, against the whole network of knowing looks that was adulthood, that seemed to reduce all feeling to a handful of predictable drives, and more than that, a part of me still balked at the enormity of what would actually physically happen. Someday.

And yet if someday never came . . .

I could still choose to sit and stew and let George get it all wrong and go away miserable, except for one thing. I wouldn't be able to avoid talking to Augusta. And she wanted me to be happy; like my father, she really did, and she didn't care if happiness came hard. That got me out of my chair and down the basement stairs.

I sat down on my stool at the end of the workbench, and George grunted another "Hi." He was painting the summerhouse

—yellow lattice, brown posts, dark red trim. The model was a good two feet long and at least a foot high, so precise and solid that I was sure Augusta, who had deliberately not looked at it, had no idea what she was getting. George looked grim, and he was doing an unbearably neat job. What I wanted to do was take the brush out of his hand and make him look at me until he saw what I meant, because I didn't know how to say it, but he left no opening for me to break into. I watched until I began to fear that speech might desert us forever; then discomfort made me stand up, move away. He glanced at me but didn't quite meet my eyes and went back to his work; from behind him I watched the back of his neck. Don't be such a coward, I told myself, and laid my hands on his shoulders. His brush kept moving for a second and then froze. I let my fingers slide down his back and was starting to put my arms around him—it took all the nerve I had—when he turned on his stool and caught me in a hard embrace. The force of it took me by surprise, made me want to say I was sorry, filled me with unexpected joy. "Are you still there?" he said, his mouth next to my ear.

"Yes, are you?"

"Can't you tell?"

"I'm sorry."

"Did I do something that. . . ?"

"No."

He deliberately held me away from him so he could look me over and then kissed me. "There," he said, looking like a different person.

"Well," I said, "you did do *some*thing." That was my little risqué joke, but he didn't get it; instantly he looked wary again.

"What?"

"Oh, George, come on."

"I don't understand."

I kissed him, peck, the most I could unless he started it, though I wanted to do more. "Do you understand that?" I said; he looked as if he did. That night he left late again.

Nothing was left to do on the model when George came over the next day but to inspect it, touch it up one last time, and unveil it before Augusta; I knew he could hardly wait to see her face when he did. The roof was made out of tin-can metal so perfectly flattened I couldn't see a trace of the hammer blows that had done it, and painted dark green in a sort of bow to Augusta's pagoda idea. The fanciful scalloped roofline she had originally drawn had been ironed out to something that wouldn't look completely absurd in New Franklin, and below it was a summerhouse that looked as though George had seen a hundred of them and extracted their common denominator. It even had the same decorations as the house: the same scrollwork brackets that held up the front and back porch roofs could be seen at the top of the posts in George's model, and over the doorway of the summerhouse was a round red medallion exactly like the one above the kitchen door. The model was as heavy as a dictionary and smelled like fresh paint. George couldn't stop admiring it, and no wonder.

We were discussing how to present this masterpiece to Augusta when I heard the doorbell ring and ran upstairs to get it. It was Jerry, who had finished repairing the shutters—the project that I had thought wouldn't be done in my lifetime—a couple of days before.

"Hi," he said. "I thought I'd stop by and see how things are going."

"Great, the model's finished."

"What model?"

"You know, the new summerhouse." I was sure I'd told him about it.

"Oh, is that for real? I thought that was just an idea."

"Oh yeah? Want to see it?"

"Why not? I've seen everything else around here."

You wait, I thought, leading him down to the basement. He and George had met before, but they only mumbled "Hi" uncomfortably. George looked the way I would have looked if I had just served dinner and no one had tasted it yet.

Jerry had been prepared to cast a skeptical eye on this model—he teased me about almost everything—but when he saw it he gave a low whistle and stopped smirking. He glanced once at George, who was standing next to it with his arms folded, and then bent down to examine it. There was a long silence while he did so.

"Mind if I turn it around?" he asked without looking up.

"Paint might be wet," said George. Jerry didn't touch the model but bent over the workbench to peer in one end of it and then the other. "Nice," he muttered, as if to himself. I could see George brighten, though he tried to hide it.

Jerry straightened up and looked George in the eye. "Very nice," he said.

"Thanks."

"What scale is it?"

"Inch to a foot."

"You do this a lot?"

"Mm-hm."

Jerry peered into the little summerhouse again, trying to see up under its roof. "What are these supposed to be, two-by-fours?"

"Yeah."

"You might need trusses, you know. Or more center posts. I'm not sure this'll quite get it."

"You don't think three posts is enough?"

"Well, it might be just enough, but it's bound to snow sometime. There's always ice storms, they put a ton of weight up there."

"I don't want any more obstructions on the inside than I can help."

"Well, that's what trusses are for. Besides, you can buy them ready-made. They have them for building garages that are about like this. Cheaper than making your own."

"What about the pitch of the roof? Do you get to order that, or what?"

"No, it's standard. I forget exactly how much."

"Hm." I could tell George wasn't happy about any deviation from his plan, though he was eating up the discussion with Jerry.

"It's pretty close to what you've got," Jerry said, looking as though he realized the same thing. "But one thing I've got to say, the roofline has to be straight."

"You should have seen the way she drew it."

"I bet. But see, even the way you've built it here is going to be more trouble than it's worth. Once you start trying to get all these angles exactly right, and then you go to roof it . . ."

Well, I thought, I could pop right now and they'd never miss me. I went upstairs and got three glasses of iced tea and carried them down. They hardly looked up when I set two glasses on the workbench. I parked myself on the stairs and watched. I had never seen George so completely in his element, not even when he was building the thing. So this was what he wanted to talk about. Did Jerry remind him of his father? After half an hour or so, when they had taken out pieces of paper and Jerry was drawing diagrams of how the various posts and beams would be joined in real life if he were constructing it, I left the basement and found Augusta outside. She had almost finished painting the repaired shutters.

"It's going to be really something when those are all up," I said.

"I know."

"Want some help?"

"Aah—it's past lunchtime. I think I'll quit for a while anyway. How's George doing?"

"He's finished. Jerry's down there with him, talking about how they're going to build it."

"So that's where he is. I saw his truck out there a while ago and I couldn't figure out where he went."

"I think you're going to get yourself a new summerhouse."

"Oh yeah?"

"All you've got to do is say yes."

"To what?"

Funny, how I had forgotten for a while what Jerry wanted out of all this. The thought that maybe he and Augusta, when I wasn't looking, were going through something like me and George was one that still didn't add up, though I could begin to understand why she might have once planned to marry him. It wasn't the marriage that was so hard to imagine but the falling in love—and there was supposed to be some sort of connection, after all. That made me think of my parents, but they didn't seem to have anything to do with the world of doubt and improvisation that George and I and Augusta inhabited. No wonder they were hard to talk to.

"Hey, you," Augusta said, snapping her fingers in my face. "Want some lunch?"

"No, I've had some, thanks. Why are you looking at me like that?"

"Just watching you float off into the wild blue. Wouldn't have anything to do with George, would it?"

"I was thinking about you and Jerry, actually."

"Huh. Well, that's a different story."

"Such as?"

"Ask me when he's not around."

In midafternoon George found me where I was helping Augusta paint and said, "Come here for a second." I followed him into the house; he and Jerry had cleared everything off the dining-room table and placed the model in the middle of it, surrounded by drawings—Augusta's sketch, George's scale drawings, Jerry's diagrams of how to carry the project out. "What do you think?" he said. They had drawn the shades so that she couldn't peek in. Jerry was sitting at the table still pondering one of his own drawings.

"It's terrific," I said, looking over the tableau, thinking, It just needs something else. "How about . . ."

"What?"

"Wait, I've got an idea." I ran upstairs to the linen closet where I knew there were some frayed and threadbare sheets too worn to use. I dug one out, found a nail scissors in the medicine chest, and tore a big square out of the old sheet; then I took the square down to George and made him paint on it the words AUGUSTA'S FOLLY. With twine from the kitchen we hung this banner from the chandelier. "There," I said.

"Go get her."

"You sure this is elaborate enough?" Jerry said, putting down the diagram he had been tinkering with. "I could have been out earning an honest living all this time."

"Okay, okay." I hurried outside again; Augusta was standing back, inspecting the shutter she had just finished and wiping the sweat off her forehead.

"There's something inside that you ought to see," I said.

"I can't imagine what," she said, putting her brush into a coffee can of paint thinner. I led her inside as if it were my house and not hers. "Right this way, ma'am," I said, at the dining-room door, and threw it open.

Augusta had the look on her face of someone prepared to be pleased, the frozen half-smile you see when people have "Happy Birthday" sung to them in a restaurant, but I saw it change to pure amazement. She stopped in the doorway as if she wasn't sure she ought to go in.

"It's okay," I said, "you won't break it."

"My God, I had no idea." She stepped up to the model gingerly and leaned both hands on the table to examine it more closely. Right in front of it was her own sketch, and she compared the two for some time, shaking her head, a smile slowly spreading over her face. Watching her, I noticed that on one of the posts George had painted a tiny heart pierced by an arrow with GS + KM inside it, and I was sure she noticed it, too. I hoped Jerry hadn't.

"George, did you really do this?" she said finally.

"Sure," he said, his voice cracking. He cleared his throat. "Sure."

"It's beautiful," she said. "It's exactly what I had in mind." George caught my eye. Sure it is, I thought. She scanned the other drawings that ringed the model and for the first time noticed the banner. "Folly, indeed."

She looked around at the three of us who were watching her and stopped at Jerry. "Well, what about it, Jer? Can you do it?"

"Why don't you ask me if I will first?"

She turned to face him directly and clasped her hands in front of her like a proper little schoolgirl, but strangely enough, when she spoke, she actually sounded humble. "Jerry, will you build me a summerhouse?" she asked.

He let the question hang there unanswered for long enough

for all of us to appreciate what a lot that was to ask. He seemed much bigger than the rest of us, even more so than usual, and I thought what a lot of nerve Augusta had. She was still looking up at him. "Okay, I will," he said. "Me and George. He's got more free time than I do."

"Thank you," she said, holding out her hand as if to shake on the deal. He took it gently, not like business, and after a second let it drop.

"George?" she said. "Do you really have time?"

"Sure, why not—I mean—it's a job, isn't it?"

"Well, I'm not going to ask you to do it for nothing. Either of you."

"You're not paying me for this," Jerry said.

"Of course I am."

"Look, you can't afford what I charge. Plus, I won't take it anyway."

"Come on, Jerry, it's—"

"Gus," he said patiently, "it'll be just like that one on the table. No strings attached."

Even Augusta couldn't look him in the eye for a second after that; I felt rude watching her, but I couldn't stop. Out of the corner of my eye I could see George, amazed. "Well, can I cook you all a dinner without you getting huffy about it?" she said. "Maybe I could even twist Karen's arm to help me, what do you say?"

"Now you're talking," Jerry said.

She started moving toward the kitchen as if to begin at once. "Seven o'clock," she said. "That way we'll have time to shop and everything, and you can go home and get dressed up."

"I can, can I?"

"Don't you want Karen to see how you really look?"

"I think he's fine the way he is."

"Just wait."

George and I, caught up in Augusta's momentum, were following them into the kitchen; George's arm went around my waist as we all four passed through the back hall. Ahead of us, Jerry let his hand rest on the back of Augusta's neck.

"Come here," I said to George, holding him back. I steered him into the dining room with me.

"What's up?" he said.

"They might have something to talk about. Anyway, have I told you how beautiful this thing is?"

He kissed me. "I never built anything that started a celebration before," he said.

George went home, Jerry went back to work, and we went to work, too. Augusta looked the happiest I had seen her all summer as she drove all the way to Shiloh to buy a leg of lamb at what she said was the best meat market in a hundred miles. On the way home she stopped at a liquor store and bought a bottle of champagne and two bottles of French wine; we got corn at a farmstand, beans and tomatoes and peppers out of the garden; we even picked one of the melons that Augusta had been jealously guarding from groundhogs all summer.

As I was snapping beans, I thought, Okay, I will ask her. Then I wasn't sure where to start; the more I thought about Augusta's life, the more I wanted to know. "What *is* going on with you and Jerry?" I finally asked.

She glanced up from where she was rubbing the leg of lamb with a cut clove of garlic. "I had a feeling I'd hear about that," she said, going back to her work.

"Well?"

She sliced a new clove.

"He's in love with you, isn't he?" I said, thinking, Is this any of my business?

"I guess he is."

I went on cutting the stems off beans. Would she go on?

"When the old summerhouse fell down it kind of . . . I don't know, when he took me upstairs I thought, Here is this man, I've known him half my life, I know he loves me, what am I, crazy?"

I kept working deliberately, not looking up, willing her to continue.

"Maybe I am. He's a good-hearted person, Jerry is, and you'd be surprised how hard that is to find. And I'm not very nice to him, I know what you're thinking. I'm not even as nice as I want to be. It's as if I have to make sure he knows what he'd be getting. If we ever did." She turned over the leg of lamb. "You like him, don't you?"

"Yeah. At first I thought he was kind of . . . uninteresting, but—"

"He grows on you."

"Yeah."

"Think I should marry him?"

I felt the whole difficulty of that question the instant she asked it out loud. "God, I don't know, I . . . it's none of my business who you marry."

"Yeah, but do you?"

"Do you want to?"

She didn't answer for a while. When I glanced at her she was cutting garlic into careful tiny slivers. My mother had always regarded garlic as sort of uncivilized, and Augusta's use of it seemed daring and Continental. "I think I don't want to enough," she said finally.

"That's sort of what he told me."

"Really? When?"

"Right after we dumped off the stuff from the old summer-house."

"You mean you grilled him about him and me the first chance you got?"

"Don't get mad at me, he brought it up. He said he thought for you it would be kind of like marrying your brother."

Augusta made tiny pockets in the meat with the point of her knife and slid garlic slivers into them. "He's a smart man," she said sadly, bending over the leg of lamb. "You can't fall in love with somebody because you ought to; that's not the way it is."

I couldn't help thinking of who she shouldn't have fallen in love with, but I had pressed my luck as far as I dared go already. "Well, what way is it?" I said.

"It happens or it doesn't. Like you and George. That never changes, you know, not really. What changes is what you do about it."

And what would I do? I hoped to God she wouldn't ask me.

"That's what made me get involved with Jim," she said, making me wonder if she had read my mind. "The same thing. It gets stronger as you get older. Or maybe you just forget how strong it was in the first place. I was in love with Jerry that way once, that's what keeps me thinking maybe I could be again."

She took down a bottle of vegetable oil from a kitchen cabinet and began to rub it on the lamb. "Or maybe I almost am," she said, so quietly that I barely heard her. "I just don't know if almost is enough." She covered both sides of the leg of lamb with the oil and set it on a rack, ready for the oven. "There."

She passed behind me to get a paper towel and wipe her hands off; then she nudged me aside with her hip so she could wash up.

We stood side by side looking out the pantry window at the garden.

"You did it, you know," she said.

"Did what?"

"Got that thing with Jim over with."

"Really?"

"I think so. It's a good thing he doesn't live in New Franklin, because I know I won't stop wanting to see him. But I couldn't keep on with it. God knows it was crazy anyway, in a place like this. I hate like hell to admit it, but there are things you can't get away with. You remember that day I went out all afternoon?"

"You mean the tennis game?"

She gave me a slight sidelong smile. "I guess you figured that out."

"I think so."

"Jerry came over before that—you were on the phone or something—and told me he knew about it. I don't know how he heard, he wouldn't tell me. He told me to forget it, made me furious. I went right to Jim's store and made up some story about who I was and why I had to see him, and we drove about fifty miles and spent the afternoon in a motel. Crazy. Sometimes I don't even know what I'm trying to prove. But we had a big fight because I said he was never there when I needed him and he never would be. I told him it was over, too. I didn't know if it was over or not, really, but just saying it was hard enough. What did I look like when I got home, anyway?"

"Well, not so great, but . . ."

"I hide things pretty well when I have to," she said. "But then I couldn't, I had to tell you about it. And if you hadn't been out there when he came back, who knows what might have happened."

"Are you sorry I was?"

"Sometimes. How can you be glad it's over when you want somebody that way? But you know what I couldn't stand, besides everybody knowing about it? It was the idea of you looking at me and thinking, Can't she do better than that?"

"I wasn't thinking that," I said, but I remembered who did: Allan, who seemed to stand behind the conversation like a ghost neither of us could mention. The angel passed over, striking us silent and making us shake ourselves as if waking up.

"This is supposed to be a celebration, you know," I said. "We'll never even get dinner ready if we stand around like this."

"I don't think George would notice if there wasn't any, as long as you were there."

I could feel myself turning pink. "You can actually be nice when you want to."

"Nice, hell—I'm right," said Augusta, putting the lamb in the oven.

"The beans are ready."

"Come on, admit it, he's crazy about you."

I opened the refrigerator to put the colander full of cut-up beans inside, and with the door between me and Augusta I said, "I hope so." Admitting that made my heart thump so I couldn't say anything more. "What else do we have to do?"

"Not much. Make salad, drop in the corn, that's about it. Maybe we should get dressed. Do you want to go first in the shower?"

"Okay." I hurried up the back stairs before the conversation could return to George and me.

I wore the same dress I had worn on my first date with George, and as I had done then, I stole two drops of Augusta's perfume;

this time it seemed to be what the occasion demanded. I even wore earrings. But when I saw Augusta dressed I felt like a child. She had on a severe black dress with a high neck and a scoop back and a string of pearls I recognized as my grandmother's; her long straight hair was down and brushed to an auburn shine, and I thought, Poor Jerry. But I could have saved my sympathy. When he came to the door I realized I had never seen him when he wasn't in the middle of work. He had a white shirt on, open at the neck, and it made his hands and face look tanned instead of weather-beaten; he brought into the house with him a faint scent of aftershave, and he couldn't take his eyes off Augusta. She made herself extremely busy in the kitchen and told him to go sit in the parlor, he made her nervous; and the wonder of it was, he really did.

George came just in time to help me set the table; we left the model where it was, in the center of everything. He had obviously just washed his hair, and it hadn't quite dried; it was still slicked down in a way that made me want to touch it. He would have kissed me, I knew, but Jerry sat in the parlor a few feet away, reading the *Post-Dispatch* like a man who had all the time in the world. He never looked up at our preparations except when Augusta came into the room. Finally every dish and glass and piece of silver was as she wanted it, with the leg of lamb on one side of the new summerhouse and a steaming platter of corn on the cob on the other, and Augusta, with a cold bottle of champagne in her hand, said, "Dinner's ready."

It was a long table, meant for six, and we four sat on the sides, me facing Jerry, George across from Augusta. The empty chairs at either end reminded me of my grandparents, Thanksgivings, Christmases—occasions of a different sort, when I had been a different me.

"A toast," Augusta said, pouring champagne for everyone. We all three raised our glasses. "Just Karen and I get to drink it. To Jerry and George."

I sipped self-consciously at the cold, fizzy wine; its bubbles tickled my nose. Surreptitiously, George touched my knee under the table.

"Now eat," Augusta said. "No more toasts. Just drink it up."

"Have you got another bottle to christen this thing with?" Jerry said, making George grimace at the thought.

"We'll do that when it's built. Do you want to carve?"

"I might as well." Jerry picked up the carving knife and fork that had been laid directly in front of his place. "I've said yes to everything else today."

"Well, I could always get George to do it. If he can build that thing, he can probably cut up a leg of lamb."

"I wouldn't be so sure about that," George said. "The only time I tried to carve something it turned into a stew."

"Pass your plate."

"Thank you."

"Tell Jerry about that girl from your high school."

"Who, Queenie? The one with the Impala?"

"The one who dyed the white mice blue in Biology."

"What are you talking about?"

"Oh, it's this girl named Queenie King, or that's what we call her, anyway. She drives a black Impala, two years old, with a 327 and black sidewall tires. Her mother used to race it at Alton Dragway in the amateur races, but she said it wasn't fast enough, so she gave it to Queenie. Anyway, one day Queenie challenged this guy to a drag after school, one of the real hoods, and of course he thought it was a big joke. This guy's got a D.A., and he goes around with his shirt hanging out all the time. He drives a

Bonneville and he thinks it's the fastest thing in St. Louis. Anyway, they met in the parking lot and—"

The telephone rang. George paused, looked at Augusta; annoyed, she muttered, "Now, who would that be, calling in the middle of dinner?" as she got up to answer it.

"So anyway," George said, "the guy gets in his Pontiac, lights a cigarette, turns on the radio real loud, peels out of his parking space—"

"Karen?" Augusta called from the kitchen. "It's for you; it's your father."

chapter 17

What could he want, I wondered, standing up; then I realized I hadn't talked to them in two weeks—not since the day I had said I was coming home. Now I remembered that both of them had asked me to call, and I hadn't done it; I had been bad about that ever since I had gotten to Augusta's. As I passed her in the back hall she said, "Don't miss the party."

I sat down next to the stove, where we always talked on the phone, and couldn't help hoping it wouldn't take long. "Hello?"

"Hello, Karen."

"Hi, Daddy." I almost wanted him to call me Miss so I could object. Was he mad at me for not calling? "Is everything okay?"

"Um . . . sure. I just wanted to talk."

"Oh."

"How are you doing, anyway?"

"Fine, we're having a sort of celebration on account of—" I was going to say "the new summerhouse" but realized it wouldn't make any sense to him. "Well, see, the old summerhouse in the back yard fell down while Augusta was working on it, and we're going to build a new one, or Jerry is, really, and this kid named George has been working on the model of it for a while now and finally finished it today, so we're having a dinner party."

There was a silence. I could picture him trying to digest all that. "You say it fell down while she was working on it?"

"Yeah, she was on top, hammering down the roof, and the whole thing collapsed."

"Is she okay?"

"Uh-huh. She sprained her ankle, that's all."

"Boy, it's a laugh a minute down there. So now, what about this George?"

"Oh—Augusta made this plan for a new one, and she hired him to build a model of it. He just finished it. It's amazing, it's got every single part you can imagine."

"Where'd she find him?" my father said, and I knew he had a pretty good idea.

"I met him at the swimming pool."

"Ah." At least I couldn't see him giving his knowing look. "I suppose when you say he's a kid, that means he's about sixteen, right, Miss?"

"Seventeen, actually."

"Mmm," he said, with an amused lilt to his tone, but his heart wasn't in it, I could tell. I wasn't sure what to say. "Does that mean you're not ready to come home?"

Oh. So that was what it was all about. No, I was not ready at all. "Well—" I couldn't get the words out; they seemed cruel. But go home? Now? Just when everything was only beginning?

"Do you want me to?" I said finally, wishing I could have kept my mouth shut.

"Well—it might help," he said.

"Help?"

"Um." My heart sank. Just from the sound of that "um" I could tell he meant it. "Well, I haven't seen your face in over two months."

"Help with what?"

"Well, the cooking, for one thing. I'm getting sick of eating mine, and your mother seems to have given it up."

"Daddy, you want me to come back so you can get me to make *dinner*?"

There was a silence. I couldn't tell if I had made him angry or not, but I was; my heart pounded with resentment. If that was really all he wanted . . .

"Okay," he said; it was as though he added, Now we'll get serious. "Forget the cooking. Sweetie—" Then he didn't seem to know what to say. "Look, things aren't so great at the old homestead right now."

"What does that mean?"

"Well . . . your mother and I are having a hard time, she— well, I don't want to blame it on her, but she never seems to think about anything but houses anymore. And making money. The more she makes, the more dissatisfied she gets. Now she's got it into her head we've got to buy a new house over in Lake Forest. She's got it all picked out, of course. This one isn't good enough anymore. She's seen an awful lot of them, and she knows what we can afford, and what's for sale, so we've got to have it. Sometimes I really don't know what she's thinking."

"I'll bet you don't want to let anybody else dig in your garden." I knew that was a feeble thing to say, but my parents had never told me directly they had troubles. I'm sorry, I said in my heart, I don't know what to do.

"Well, it's more than just the garden."

"*Just* the garden?"

But he wouldn't be teased. "How would you feel about moving?"

"God, I don't know," I said, before I remembered that I

wasn't supposed to throw around the word "God" like that at home. My father didn't seem to notice. "I mean—does Mom really truly want to sell the house?"

"Yes."

"Well, what if no one else does?"

"I think she's pretty set on getting what she wants."

"Oh." The word came to me finally, as if I were taking a test in French: this is a fight. My parents are having a fight. And my father wants me to . . . What? Stop it? Make it come out his way? From the dining room I could hear Augusta and the others laughing at something, maybe the end of the drag-race story, and resentment swept over me again. "Does she want me to come home?"

"Of course," my father said—the old answer. Of course we love you. Of course we want you to be happy.

"What am I supposed to do about all this, anyway? You know she won't listen to me if she's really made up her mind."

"You don't have to do anything, Karen, I just . . . miss you, that's all."

But can't you take care of this without me? I thought. There was nothing I could say, no way on earth to tell my father about me and George, or even make him understand what the new summerhouse meant. Let alone the summer itself.

"Karen?"

"Yes?"

"There's something I've got to tell you. I don't want to scare you, but—it's more than the house. You know when you went away, your Mom sort of claimed it was for your own good so you'd stop thinking about Rodge? Well, maybe it worked, but really it was for us. After all, you'll be going to college in a couple of years, and we thought it would be good for us to be alone with each other for a while. Kind of to see if we could remember what it was like. I didn't really want you to go, but in a way it seemed like a good idea."

He paused as if he didn't know what to say next, and I could hardly breathe.

"I don't want to burden you with anything," he said. I closed my eyes, pulled my knees up against me, and hugged them with my free arm.

"I guess some things have been bottled up for a long time," he said sadly, and then there was a silence. I sat there locked in fear, and back in Evanston, I had a feeling, so did he. "It seems to me," he said finally, and stopped, and I was almost certain he wouldn't go on. His voice was barely loud enough to hear over the long-distance lines. "It seems as though we've forgotten why it was we got married to each other," he said, as if forcing himself to recite a sentence he had memorized late at night. "That's what it's all about. All this about houses is just something to do. Something to fill up the time. That's what I think. You'll have to ask her."

I opened my eyes and looked around at Augusta's kitchen. I'll have to ask her that? No. It won't happen.

"I think she really believes a new house will make her happy. She's sold so many of them to other people that way that she finally sold herself."

What about you and your garden? I thought. What about Augusta and hers? What about this place? What does make people happy, anyway?

None of them knew, not one bit more than I did. And yet, in a kind of singing inside me, like defiance, I knew, I was absolutely certain, that despite all their problems I would figure it out.

"You still there, sweetie?" he said. He hadn't called me "sweetie" so often in years.

"Yes."

"Are you all right?"

"I'm okáy, Daddy."

"Do you want to ask me anything?"

"No." That sounded too abrupt. "Not right now."

"Well, think about it, will you?"

"You mean about coming back?"

"Yes."

"Okay. I'll call you up. This time I really will."

"It's almost time for school to start, anyway."

"I *know*, you don't have to remind me."

There was another silence; I looked up at the kitchen clock. Almost nine o'clock already.

"I love you, Miss."

"Karen," I said automatically. Then, with an effort, "I love you, too."

"Have a good dinner party."

"Bye," I said, thinking that dinner was probably over by now, and I wasn't even sure I cared. I had to get up from the chair by the stove to hang up the phone. Then I stood looking around me, at the metal-top kitchen table with its spindly black design against the chipped white enamel, the Hoosier Kitchen that served for a cupboard. Things so familiar I hadn't truly looked at them in weeks. I wanted to hold them somehow, or hold myself to them, as if the sheer weight of the house and its memories would anchor me in New Franklin, would entitle me to say, "This is home." And the harder I tried to hold on, the faster I slipped away.

Forgot why they married each other. It was none of my business, nothing I even wanted to know, and yet if it was forgotten, where was home?

And was I their memory? Maybe they thought so, or my father did. But it wasn't their lives I was born to live.

I could feel "goodbye" coming toward me, the moment when I would have to acknowledge that I was going back, and as if I could run from it, I turned away from the kitchen, from my father's call, and hurried back to the dining room.

"Like I told George," Jerry was saying, "all you have to do is change the roof a little bit."

"A little bit?" Augusta said. "He already redesigned the whole thing. Have you looked at my drawings recently?"

"Uh-huh," Jerry said, with a hint of a smile. Augusta raised one eyebrow at him, started to speak, thought better of it. "Now all that's left to do is make it really straight on top instead of sort of bowed the way it is now, and it'll actually work."

Augusta sat back in her chair and looked at the model for a moment. "Well, you're building it," she said.

Jerry cut a piece of meat and ate it, looking vindicated; George picked up his knife and laid its straight back along the peak of the model's roof. "See? It won't be that different anyway," he said.

"Suit yourself," Augusta said, as if nothing ever happened according to her specifications. "How's Steve?" she said to me.

"Okay."

"Any news from the suburbs?"

"My mom wants to buy another house."

"You're kidding."

"No."

"Another *house*? God, the one you've got's enough, isn't it?"

"I guess she just wants a change, I don't know."

"But you've only lived in that one—what?—five years, right?"

"Look, don't ask *me*, call her up. I don't read her mind."

"Mmm," Augusta said, giving me a look that said, So you're going to be like *that*, are you?

"Whatever happened in the story about Queenie, anyway?"

"Oh, she beat him, of course. And then on the way home from the race he had a flat. It turned out he didn't have his lug wrench in the car, and he and his friends had to walk home."

"Tell her what she said the next day."

"Oh, she ran into him in the hall and said, 'I always thought you guys just unscrewed them with your teeth.'" Augusta and Jerry chuckled the way people do when they hear a punch line over again. I smiled, too, aware of smiling, aware of being aware, separated, already partway gone. I wanted to get Augusta alone and tell her the real news, but as she poured more wine in everyone's glass I knew that was impossible.

"So tell me," she said, "just where does this thing sit in the back yard, anyway? It's a lot bigger than the other one, isn't it?" Jerry and George exchanged a look.

"You could put it that way," Jerry said.

"Okay, so here's the back porch," she said, laying her spoon down parallel to the model. "Right? And then—"

"No, it's turned some," George said.

"Turned?"

"The summerhouse. It's a little bit diagonal toward the house. At least that's the way I've been thinking of it."

"You're kidding."

"That's not a bad idea," Jerry said. "But the question is, how far away is it? Now see—" He moved his water glass to a spot in line with Augusta's spoon. "Okay, imagine that's the inside corner of the porch, where you go into the kitchen. Now, the kitchen sticks out about like this." He put down the salt shaker.

"Wait, it doesn't come out that far," Augusta said. "That's way too big. That makes it look as if the kitchen fills up the whole back yard."

"No, it doesn't, the yard goes back about to where Karen's chair is."

"Oh, come on—I've lived here my whole life, practically. You think I don't know how big the back yard is?"

"You're not paying any attention to the scale—you see how big that model is? The way you've got it, it's about five feet from the back porch."

"Maybe I want it that way," Augusta said, looking as if she was trying not to laugh, and I recognized what she was doing: she was flirting with Jerry, amazing as that seemed.

"Maybe you do," he said, meeting her teasing look. "I wouldn't put it past you."

"Okay, so according to you it's over there where Karen's plate is or something, right?"

"No, Karen's plate is the garage. It's right about—there," he said, pushing the model toward George until it touched his glass. "Dangerous around here," George muttered to me.

"I've got an idea," Augusta said. "Instead of knocking everything off the table, why don't we go and actually look at the back yard? Or is that too easy?"

"Okay by me."

"Do you guys mind?" she said to me.

"Go ahead."

"Don't drink up all the wine while we're away." She and Jerry got up; she leaned over from behind George and picked up the model. "Might as well take this." As they passed through the kitchen I could hear her saying, "Now, Mr. Reese, we'll see who knows where everything . . ." The sound of the screen door closing drowned her out.

For a moment it was like George's and my first date, but harder. Here we are alone, what are we going to do? I cut a piece of meat, ate it, realized I hadn't wanted it. It was too rich, too garlicky; it made me feel stuffed, even though I had hardly started my dinner when my father called.

"Are you okay?" George said.

"Sure."

"Well, you don't act like it."

"What do you mean?"

"You haven't said a thing since that phone call." He sounded almost reproachful.

"Sure I have."

"If you don't want to say anything, don't," he said, sounding hurt.

Since when do I have to tell *you* everything? I wanted to say, but all of a sudden getting angry didn't make a whole lot of sense. I had a secret of my own this time, to tell or not tell. Hadn't he told me about him and his mother, and how he couldn't believe in God?

"My parents are having a fight," I said, looking at my plate.

George took a drink of water. "I knew it," he muttered, half to himself.

"You didn't either."

For one moment he looked at me, as if over the barrier of some kind of pain; then he turned away and seemed to go into himself. "What's it about?" he said finally, sounding as if he didn't want to know.

"He didn't really say. I mean, I guess it's true, she wants to sell the house, but he says that isn't actually what it's about."

George fiddled with his salad fork. "It's never about what they say it's about, anyway."

"George, you don't know everything. You've never even met my parents."

"You'll see."

"Sometimes you drive me nuts," I said, getting up. I wanted to whack him with something, pour water on his head—it was just like the impulse to throw him in the pool, and I had to get away before I actually did it. I went into the parlor and peered out one of the front windows, leaning my forehead against the screen. There was the street, as peaceful and noncommittal as ever; behind me I could feel George watching me from the table, trying to decide what to do. Stay away for a minute, I thought in his direction, just leave me alone. All of a sudden, leaning there, I was afraid I would cry, and I couldn't bear to have him see me do it. I wanted him to hold me, but I was sure I couldn't stand it; if he felt sorry for me I would punch him. Why hadn't they ever told me? I squeezed my eyes shut, but a tear leaked out, down the side of my nose, and I tried to wipe it away surreptitiously; then I couldn't keep myself from holding on to the windowframe and crying, all the time thinking, If he touches me . . . But George didn't make a sound.

Why did people hide everything, never tell until it was too late? Had this been going on for years? But if it had, I didn't want to know. Then nothing would have been what it seemed.

The crying passed over, tapered off. When I could move without upsetting the precarious balance that was keeping me from giving in to sobs, I made a dash for the front door of the parlor, keeping my back to George, through the front hall, up the stairs to the bathroom, and locked the door. Deliberately I avoided looking in the mirror to see what a mess I was, blew my nose over and over, splashed cold water on my face and toweled myself until I was sure the attack was done. Then I sat down on the edge of the bathtub; for a minute or two I stared into space, recovering and thinking of nothing, and then the sound of crickets from outside came flooding in. A few pale moths materialized at the screen and attached themselves as if they wanted to watch me.

Had I known it all along?

Or was I just telling myself so, now that I knew?

If they stopped being married . . . but I couldn't imagine that. I would have to go home, despite George and being in love, despite the summerhouse getting built and whatever was happening to Augusta and Jerry and everything that I finally knew I wanted. All of it was away from me, apart, pushed back with one careless shove—not of *my* doing. I resented that fiercely, furious at them both. But I had to go home.

"Damn it," I said out loud; the sensation of my voice in my throat almost made me start crying again. I sat and struggled with myself, holding back sobs while a part of me said, But it was just the *beginning*, I won't get to see the summerhouse get built, I'll probably never see George again, why now, why couldn't they just get along?"

Somewhere outside, there was a sound like hammering. Could it be that. . . ? No, that was impossible. I stood up to look in the mirror and see what this feeling looked like, to see if I was a different person. My eyes were red, but otherwise I could hardly tell that I had been crying. No one would know; maybe that meant it was not so bad. Or maybe it meant that people went around with more inside than anyone else dared to find out. Like my parents. I buried my face in the cool dampness of the washcloth again, dried myself off, took a deep breath, and unlocked the bathroom door.

The house was silent. Our party had lived out its short life, even before dessert. Stop feeling sorry for yourself, I said inside, but it didn't help.

From downstairs I heard a few random notes from the old piano. George, wandering around wondering what to do with himself. Looking miserable, I could just imagine. If some strangers were asked to decide on the spot which of us had trouble in the family, they'd be sure to pick George.

When I came in, he was in the back sitting room, looking out the window, pressing his forehead against the screen as I had done a while before. He looked around, again as if he were the one in pain, and then went back to peering out. "I don't know what they're doing out there," he said.

"Maybe they don't want you to."

"Oh." He turned to face me. "Really? You mean they're—?"

"I don't know what they are, but I don't think it's any of our business."

"Sorry," he mumbled, like a kid who's been yelled at by his mother.

"Oh, stop it," I said. "Stop moping around. You're driving me crazy."

"Sorry," he said again, even more softly. He was watching me now, carefully, as if I might be dangerous, and that made me even angrier. "And stop saying you're sorry," I told him, knowing how unfair it was, knowing it wasn't his fault. For a long moment we stood staring at each other like people losing their balance; panic churned inside me, a helpless feeling of being out of control, driving George away when that was the last thing I wanted and yet not being able to stop.

"It's really bad, isn't it?" he said, and something inside me uncoiled, released me to look away, sit down in the old ratty armchair where no one ever sat.

"I guess so," I said. I sat bent forward with my elbows on my knees, looking at the floor. "I don't know how bad it really is."

"I mean for you."

I nodded without looking up. George sat down on the arm of the chair and put his hand on the back of my neck, just rested it there lightly but steadily; I closed my eyes and didn't move, didn't do anything for a while but breathe and feel that touch. Don't leave, I thought, but what I finally said was, "I've got to go home."

He didn't respond, and I didn't dare look at him; then his hand moved, rested on my shoulder instead. "Yeah, I thought so."

"I really don't want to, but—"

"I know." He got up, wandered away. When I looked up he was standing with his back to me, his hands jammed in his back pockets. "When?" he said. I hadn't even thought, but as soon as he said it I knew.

"I think I'd better leave tomorrow."

He turned. "To*morrow*?" He was outraged.

"Well, my father—"

"Tomorrow?" he said again, his face squinched up in a kind of ecstasy of disbelief. "You're just going to—" He seemed to search for an adequate word and, with a gasp of exasperation, not find it. "Leave? Like that?"

"I can't help it."

"God, I don't believe it," he said, turning away again. He went to the piano, aimlessly hit a note in the bass, and held it down until it died away. "I don't believe it," he said again. For one instant, as he stood with his back to me, I thought we had traded places and now he was trying not to cry, and that got me to my feet and across the threadbare rug. I put my arms around him from behind, as I had wanted him to do to me, and after a moment he covered my hands with his.

"Don't go," he said.

"Stop. It won't help."

He pulled my hands away, loosened my grip on him, turned around to hold me face to face, and we stood that way for some time. The night sounds kept on as always. I thought I heard

Augusta's voice from out back saying, "Hey, Jerry," but I didn't hear an answer. I started wanting George to kiss me, but it was as if he never had, even though our arms were around each other; there was some kind of embarrassment between us, and I had a funny feeling I would have to break the spell. How did boys do these things, try to kiss girls when they didn't even know if it was all right to do it or not? I was leaving the next day, and I knew George wanted to kiss me, and still I barely dared to turn my head and kiss him tentatively on the lips.

As we kissed, a part of me turned toward him, toward wanting more, but the heaviness in my heart wouldn't go away, like a force of gravity in the direction of leaving. I was in George's arms, kissed by him, touched by his hands, and yet now of all times, when I would probably never get to do this with him again, I wasn't really in myself to feel it. I pulled away, thinking of leading him to Augusta's study, turning out the lights. But why did he look hurt?

"Do you want me to go?" he said.

"No, why would I—what's wrong, anyway?"

"What's *wrong*?" He stared at me full of reproach. "God. I'm in love with you, that's all."

My heart leaped in a kind of painful happiness; I had almost forgotten, in the midst of everything else, dreaming of hearing those words said to me, unfolding the scene in my heart in a patient and somehow sad ecstasy night after night, or in stolen moments of privacy when heat paralyzed the middle of the afternoon. Never like this, though—always at the end of some painfully perfect conversation that I could not stop rehearsing, and always I didn't know what to imagine next, whether I would have the courage to say the same, but if not now, when was I waiting for? George looked almost guilty; I put my arms around his neck and held on. "I don't want to leave," I said against his shoulder. "I really don't." Come on, say it, I pleaded with myself, but though we both waited for them, the words wouldn't come.

"What do you have to do?" George said finally, when the silence had become awkward.

"Do? Just talk to them, I guess. I don't know."

"I mean right now."

Kiss you a lot more, I thought. Tell you I love you too. "I suppose I should pack," I heard myself say, despising the cowardly practical self that could think of such a thing at that moment. And now that I had mentioned packing, my departure seemed horribly real. "Want to come up while I do it?"

George gave me a long look that I didn't understand at first. "Sure."

chapter 18

As soon as I knew what I had said, it was too late to take it back; the knowledge of George behind me, following me through the front hall and up the stairs, and what he thought I had meant, and what I might have meant, and what I wanted and didn't want, made my heart pound and weakened my knees, and each step was a new indecision. It was a slow, teetering journey; I hardly dared to breathe, and the faded stripes and flowers of the old wallpaper stuck out at me with inconsequential vividness. Behind me George's footsteps echoed mine, as if he didn't dare take each step until I did. If I could have said, "I didn't mean . . ."—but I wasn't sure that that would be the truth.

Once we got through the door of my room—purposely I didn't shut it—I at least had something to do. I darted to the closet and pulled out my suitcase with as much haste and banging as I could; then I threw it open on top of the bed. I pulled out the top drawer of my dresser and there were my panties and my brassieres; I could feel myself turning red. You idiot, I told myself, he's seen them on you—the bras, anyway—he's even seen you without them on, sort of, seen whatever he could see in the study with the lights off. Thinking that made me want him

to touch me and fear my own desire. Of course I would let him—
I would be mortified if he didn't want to—and then where would
we stop, this time, so very probably the last? As fast as I could,
I grabbed up the underwear and threw it in a heap into my
suitcase; George was perched awkwardly on the windowsill
behind me, in the back corner of the room, and I took momentary
comfort in the thought that he couldn't see through me. I pulled
some folded-up pants out of the next drawer and laid them on
top of the pile, covering it up. Decency. But, God, I wanted this
over with. I didn't care if my things got wrinkled; I had all the
rest of my life to iron them back in Evanston. It would be an
excuse to hide in the basement from my parents' troubles, whatever they were. Recklessly I went to the closet and pulled out
the clothes that were hanging there in one armful, extracted the
hangers and dropped them on the closet floor, threw the clothes
in my suitcase any old way. From under the bed I took my
sneakers, beat them together to knock the caked dirt off them,
and wedged one on each side. That left almost nothing—a few
things in the bathroom, the clothes I was wearing, my ticket
that still sat on top of the dresser. To think that it could be
done as fast as that, that all along so little had stood between me
and going back. I closed the suitcase with an effort and put it
on the floor, and now there was nothing left, either, between me
and George.

I couldn't look at him. Not alone in my bedroom, alone in the
house, for all I knew. Where was Augusta, anyway? I had lost
all sense of time; fifteen minutes could have passed since she
and Jerry had gone out into the back yard, or three hours. I could
not help thinking of what she had said to me in the middle of the
night—"If you want to take him to your room some night, don't
stop because of me." I had informed her that I would never do a

thing like that, and now here I was, scared and feeling terribly unprotected. I went to the front window because it was far from George, and when I looked out I saw that there was no Buick in front of the house. Nothing to stop us. Underneath our clothes we were naked, and I had asked him to come upstairs.

George's footsteps crossed the room, and I turned at the last moment as he put his hand on my neck; his other arm went around my waist and he kissed me. "Not in front of the window," I said, and in one motion I broke away from him and before I could think better of it closed the bedroom door and turned off the light. At least that way I could breathe. I stood with my back against the closed door and tried to gather myself, to know what I wanted, my eyes adjusting to the dimness. Reflected streetlight glanced off the ceiling, and against the windows I could see George's silhouette, but I couldn't make out his face yet. The light that had been in the room dispersed on my eyes in random sparkles that meant nothing. He came to where I was and held me pressed against the door, kissing my mouth and my neck; I kissed him back under the cover of the darkness; I was darkness and so was he, not Karen and George, not fifteen and a half and seventeen, not part of any daylight world. Night came to us, the self inside ourselves. I could feel him pressing hard against me, and I pressed back with my hip, unthinking, until I realized what I was doing, and that scared me out of it. But I did want him. I wanted something. He took my hand and tried to lead me toward the bed, but after one step I wouldn't or couldn't go, and he stopped trying and kissed me again. We were standing still, but I could feel his body pulling in that direction, and at one point we almost lost our balance and had to catch ourselves.

"Stop a minute," I said. His hand had been caressing my back and my hip and sliding up the front of my dress, over my breast, and every time he did that I turned slightly so that it would be easier for him to touch me. The feeling of that touch traveling over me made me dizzy, and I wanted his hand to stop at my hip or my breast or the small of my back and just stay there. Just touch. But I couldn't say that. And yet I could do something else that was more daring: I turned my back to him and bowed my head slightly and thought as hard as I could, Unbutton me. I was sure I had felt his fingers pause over those buttons, felt him almost resolve to do it and then not dare.

He had a hard time with the buttons; it took him so long to undo me that I had time to be scared again, time to be flooded with doubt. When he got low down on my back, so low that he would reach my panties on the next button, or the one after that, and the dress would be able to slide over my hips and off, I couldn't let him go on; I whirled around and held on to him, to stop him, and his hands slid up my naked back and unhooked my bra. He had done that before, downstairs, but here in my room, a few feet from my bed, it was not the limit of possibility. He stood back from me and tried to ease the straps of my dress and my bra over my shoulders, to unclothe me in one motion, and I put my hands up and prevented him. "Wait," I said, not knowing for what. "Just wait, can't you?"

He took a step back; I couldn't read his face. I sat down on the bed, arms crossed over my chest, hands holding up my straps, and stared at the rug. Don't get pregnant, I remembered Augusta telling me—how could I forget?—but how did she think I could do what might get me that way, just decide one night that the time had come? Had it been that easy for her to go over that edge? I couldn't even stand to think about it very hard, and yet more than anything I wanted him to touch me. Without looking up I took my hands away, straightened my arms, and let my dress slide down, and deliberately, knowing what I was doing, freed my arms from the dress and the straps of my brassiere. I even dropped the bra on top of my suitcase, bending forward to do so without looking at George, but I couldn't straighten up and show myself to him; I crossed my arms over my breasts again and turned and lay face down on the bed, half on and half off it, my feet still on the floor. Behind me I heard the soft sound of a piece of clothing falling to the floor and thought, Oh no. What if he takes off his belt? What do I do if I hear him unzip his pants? But there was no sound at all for a moment. Then George sat down on the bed beside me, put his hand on my shoulder and gently turned me over. I had seen him with his shirt off many times before, seen his swimmer's body at the pool, more nearly naked than he was now, but still I could hardly look at him, could not bear to have him study me, and I pulled him to me to avoid his eyes and for the first time felt the weight of his body on my own.

It was a while before I could relax my grip, let him kiss me, let there be space between us so we could look at each other; somehow the touch of our bodies was less intimate than being seen. When our eyes met, it was in a kind of admission, almost guilt. We are here together, I am showing myself to you.

For an immeasurable time he caressed me, and I lay with one hand curled behind my head, the other on his ribs, not quite able to caress him back. I could only look at him for brief moments; it was much easier to close my eyes and just feel. It seemed he would never tire of touching me the same ways over and over; sometimes my breasts and my nipples were almost numb from being caressed, and then sensation would come in a wave, and a self-consciousness would follow close behind.

He began kissing me, pressing against me again, his hand

moving down over my hip and onto my thigh; over and over his hand made the journey down me as far as he could reach and back up. My feet were still on the floor and my back was beginning to ache from the position I was in; when I moved a little farther onto the bed, he moved with me and reaching down, he took hold of the skirt of my dress and began to pull it up. Involuntarily I swatted his hand away, and we both froze.

Hadn't I been wondering when he would dare do that? When his hand would rest on my thigh without that material between? And then slide to the inside? And yet if he did—if he touched me there meaning to do more, to do what I couldn't imagine, it felt as though some part of me would shrivel up or contract like a clenched fist. No matter what some of my daydreams had hinted at, the hardness of him pressing at me through his pants had never been part of them. I had him by the shoulders, holding him away from me, and we were staring at each other; it was almost too dark to see his face, and as I stared at him he seemed to change from moment to moment, becoming people I didn't know.

"I can't," I said.

We held each other's shifting gaze. "Why not? Are you afraid she'll catch us?"

"God, is that all you're thinking about?"

George turned away from me as if I had slapped him and lay down on his back, his hands at his sides, staring at the ceiling. "No, it's not all," he said, and was silent; I could feel resentment, frustration, coming at me like heat from an open oven. I sat up, but he wouldn't look in my direction. He lay diagonal across the bed, compact and definite, still wearing his white pants and his good shoes. The white of his pants and the bedspread made his tan body seem dark, foreign, and I wanted to touch him somehow, but I didn't know how after everything that had happened, and I remembered what he told me downstairs, before we had done all this. Was this the answer I had tried to give? Was it always about courage, no matter where you turned? I moved over to him and knelt next to him on the wobbly bed, leaned forward and propped myself on my hands, one hand on each side of his head, forcing him to look at me, dimly aware that my breasts were close enough to him to feel the heat of his body. "I love you," I said, and then I couldn't look at him anymore. I would have gotten up, but he grabbed my arm and pulled me down beside him so that I had no choice but to stretch out my legs, and there we were, lying on the bed in each other's arms, not quite lovers and not quite not. He kissed me, surprising me with his gentleness, and for the first time that night I felt close to him.

We lay on our sides facing each other, kissing, and without meaning to, almost without knowing it, we went over the horizon, ceased to be aware. At some moment I awoke and realized I had been sleeping, saw George next to me still asleep. Something had happened in my heart as I lay there breathing next to him for a time no one had kept track of; we had trusted each other with our unconsciousness, our presence without guard, and this had never happened before in my life or, I was almost certain, in his. Now George was like no one else in the world; where my body had been lying against his felt natural, taken for granted, and as I watched him sleep I could take advantage of his unawareness and tentatively caress him with the lightest of touches, hoping that somewhere inside a part of him knew and might even remember. Hoping, even, that my touch, light as it was, might wake him up. If he awoke, I thought, if he tried now to unbutton the rest of my buttons, I would not stop him. I would still be more than halfway embarrassed and scared, but I would not say no. As if in the magic looking-the-other-way of night a moment had come when we could do anything we wanted, and its coming had waked me up.

But George still slept, and I could not begin it; if the gliding of my hand over his chest did not awaken him then, some rule seemed to say, it wasn't meant to happen. I could do no more. Gradually, against my wishes, the moment passed.

I began wondering what time it was, where Augusta was—there was not a sound from the rest of the house—and what was happening to her, what George's grandparents would do to him when he finally got home. The thought that this would end in some sort of punishment made me feel helpless and furious, as if we were not entitled to our lives, and the resentment made me too restless to lie still; I had to get up. Automatically I picked up my bra and put it back on, slipped the straps of my dress over my shoulders. What time *was* it? Some time beyond late, past the middle of the night, a time when everybody in New Franklin, except maybe Augusta, slept. Though it was still full dark, I would not have been surprised to notice that the sky was beginning to lighten—and then, I realized, I could say that I had spent the night with George. The thought filled me with surprise and tenderness. I looked down at him, and as if he knew he was being watched, he stirred, flung one hand back behind his head and arched his back slightly. He let out a sigh and opened his eyes, looked up at me. Did he remember that I had told him I loved him? Or know that I had caressed him, or sense somehow the opportunity that had come and gone?

"Hi," I said, because I didn't know how to say anything more.

"Hi." He sounded sad, as if he did know what we had missed. Or maybe just bewildered. He sat up and didn't seem to know what to do now that I was dressed, almost, and he was not. He leaned forward and picked his shirt up off the floor, slipped it on and buttoned it, not looking at me. I had a feeling he wished I would stop watching him, but I couldn't; I wanted to devour the moment. When he had buttoned his shirt I sat down next to him on the edge of the bed, turned my back and said, "Now me."

He sighed again; instead of buttoning me, he put his hands on my shoulders, ran them down my still-uncovered back. He put his arms around my middle, under my dress, and held me tight, rested his face against my shoulder for a long moment; I could feel his breath on my skin. I was almost ready for everything to begin again; then he let go of me and slowly buttoned me up. When he finished he held my hair away from the nape of my neck and kissed me there, and the thought of going away was so unbearable for a moment that I wanted to cry.

He stood up, looked around the room as if he had misplaced something. "God, what time is it, anyway?" he said.

"I don't know, are you going to get in trouble?"

"Am I ever. I don't know what they'll do when they realize how long I've been out."

"Maybe they won't notice when you come in if you're quiet."

"Maybe," he said, not sounding convinced. "It doesn't really matter, I'm always in trouble over there. Anyway, it's worth it." He mumbled the last few words, but I heard them.

"I'm glad." If only there had been more to be glad about, if the day of my departure would not begin when the sun came up.

"What about you?" George said. "I mean, aren't you going to get in trouble too?"

"With Augusta? I don't even know where she is. Besides, it's okay with her."

"Really?" In his voice I could hear how impossible that seemed;

when would there ever be another chance like this? Never as long as I was at home, that was for certain, and now I was going there. Being in my room with George was suddenly intolerably sad.

"Let's go downstairs," I said. The thought of brushing my hair crossed my mind, and I dismissed it.

The living room was dark, and darkness was what we had grown used to; the light coming up the front and back stairs seemed excessively bright.

"Do you think she's in there?" George whispered, meaning Augusta's room. He was right, she could have come in and gone to bed while we slept, but somehow I knew she had not; the silence of the house said that it was occupied by no one but us.

"Don't worry about it." We crossed the living room and went down the back stairs; the hall light made me squint. In the dining room nothing had changed; the plates and glasses and silver still sat where we had left them, under the bright light of the chandelier, as if we had all left the table for a moment and were intending to resume the dinner party a second later. But that had happened back in what was already the past.

"She must not be here," I said. "She never would have left all this sitting out." Automatically I picked up a couple of plates and carried them to the kitchen; George did the same, and as if by an unspoken plan, we methodically cleared the table, dumped the scraps in the garbage, piled the dishes by the sink, emptied the wine that was left in the glasses. I drank a sip but it no longer tasted as good to me as it had. I wrapped the rest of the lamb in tinfoil and put it in the refrigerator, and George, without my saying anything, took the roasting pan and squirted detergent in it and ran water in it to soak. He must have learned how to clean up from his mother, the way I had learned yard work from my father. Everything was cleared away, under control, and George was turning on the hot water to wash the dishes; I felt we had crossed over a bridge to the world we were accustomed to, but I didn't want to go all the way back. It was almost five in the morning. "Don't do that," I said, breaking a long silence. "We'll do that tomorrow."

"It is tomorrow," he said, turning the water off.

"Let's go out back."

He dried his hands on the dish towel and followed me out the door; the back door had stood open all night, with only the screen between the kitchen and outdoors. I held it to make sure it didn't bang shut.

Now it was just possible to tell that it would not be night much longer; the darkness had thinned, become chalky, although the sky did not seem to shed light. Out in the middle of the back yard Augusta and Jerry had pounded some garden stakes into the ground—it had been hammering I had heard. What in the world had they been doing?

"You know what that is?" George said, as if I had spoken out loud. "That's the summerhouse."

"What? Oh." Of course, what else? They must have been out there arguing over where to put it and pacing it off. So this was where it would be. Unless my eyes fooled me in the near-dark, it did sit slightly diagonal to the house; I wondered if George was pleased to see that. It was big, bigger than I had realized, and I wondered if Jerry—and George—would get it done before the next time we came down. Whenever that would be, and whoever would come. George wouldn't be there, I knew that. He would be a senior in some high school in St. Louis, and his mind would be on going to college, on getting away from his mother—not on me.

Or would it?

"We could be the first people to use it," I said. "If we could find the lawn chairs." They were sitting by the grape arbor, their plastic webbing frayed but still intact. George carried them into the space inside the four posts, and we sat down gingerly, feeling the dew on the battered aluminum arms of the chairs. Everything in the back yard, as we sat there holding hands, was shades of gray and black, barely beginning to take on color. In the corners of the yard, in the brush pile and beneath the leaves of the garden, night still lurked.

"It's nice in here," he said.

"Cool and shady."

In the east, now, a specific part of the sky was beginning to change. Sitting there with George, I thought about Augusta's night with Allan on the bus and what had happened when they got to Champaign and then later when she went to New York . . . they had both missed their chance. And had I? Or hadn't this been a chance, not just yet? The contact of his palm and mine seemed as intimate as any other for a moment, and in the dawn air I could feel myself a person who had made choices. If George and I hadn't made love, it had not been because someone else forbade it. If there were another night, I thought—but then, if the moment came again and I did not say no, how would I ever leave, how would I bear it when I had to after all?

"I don't want to go," I said.

"I know." Why did he always say he knew? But I wanted him to, wanted him somehow to understand what was in my heart. Maybe he did know, maybe that was why I loved him. Being able to say that to myself was like a secret fortune, as if I had inherited a million dollars and no one knew it but me. Except George. Maybe he even understood what I had almost wanted.

"I'll have to go back to St. Louis," he said. "Pretty soon."

But I couldn't help thinking of that irreplaceable time before "pretty soon" would come. "What happens then?"

"Oh—school." He sighed. "Home life." I knew what that meant.

"Do you have a girlfriend?"

He waited until I felt his eyes on me and looked over at him. "You."

I leaned over to him and kissed him, a real kiss, not a peck, the first time I had been able to be the one to begin it. Just in time; when I looked up, night was over, whatever magic it possessed had begun to give way to day. George seemed to see it too, feel the change; I could tell when the thought of his grandparents came into his mind. "I'd better go," he said. "If I go now I still might be able to sneak in. They get up real early."

I didn't want to say okay, to agree to his leaving, but I knew he was right, and there was no holding back the moment anyway. I stood up and so did he, and still holding hands we slowly crossed the side yard. I was trying to think of what to say. We stepped down the slight slope of the front lawn where it met the walk, onto the sidewalk itself, and I knew I would have to turn back somewhere, but at each step I wanted to stay with him one step more, as if at the last minute—no, the last second—something could snatch departure away if only I refused to give him up. But when we reached the corner we had to stop, know what we knew, give in.

"I hate this," he said.

"Me too." Don't cry, I ordered myself. He pulled me into an embrace, and for an instant I wondered if someone would see us, and then I just held him and didn't care. Come back, I thought, come back, as if he were the one leaving and not I. He kissed me and looked me in the eye and said, "I'm in love with you."

"I know—I mean—" I had to stop and swallow.

"What do you mean?"

"I love you too."

He put his hand on the side of my neck and looked at me for a long moment. Then he shrugged and shook his head slightly; a sad, fatalistic look crossed his face as if he were just about to cry. "Well, goodbye," he said.

"Goodbye," I answered, but my voice wouldn't work and it was no more than a squeak. His hand dropped away from me, and he turned and began walking away, fast, as if he knew the moment for decision had come. I wanted to run after him and beg him to come back, like a child to another child when she isn't through playing, but it was way too late for that.

"Write to me," I called, when he was across the street. He turned; was he trying not to cry?

"Okay," he said, just loud enough to hear.

I had a terrible thought. "But you don't know my address."

"I'll find out from Augusta."

For an awful moment we just stood and looked at each other across the empty street; then he took a deep breath and turned away and kept going. He's stronger than I am, I thought. But I watched him go without calling to him again. He got half a block without looking around before I could turn away.

chapter 19

I walked back up the block in the cool lemony first light trying not to feel George disappearing behind me, my back and his back getting farther apart, trying not to think that we would never again touch as we had just a couple of hours before. Now I wished helplessly that I had dared to awaken him. Inside me regret was like an animal pacing.

The green of the shutters was a color now, standing out against the brick of Augusta's house, not just a shade of gray. And it was my house, too, after everything. I didn't want to leave it. They could go ahead and sell the place in Evanston for all I cared.

In front of the house I saw the Buick in its accustomed place once again, and in it, Augusta. From the back as I approached, it looked as though she was just sitting there staring straight ahead, as I had done on the night when everything changed. New Franklin was as still as could be.

I opened the passenger door and looked in; she turned toward me without seeming surprised. "Get in," she said.

"How long have you been here?" I asked, settling into the seat.

"I don't know. A good while. What are you doing out here, anyway? Are you okay?"

"No." I surprised myself by being able to say it.

"No?" Augusta rested her hand on my head; I didn't look at her but stared ahead, like her, at the lightening street.

"How about you?" I said to the dashboard.

She thought for a moment. "That depends on what you mean by okay."

We were silent. I thought of how much I needed to tell her about what had happened since we sat down to dinner, and how much I would keep to myself. And what about her, all that time?

"You went somewhere, didn't you?"

"Went for a drive. With Jerry. We staked out the summerhouse beforehand."

"I saw."

"Mm." She took a deep breath and exhaled it in a sigh. "He asked me to marry him again."

That took my mind right off me. "And?"

"If it hadn't been for that damn summerhouse I might have said yes." Much as I felt bad for Jerry, I was relieved. She couldn't marry him, I knew that. "But it would have been like paying him back. God, I don't know. He's a wonderful man."

"But."

"Yes. I wish I wanted him. And I really tried, too. It worked for about thirty seconds, but after that . . ." Augusta slumped down in the driver's seat and let her head loll back on the upholstery. "Not a nice moment," she said, closing her eyes.

I looked away, not wanting to imagine too clearly what she was telling me about. "Is he still going to build it?"

"I don't know." She almost sounded as though she didn't care. So things were that bad. "Maybe he's had it with me forever. If he wants to do it he will, I guess."

"I hope he does."

"Why?"

"Because he's your friend, I suppose."

"Maybe being my friend is not a job he wants anymore."

"Where else is he going to find somebody like you?"

She looked over at me and seemed to be tempted to smile. "Know-it-all," she said. "Where'd you learn to talk like that?"

"Guess."

"I don't know." She leaned back and closed her eyes again. "Teenagers just don't have any manners these days." Augusta sounded as though teasing took more energy than she had; I didn't answer.

"What are you doing out here at this hour anyway?" she said, when she realized I wasn't going to go on. "Checking up on me? I'll bet you've never gotten up this early in your life."

"Saying goodbye to George." In the special silence that followed that remark the longing came back, flooded over me.

"Oh," she said, sitting up and looking me over as if she expected to see some visible alteration. "Really."

"We didn't, if that's what you want to know."

"Is that why you're not okay?"

Well—it *was* part of it, wasn't it? But I couldn't explain that the right way, even to her. "I've got to go home."

"Home? You mean it really was goodbye? What is this, Breakup Night or something? Why do you have to go home?" She sounded more annoyed than anything, as if at a dumb idea that a few minutes' talk would take care of. I wished that driving me to a ball game would do the trick again.

"My parents. They're doing it, too, maybe. Splitting up, I mean." How could I say the words so casually, as if I didn't care, as if I were somebody else sitting outside me on the curb and moving my lips by remote control? Except maybe that was the only way they could get said.

"That was what that call was about?" She sounded hurt, reproachful.

"Sort of. I couldn't just stop everything in the middle of dinner and tell you."

"What did he say?"

"He said"—I didn't want to bring out the words—"they forgot why they got married to each other."

"Oh brother." She turned away from me, looked up at the sky. The look on her face confirmed my fears. "Was Cheryl there?"

"I didn't talk to her, but . . ."

"She hasn't moved out?"

"God, no, it's not that bad." Did Augusta think everything could fall apart as easily as that? And was she right?

"What else?"

That made me feel as if she were filling in the blanks on some form. This is our family, I thought, your sister, my parents. "I don't know, she works all the time. He didn't really say what else."

"It figures."

"So you know everything too, is that it?"

"I've known her for thirty-five years and Steve for eighteen."

"Okay, then you tell me what's going on at home."

"I'll tell you one thing, they're not talking."

I had to look away from her, up the front walk toward the house. Of course she was right.

"I'm sorry," she said. "I don't want to argue about this." She put her hand on my shoulder, rested it there lightly as if to tell me she was there if I wanted her. "How's Steve?"

"He didn't sound happy."

*　*　*

We sat in silence until I realized the angel had passed over and wondered momentarily what time it was.

"He didn't say I had to come back right away, but . . ."

"Well, I'm sure he needs you there. They both do."

"I'm not going to solve their problems for them, that's for sure."

"Did he ask you to?"

"Well, sort of—about the house. But she's not going to change her mind about that for me."

"Or anyone, probably," Augusta said, and for an instant I resented that on my mother's behalf, but she was only echoing my own thoughts. "She sure does like control. Just like me."

And look what it's gotten them, I thought. Augusta and my mother seemed, in that light, more like sisters than I had ever thought before. And I was like them—of course I was—but like didn't mean the same. I was partly my father, too, someone they'd never be. Maybe never even understand. Quieter than either of them, less direct. Thinking, I could feel myself pulling away from all of them, all my loyalties strained by differences that might never be resolved. I would never be any of them, or any adding up of them. For a moment I felt permanently alone.

"I'll miss you," Augusta said, sounding as if she had been trying to think what to say.

"Miss you too," I mumbled.

"And George, I'll bet," she said, and I was grateful, because I couldn't have brought him up even though I wanted to.

"Yes." I slept with him, I thought in wonderment, though the words didn't mean what anyone would think if I just said them. I wanted to tell her how I had been close to him when I woke up and watched him sleep—she was the only person in the world I could tell—but I couldn't find the way to begin. In place of that secret I wanted to tell I could feel another rising in me, one I hadn't intended to reveal to anyone, least of all her. But I had to say it before I could leave. "I've got to confess something."

"Only if you want to," she said, and I knew she thought it was about George.

I made myself speak. "I read one of your letters I found in the basement. It was from Allan."

Her hand left my shoulder; I couldn't look at her, but I could feel her eyes on me. What's she going to do to me, I thought. "You found it, you say? Just by chance?"

"I was poking around. While George was working. I didn't have anything to do."

"You must have poked pretty hard to find those. How come you only read one?"

Now I knew how her students must feel when she reprimanded them in class. "I'm sorry, I—" didn't mean to? That was some excuse. Of course I meant to, I thought, filled with shame.

For a painfully long time neither of us spoke. "Well," Augusta said finally, "I guess I asked for it."

"I'm really sorry."

She ignored that. "You've already heard everything else about my life. What was in the one you read?"

If there was anything I couldn't repeat, it was that. I cast about for a way to say it. "It was the one he wrote in the middle of the night."

"That's when he writes all of them," she said. "It doesn't really matter which one you read, anyway. They're basically all the same."

"It's so *sad*," I said in a kind of protest, unable to stop myself.

"It's life, it's the way it is."

"I couldn't stand it."

"Then don't let it happen to you. If you can help it." She

didn't make helping it sound easy. Should I have made myself wake George up? If I had been Augusta, I would have—but I wasn't. That got too complicated to figure out.

"Isn't there anything you can do about it?" I refused to accept the idea that it was too late.

"What would you suggest? Poison his wife?"

"Why did he marry her, anyway?"

"That's his problem," Augusta said, as if there would be no more on that subject, but then she relented. "Maybe he gave up on me—why shouldn't he? I don't know why he's still in love with me, I really don't."

"Same reason Jerry is?"

She gave me a surprised stare. "Which is what?"

But there was no way to put it in three words, even though inside I thought I knew. "I don't know what it's called."

"Well, if you figure it out, write me a letter."

I wanted to ask if she was as in love with Allan as he said she was, and how she could live with it, but I didn't dare.

"You know something?" she said. "You're the only person who knows about this. I mean, in the world. Except me and Allan. I never thought anybody else would."

"I'm sorry, I shouldn't have read it, I know that."

"No. Don't be sorry. I'm not. It's kind of a relief."

Not to me, I thought, but then that seemed silly. Was there anything to be gained by not knowing?

"Maybe I would have told you eventually, anyhow. Unless you got sick of my stories and refused to listen."

"I wouldn't do that."

"You know, I forget you're fifteen sometimes. I hope I haven't . . . said things I shouldn't have."

"I forget sometimes, too." And I had Augusta to thank for that.

"You wouldn't consider maybe telling me what happened last night, just sort of in a general way, to keep me from dying of curiosity? I mean, you know all of my secrets."

"We fell asleep." That sounded flat, all wrong. "Together, I mean."

"Ah, together." Her words sounded the slightest bit teasing, but tactfully she kept her gaze straight ahead. She nodded to herself as if she knew what I meant instead of what I had told her. "I'm happy for you," she said. "Don't tell Cheryl or she'll have my neck."

"What do you think I am, crazy?"

"You're the sanest person in this car, but that isn't saying much."

"Together" still echoed in me, full of wealth and loss, pain and consolation. "You have to tell him my address—don't forget. He said he would ask you."

"Okay."

"It's important."

"I know it is," she said, and I believed her, but how much good could letters do?

"I don't know when I'll ever see him again."

"Get him to meet you here next summer."

"Sure. He won't even remember who I am."

"Want to bet?"

"I'll tell you what he'll remember—his grandparents are probably going to kill him for staying out all night."

"Oh, who cares about them? Next time we'll invite him to stay with us."

"And you really think my parents would stand for that? Come on." It was a piercingly wonderful thought—too exciting to happen; even thinking of such a thing was a scary, illicit pleasure.

Perhaps there was no limit to how many fantasies like that Augusta had up her sleeve.

She sighed resignedly. "I suppose you're right. Tell you what, though. When you come back you'll be sixteen, you'll have your license, right? I've been thinking maybe I'll just give you this car. You look kind of nice in it. I like the idea of you driving into the school parking lot in this thing, and anyway, it doesn't have much trade-in value. I've been thinking of buying a Volkswagen."

"Wait a minute—give me the Buick? Are you serious?"

"Can you think of a better person?" Augusta looked away after a moment, ever so slightly pink under her tan, and I realized she was embarrassed. Maybe this dumb idea of a Volkswagen was just an excuse, her way of making things complicated as usual. I moved over on the seat and gave her a hug; with one hand she held me hard around the neck and with the other she patted me on the back, quick light pats as if she thought someone was watching us. "Don't go getting sentimental on me," she said, "I can't stand it."

"Tough," I said, but I let her go. We sat shoulder to shoulder on the Buick's big front seat, like a couple on a date. As if we had been out all night and still didn't want to say goodbye.

"Thank you," I said.

"Oh, you're welcome. It's not that big of a favor anyway; you won't believe how much gas this thing takes."

God, she was stubborn. "I mean for everything."

She sighed and put her arm around me. "So you're really leaving, huh?"

I brought my right hand up to touch hers where it rested on my shoulder. "Yes."

"Damn it," she said. That was my Augusta. "Well, I suppose

if you are, you are. I think there's an early train, you'd better call and find out when. Are you packed, or not?"

"Just about."

"Hell of a time to leave," she said. "Just when the grass needs cutting."

"The grass always needs cutting," I said. "Think of all the work you can get out of me next summer."

"Go call the station. I think we've got just about enough time to make the train."

I put my foot out the door of the Buick, couldn't bring myself to move farther. "God, I hate to leave."

"Don't talk about that, go on."

I got out of the car and shut its heavy door behind me, walked up the uneven bricks of the front walk for the last time until—when? It felt good to talk of next summer, to take it for granted, but who could say what might change by then? It seemed too far off to be real; I would be someone else. And so would George, and nothing could stop it. The memory of making him kiss me crossed my mind as I passed a certain place on the walk that no one would recognize but me.

The inside of the house was dim, making me realize that full day had come while we sat and talked. The kitchen clock said six-ten. Twelve hours ago we had not even sat down to dinner. I dialed the train station in St. Louis, and as it rang and rang I looked around the kitchen. We had done a pretty good job of cleaning up; Augusta would have a big stack of dishes to do, but that was all. The back door still stood open to the outdoors; I realized that we had never replaced the little gadget that was supposed to keep the screen from banging when it shut, after saying that we were going to fix it every day. Finally Union Station answered. There was a Chicago train at eight.

Well, this time we would make it, like it or not.

I went up the back stairs, noticing as I did every time that the railing was a little wobbly at the top; that seemed like exactly the way it should feel. Everything in Augusta's house and around it seemed to be alive and in its right place—even me. I stood in the middle of the living room and felt New Franklin surrounding the house, its air and its sounds entering the open windows. Even time came in there, a particular kind of time, that was memory and the present at once. A life could turn on this—on being at home—Augusta's had, hadn't it? And it was imaginable that mine could, too.

But things I couldn't imagine lay ahead. We had to go, I had to face them. I collected my things from the bathroom, dragged my hairbrush through my hair, tucked my train ticket into the pocket in the top of my suitcase. The bedspread that George and I had never pulled back was rumpled from our night on top of it, and I did not straighten it. I didn't want to be the one to erase that mark of whatever we had shared; perhaps when Augusta saw it she would know what it meant, think of us together before she pulled the covers square again.

I stood at the top of the stairs with my suitcase, ready to go; then I set it down. We could spare another moment for me to say goodbye. Or not say it, since I would always be back, because it made me happy, because I would choose that; because it would be my life, my own. If only I did not forget what was in my heart.

Outside I heard Augusta's steps on the porch. She opened the front door and looked up at me; we were equals for a moment, I saw it in her face.

"What time's the train?" she said quietly.

"Eight."

"Well, come on, we'd better go. Are you ready?"

"I guess so."

As I descended her look changed; she watched me in a kind of proprietary way and took my suitcase when I reached the bottom.

"You don't have to carry that."

"I know, silly."

Outside, the sunshine was not hot, and yet heat lay waiting in its brightness, the long story of another day.

When we reached the car, Augusta opened the trunk and put my suitcase in; then she went around to the driver's side. I opened the passenger door; why were we hesitating, looking at each other over the roof of the Buick?

"I'll drive this time," she said. She did not roll up the windows as we pulled away.

LOWRY PEI was born in Chicago, grew up in St. Louis and went to college and graduate school at Harvard and Stanford. He has taught writing and literature at the University of Missouri, the University of California at San Diego, and Harvard University; his fiction has appeared in *Stories*, the *Ohio Review*, the science-fiction anthology *Edges* and *Best American Short Stories 1984*. In 1984 he was a finalist in fiction in the Massachusetts Artists Fellowship competition, on the basis of a chapter of this novel. He is currently director of writing at Simmonds College and lives in Somerville, Massachusetts.

VINTAGE
CONTEMPORARIES

"Today's novels for the readers of today."— VANITY FAIR

"Real literature—originals and important reprints—in attractive, inexpensive paperbacks."—THE LOS ANGELES TIMES

"Prestigious."—THE CHICAGO TRIBUNE

"A very fine collection."—THE CHRISTIAN SCIENCE MONITOR

"Adventurous and worthy."— SATURDAY REVIEW

"If you want to know what's on the cutting edge of American fiction, then these are the books you should be reading."
— UNITED PRESS INTERNATIONAL

On sale at bookstores everywhere, but if otherwise unavailable, may be ordered from us. You can use this coupon, or phone (800) 638-6460.

Please send me the Vintage Contemporaries books I have checked on the reverse. I am enclosing $ _____ (add $1.00 per copy to cover postage and handling). Send check or money order—no cash or CODs, please. Prices are subject to change without notice.

NAME _____

ADDRESS _____

CITY _____ STATE _____ ZIP _____

Send coupons to:
RANDOM HOUSE, INC., 400 Hahn Road, Westminster, MD 21157
ATTN: ORDER ENTRY DEPARTMENT
Allow at least 4 weeks for delivery.

005   38

VINTAGE
CONTEMPORARIES